AN ADVENTURE THROUGH THE TOGETHERWOOD

Sean Anderson

D0731654

RIVERSONG
BOOKS

An Imprint of Sulis International Press
Los Angeles | Dallas | London

Chapter 8 originally appeared as "Redemption in the Thorny Thicket" in <u>2022 Best Short Stories: Riversong Contest</u>, published by Riversong Books, an imprint of Sulis International Press.

ISBN (print): 978-1-958139-13-4
ISBN (eBook): 978-1-958139-14-1

Published by Riversong Books
An Imprint of Sulis International
Los Angeles | Dallas | London

www.sulisinternational.com

CONTENTS

1.
A New Path and an Unexpected Box

After spending the early morning playing in the cool October sunshine, 11-year-old Eleanor was ready to leave the woods and return home. The path beneath her feet was a mixture of hard mud and bright leaves. On both sides of her were rows of trees, their branches poking up at the clear, blue sky above. She walked slowly, humming a favorite song to herself. She could hear the occasional chirping of birds, the gentle rustle of a breeze, and the occasional drone of a plane. A little tired but content, Eleanor looked forward to enjoying the rest of her weekend.

It was to the forest that she went when she was not spending time with her family or occupied with schoolwork. Here, under the cover of the towering trees, she felt free to explore to her heart's content. She was very happy to take one of countless paths, following the bends of a quiet creek, placing her hand on the moss of her favorite log, or climbing up a slope to find herself at a clearing where everything below looked completely different. When she was here in the forest, the world felt big and full of mystery.

Now close to her home, Eleanor approached a familiar fork in the path. Father, as she knew, had sternly instructed her to always proceed left here. He had told her in the past that going right led deeper into the heart of the woods, and that it was unsafe to go there. She knew this well. So, eager to return to the soft armchair in the living room and the novel she started only yesterday, she turned left and continued on her way. But she soon stopped.

She stood still, listening. Yes, she thought to herself, it indeed was! With a quick turn around, she looked for where the hooting sound was coming from. Her eyes scanned up one tree and then another. Then she finally saw him on the branch of a tree not far off.

Perched up high, looking at Eleanor with an inquisitive expression, the great horned owl had wide yellow eyes and long eyebrows. The dense feathers of his wings were light brown. He stood still, occasionally hooting. His face ruffled lightly as he looked about. He continued to stare at her.

Beaming with delight, Eleanor walked back the way she had come, wondering if she might not be able to make a new friend. She soon returned to the fork, and realized she would need to go the other way in order to meet the owl. She felt apprehension as she remembered what Father had told her. Telling herself that she would only go a few dozen meters to the owl and then turn around and return home, she decided to continue.

Because she was anxious that the owl might fly off at any moment, she took each step slowly and cautiously so as to make little noise. The owl remained in place, no longer hooting. She saw now that he was perched on a jagged branch that had lost all of its leaves weeks ago. Once she was close to the base of the tree, she stopped and raised her head up to behold him.

Suddenly, the owl raised his wings and flew away from the tree. He stayed low to the ground as he traveled, hooting and flapping magnificently. Eleanor stood still and watched as he soared over a massive fern plant nearby. She ran to follow him, feeling her heart beat in her temple. As she moved around the fern, she saw something that astonished her.

Meters away, sitting in a small clearing, was a giant cardboard box. Its walls were light brown and appeared worn. The owl was perched on top of one of the box's flaps. Eleanor took several slow steps towards it.

Where, she wondered, had it come from? She was able to remember boxes in the living room every now and then, such as when her family had purchased a new bookshelf to assemble. Yet, why would there be one out in the middle of the forest with the trees and ferns? She turned around and was able to see the fork in the trail not far off. She started when she heard another hoot sound. Still walking slowly, Eleanor moved towards the box until she was able to place a hand against one of its flaps.

The owl continued to be still. Hoping to be just a little closer to him, Eleanor held the cardboard flap, raising one leg and then the other until she was standing inside of the box. She smiled. It felt very funny to her to be standing in such a thing in the middle of the woods.

Suddenly, the owl flapped his wings and soared once more back into the sky. Eleanor thought she was able to see a slight gleam in his yellow eyes before he disappeared. The box began to shake forcefully. All of its flaps closed at once. Losing her balance, Eleanor stumbled and landed on her knees. Once all of the flaps closed, everything became dark, and she was no longer able to see.

2.
TWO HOPELESSLY LOST PETS

Terrified, Eleanor wrapped her arms around her knees. She remained in darkness for a moment. Why, she wondered, had the box shaken and closed? Was there now someone standing outside of it and waiting for her? Everything seemed still and quiet. She placed her left hand against the cardboard ceiling and saw a sliver of light form on the ground. Now, pressing with both her hands, she was able to push the flaps open with ease. She was relieved to see the morning sky again and breathed a loud sigh of relief. But when she stood up and looked around, she no longer recognized where she was.

The box, she saw, was no longer sitting in the clearing as before, but instead in a small creek. Each of its sides was wet, turning a darker shade of brown. With each passing second, the entire box became wetter and less sturdy. Nervous that her feet would become wet, Eleanor climbed out and took several steps to solid land.

As she looked around, Eleanor realized she had no idea of where she was now. Despite her many trips and expeditions through the forest, nothing she saw now was familiar to her. She felt panic as her chest began to tighten. She ran towards the box, picked it up, and placed it on the ground away from the quiet creek. She jumped inside of it and closed the flaps, hoping she would return home. But when she opened them once more, she saw that she was still in the same place. She jumped out of the box, noticing how its walls bent easily after soaking up water. Sitting at last on the ground away from the creek, Eleanor placed her palms to her head and cried.

Why had she not listened to Father? If she had only ignored the owl and taken the normal path she would now be home, sitting comfortably with her book, some apple slices, and her parents close by. She would be feeling cozy and warm, rather than having her socks be slightly wet and dirty. For a few minutes, she sat alone and wiped her tears.

Minutes later, Eleanor was surprised to hear the faint sound of voices behind a rock. She closed her eyes and was able to hear what was being said:

"You need to face it, Dax. We are stranded out here, with no idea at all of where to go and no chance to survive, and it is completely your fault! It might as well be all over now."

The voice was high and shrill, talking quickly. It sounded to Eleanor like a female. A second, male voice responded:

"I didn't mean to do anything, Claire. I just wanted to have fun! You like fun too, right?"

In the distance, moving slowly, Eleanor could see who was talking. However, she was unable to believe what was taking place before her eyes.

There was a small tabby cat and a black Labrador retriever. The cat was orange, moving silently as her tail slowly swayed in the air. The dog was panting and taking big steps, his tongue hanging out as he wore a big grin.

"Do I like to have fun?" the cat continued. "Yes, I do. As a matter of fact, my favorite form of fun is called 'staying alive'. Are you familiar with it?"

The dog came to a halt and appeared to be in deep concentration. "Hmm. I think so. That sounds really fun!"

The cat closed her eyes and opened them several times slowly. She continued with a harsh tone, saying, "None of it matters. We are lost and it is your responsibility. All I wanted to do was take a nap on the back deck. You had to go ahead and convince me that we should go explore the woods. Well, how did that end for us?"

"I'm really sorry. It won't happen again next time."

The cat's tail began to move quickly as her ears perked up. "You know what? You're right, Dax. It is true that this won't happen again next time. Do you want to know why it won't?" She moved her face very close to the dog. "The reason this won't happen again is because we are not going to live through this in order to have the opportunity. We are going to be out here all day, and then when night comes we will be cold, hungry, and abandoned. Eventually, you and I will disappear forever and no one will ever know what happened to us." The cat slowly raised a paw and tapped it on the dog's nose, causing his grin to shrink. "Are you happy? Was it worth it to chase the squirrel or the ball or whatever it was that got you so eager to drag me out here, Dax? Are you happy I joined you in climbing inside of a stupid cardboard box? You dogs are all the same. Always running in circles, easily amused, thoughtless."

The dog looked puzzled. "But what's wrong with being amused?"

The cat sighed.

"We can get out of here," he continued. "I know we can!" He tilted his head back and raised his nose to the air. "I smell the way out of here!"

With eyes closed, the cat replied, "You always say things like that, but we both know it isn't true. You have no idea how to get out of here, just like you have no idea how you got into here. I don't want you to smell the way out of here. I want you to see the way out, and then I want you to place one paw in front of the other, and do that over and over again until you lead us to my bed, so I can take a nap."

The dog grinned again. "Claire, I know we can leave here. I bet we are close! All you have to do is trust me."

The cat's eyes lit up. "Trust? You want me to trust you after all this? That's it. I may like to sit around and sleep, but I need to do something about this. I need to at least maintain the illusion that we aren't doomed." She walked away from the dog, moving the opposite way from where Eleanor was still sitting.

"Wait! I can figure this out!" he cried.

"Whenever you do figure it out, go ahead and howl. I'm not going to hold my breath, though."

The orange tabby named Claire moved silently along a nearby trail, which was surrounded by trees on every side. Within seconds, she vanished behind a green cloak formed by the many leaves. Up above, the sun continued to shine.

The dog bent his legs and placed his head low on the ground. His ears flopped on top of his head. "I don't like to be alone."

Eleanor felt sorry for Dax. Why was Claire being so unkind to him? It seemed that she lacked understanding. As Eleanor looked at the dog, she felt immense relief in knowing she was not the only one lost, as though a weight on her shoulders had been lifted. She took several steps around the rock and approached him.

"What is that?" he asked. "Is it a squirrel?" The dog turned to look at Eleanor. "Oh," he grinned. "You're a human. I like humans! What's your name?"

"How are you talking to me?" Eleanor asked.

"I can talk by opening my mouth. I like talking to friends," he said, still grinning.

Eleanor took several more steps towards him, hearing the squishing sound of her shoes landing on the wet forest floor. "But you're a dog. You can't really be talking, can you?"

8

"Why can't I talk to you? I don't get it."

"Because dogs don't talk," she said confidently.

"Oh," he said. "I didn't know that."

"Is your name Dax?" Eleanor asked.

He nodded his head and continued to smile and pant. "My name is Dax. I am a dog and not a cat. What is your name?"

She laughed and said, "My name is Eleanor."

Now Dax's tail was wagging even faster. "It is nice to meet you, Eleanor. I like humans! Claire and I have two humans who own us. They are nice to us! We are trying to return to them, but we are very lost right now."

"I see that."

"I have a question to ask you, Eleanor."

"Please ask," she beamed.

Dax spread his front legs out and asked, "Do you have anything to play fetch with?"

Eleanor looked around. Planted nearby in some wet dirt was a broken branch. She walked over, picked it up, and threw it with all her strength past Dax. His face lit up with joy, and then he spun backwards to sprint after it.

"I've got it! I've got it!" he shouted. He ran away like a stone flung out of a catapult.

Eleanor watched him soon disappear. "Dax…where did you go?"

A moment later, he was nowhere to be seen. Save for the occasional chirp of birds or the rustle of wind on the ferns, there was no sound. Eleanor looked at her shoes and noticed the dirt all over her arms. She was feeling cold.

"Dax?"

Then, to Eleanor's right side, she saw a fern explode as its light green leaves soared into the air. Something black zoomed past.

9

Seated before Eleanor, tail wagging, was Dax. He opened his mouth and dropped the stick in front of her.

"Here it is! I brought it back to you!" he cried.

Eleanor smiled. "That is wonderful, Dax!"

He nodded, grinning.

"However," she continued, "don't you think we should go find your friend Claire?"

Dax tilted his head slightly to the side. "Does that mean you don't want to play fetch anymore?"

Eleanor folded her hands and replied, "It's not that I don't want to, Dax. I just think it's best that we all stay together. Both you and I are lost. Claire is your friend, and so I think we should go find her. Don't you agree?"

"I do agree! Claire and I are great friends."

"Whenever we do get out of here, we will certainly play fetch more!"

"I would like that!" Dax shouted. "But I have a problem, Eleanor. Claire was upset with me. She kept saying something to me…which was…" He closed his mouth and squinted at the ground. "Hmm…that's it! Claire said that she and I were 'two hopelessly lost pets'. She said that it was all my fault. Now I don't know what to do."

Eleanor crouched down to look directly at Dax. "It may be true that you two are lost. But you are no more lost than me, and I know that if the three of us work together, we can find our way out of here. Right?"

"Yes! You're right!" Dax spun around instantly, his tail wagging. "Where do you think Claire went off to?"

Taking a few steps past him, feeling the soft ground beneath her feet, Eleanor pointed her finger and said, "I think I remember seeing her go off that way. How about we go past those ferns over there?"

"OK!" he exclaimed, speeding past the ferns and disappearing.

"Dax!" she called.

His head appeared on top of one of the ferns. "Huh?"

Eleanor giggled. "We already lost Claire. I don't need to lose you too, now do I?"

Dax shook his head slowly from side to side.

"All right, then. Let's go find Claire!"

Though Eleanor had been afraid and sad when she first climbed out of the box, meeting Dax and playing fetch with him cheered her up considerably. She didn't feel as alone anymore, sensing that by working together with him and Claire, they would be able to find their way home. Though she was shocked at first to see them talking, she certainly was glad to be able to converse with someone. By comforting and encouraging Dax, she found that she also started to feel better.

Past the ferns was a trail, wide as a road, curving left and then right, continuing as far as the eye could see. The different shades of green in the many trees varied, some as light as the ferns lining the edges of the trail, others as dark as the bushes. In contrast to the dark brown trail, the bark on the trees was much lighter, a slight maroon. Every now and then while walking, Eleanor could see a bright, splendid glow of sunlight break through the edges of the tree branches, filling the canopy with light. Eleanor felt an occasional breeze against her legs, as though the wind was pushing them forward. Slowly, her clothes were drying off as the river water dripped onto the trail below.

Dax continued to pant as he occasionally would lower his nose near the ground and sniff. He moved steadily.

"I can smell her," he said. "If we keep going this way, we will find her."

"That means she can't be too far off," Eleanor replied. "You dogs sure do have a good sense of smell!"

"We do! Claire is a cat. I know what cats smell like, so this is easy."

"What do cats smell like?"

Dax stopped walking. "Cats...smell like cats. Not like dogs, not like hamsters, not like parrots."

"That makes sense," she said with a smile.

"Her smell is getting stronger!"

Eleanor placed her left hand on her head. "Is it true that all cats and dogs can talk? I am still having trouble understanding this."

Dax answered, "I don't know. Cats and dogs talk all the time. I don't know how often humans bother to listen to us."

Eleanor shrugged. There must be a different explanation, she told herself, for why she was having a conversation with a dog. But what was it? She decided to change the subject and continued, "How did you two get lost here?"

"There he is!" Dax shouted as he jumped off the trail. Eleanor turned to look for him and saw a butterfly appear on the trail, followed by Dax crash landing next to it.

"Stay still! I just wanna play!"

The butterfly hovered in the air for a moment before rising up in the air and vanishing behind a tree.

Crouched now at the base of a tree with his legs spread out, Dax turned towards Eleanor, and said, "Oh...that's right. We were looking for Claire, weren't we?"

"That's right," she answered with a smile.

At that moment, they both heard the faint sound of a meow.

"What was that?" Dax asked, looking concerned.

Eleanor answered, "I think it was a cat. Dax, that must be Claire!"

"We are looking for Claire!"

12

Standing still, Eleanor raised her hand to her ear. "It sounds like it is coming from this direction," she said, pointing again.

"Let's go look!" Dax shouted.

They stepped off the trail and approached a wall of jagged tree branches. Eleanor crouched down low and worked to lift the boughs up in order to create a path forward. Dax bolted through. Feeling the poke of branches from every direction, Eleanor grimaced. She slowly raised her feet up and moved through. Every now and then they would hear another meow, if only a little louder than before.

Dax's ears soon perked up. "Where is she?"

Having removed another sharp tree branch, Eleanor replied, "I'm not sure. But we must be getting closer."

"We're gonna find you, Claire!" Dax yelled into the quiet.

"Is that so? Have you bothered to look up yet?" a voice called from above.

Both Eleanor and Dax raised their heads upwards and felt another gentle, cool breeze.

High up, past many layers of pointed branches, sat Claire on a narrow limb, frowning.

"Claire!" Dax hollered. "We have found you, Claire! We did it."

Rolling her eyes, she answered, "Finding me is a great place to start. But if that is all you were planning to do, I can't say I feel very relieved."

Eleanor raised a hand to a forehead as she focused her gaze. "We can climb up to get you, Claire."

"Yes we can! Yes we can!" Dax's tail was wagging wildly as he squatted.

Claire continued, "All I wanted to do was climb up and get a better view of this forest. I thought I would be able to see the way out from a higher elevation. But unfortunately, as great as I am at climbing, I've never been one for getting back down."

She sighed. "I thought I might be able to find a way back down, but I was mistaken. Now I really am stranded forever."

Eleanor lowered her head to look at the base of the tree. Its trunk was wide and sturdy, reminding her of the fence behind her yard. When she considered climbing it, she felt nervous. She then looked at Dax, who sat still and continued panting, his pink tongue hanging out of his mouth.

"I think I could try to help you down, Claire," she said finally.

Turning her orange head down, fur bristled, Claire answered, "Would you? That would be lovely."

Resolving to not let her fear prevent her from trying, Eleanor walked towards the tree. She grabbed a branch with both of her hands, holding her breath as she pulled herself up. She felt the wood gently bend as she tried to not imagine it breaking. Dax continued to sit still, looking at Eleanor eagerly.

"As much as I appreciate you making the effort to rescue me, I do need to say that I would prefer being saved today if at all possible," Claire called.

Eleanor turned her head up quickly, feeling a small branch poke the top of her head. "I'm coming…" she whispered to herself.

"What was that?"

"I'm coming!" Eleanor cried as she held on to the tree bough with all of her strength.

For the next few minutes, she climbed in silence, knowing intuitively where to place her hands and just how much strength to use to pull herself up. The cool breeze brushed her clothes, reminding her of how frigidly cold October at times could be. With a twisting motion, she worked her way towards the back side of the tree. Steadily, she watched as the views around her transformed, as the dirty ground below grew smaller beneath her. When she stopped to catch her breath, she was able to see in the distance the line where the land met the ocean, beyond which was a blue expanse. It reminded her of her house, which was painted dark blue. Eleanor thought of how she wished she were back home, that she had obeyed Father. She knew, however, that such thoughts were of no use. She turned and saw that a nearby series of hills soon became tall mountains, going from the sea through the many layers of forest, all the way towards the very tree she was climbing.

Normally, climbing trees was something she greatly enjoyed doing. She could imagine the ones she had scaled in her neighborhood with her friends. But as she surveyed this forest, where trees sprawled out as far as she was able to see, she could not help but think that something was different about this place. She saw no cities, no roads, and no cars. Where was her home?

"Great job, Eleanor!" Dax yelled. "You climb just like a cat!"

"Let's hope she doesn't climb down trees like one," Claire grumbled.

Noticing that the branches were becoming shorter and thinner, Eleanor tried to grip them more tightly. It seemed now there were fewer and fewer of them to hold. She could feel her feet pressingly firmly on a particularly delicate bough. The breeze blew against her even more strongly now than before. The coldness stung her cheeks slightly. Dax appeared smaller and smaller down below.

Eleanor realized all at once just how quiet the forest had become. She became still, neither climbing up nor going back down. She looked away from the tree and felt a knot in her stomach.

"Your name is Eleanor, right?" a voice asked.

Turning her head upward, she answered, "Yes, it is."

Claire was not far from her anymore, no more than five meters. Tail swaying slowly, she said, "Well, Eleanor, I have to say I really am hoping you are able to get up here. It would make my day, in fact."

Feeling tension in her right arm as it reached out to grab a bough, Eleanor said, "I will be right there."

She used all of her strength to pull herself up from each branch. Moving too quickly to think about how high up she was, Eleanor instead focused on reaching Claire. The sound of the breeze filled her ears as she heard all the trees rock together. At this point, the tree was much thinner, no wider than the mast of a ship. Eleanor felt the pain of a branch scrape against her forehead. Frustrated, she crouched down on her legs, lowered her head, and sighed.

"Were you really planning to get this close just to give up?"

Eleanor raised her head once more and looked into two dark green eyes. Claire was crouched on a branch just slightly above her.

Choosing to smile, Eleanor said, "No, I was not going to do that! How are you, Claire?"

Claire raised her left paw to scratch behind her ear. "I guess better now that you're here."

"That's great. How do we get down from here?"

"Even though you're a human, you should still know that we cats, while remarkable climbers, are completely unable to get down from things unless we jump." She lifted her gaze to the other trees. "As you may understand, jumping from up here isn't much of an option."

"Yes," Eleanor nodded. "That makes sense."

"Here is what I say we do," Claire continued. She reached a small, bright orange paw towards Eleanor. "I am going to work my way towards you. I will pounce onto your knees, trying not to have my claws out too much. Then, if you can hold me very tightly, you can use your other arm and move your legs very slowly to bring us back down to safety." She moved her head to lock her eyes with Eleanor's. "Sound easy enough?"

Nodding again, Eleanor answered, "Easy enough for you, maybe."

Claire closed her eyes and wore a small smile. "That sounds perfectly fine to me."

Eleanor secured herself by holding two boughs and steadying her legs. She tried to create a spot for Claire to land.

"Are you ready?" Claire asked.

"Yes, I am."

They both remained still for a moment. Eleanor felt the entire tree lean slightly to the side as the breeze picked up.

"I am ready," Eleanor continued.

Claire was not looking at her, but beneath her, towards the ground far below. "I know you are. I just wish I was, too."

"Don't worry," Eleanor said. "I will catch you, and we will be down in no time at all. You can trust me."

"I suppose so. I really don't have a choice."

Claire repositioned her paws on the branch and Eleanor heard the sound of her claws scrape against it. Then, in one full motion, Claire leapt towards Eleanor, her claws pressing into her thighs. Holding on to the branches with all her strength, Eleanor cried out in pain. The two of them together shook a few times as the branch bent and bounced. Seconds later, they were still again.

Eleanor and Claire both laughed. "This is terrifying," Claire said as her tail pressed against Eleanor. "But I haven't died yet."

"True," Eleanor replied with a smile. "Now I will take us back down to Dax."

"I'm down here on the ground!" his voice called below. "She can help you, Claire! She is the best at fetch."

17

Somehow, Eleanor felt that she was even higher above the ground now than before. She noticed that few other trees had branches that reached up quite as high as where they were. She sought to remove such thoughts from her head and instead maneuvered her hand slowly down in order to hold on to a bough near her knees. While holding it tightly, she blinked a few times quickly, feeling a furry tail brush against her face.

"Sorry," Claire said, "sometimes I forget where it is."

Eleanor remained focused on the task at hand. Very gently, she slid from the current branch she was sitting on towards the one directly below it.

"You're doing wonderfully!" Claire exclaimed. "Please keep it up. Don't think about the fact that if we fell from this high up, we would break every bone in our bodies."

Eleanor felt her feet land on the new branch as she lowered her entire body with Claire down onto it. With her knees bent, she looked for a new one to hold, and then carefully slid her feet out so that she was sitting. When necessary, she momentarily let go of Claire so she could use both of her hands.

"Well done," she said to Eleanor. "Now do what you just did a hundred more times."

Eleanor felt quite confused. Was Claire joking? It seemed that much of what she said was very unkind, harsh even. Was there something Eleanor was failing to understand?

"I can certainly do that," she finally answered.

So they continued in this way. Eleanor would look down, trying with all her might to not think about the distance that still remained. She would grab a branch below, shake it slightly to ensure it would be supportive enough, gently lower her feet onto a different one, and then maneuver her entire body so that she was now crouched on the new branch, all without dropping Claire. Once her knees were bent and she felt secure, she would hold a branch and slowly slide her feet out until she was seated, ready to repeat the entire movement.

On several occasions, Eleanor did not lower herself quite so elegantly. She would then feel a sharp pain in her legs as Claire used her claws to help stay in her lap. During these moments, Eleanor held on to the branch below with all of her strength. She knew that, no matter the pain, she needed to be slow and careful in order to keep both of them safe. At one point, she reached for a branch only to find, upon bending it, that it broke, with a small strip of wood falling down below.

"Don't be like that stick!" Dax shouted. "Don't fall!"

After what felt like an eternity, Eleanor looked down and realized that they were now not terribly far from the ground. Smiling to herself, she heard Claire say, "Don't get excited. It only takes one fall to make everything come crashing down."

"I suppose you are right."

Overjoyed by the fact there now seemed to be more branches available to choose from, which were also much thicker, Eleanor continued to move cautiously. Just as she saw a bough that seemed suitable, the wind suddenly picked up, blowing harshly against the tree. All of the tree branches were bent by the powerful breeze. Eleanor heard the loud hush of wind and she held on to the branch with every bit of strength she had. She could feel the piercing pain of Claire digging her claws into her thighs.

Eleanor, despite her best efforts, was unable to hold on to Claire.

The shrill sound of a cat screeching filled the forest air as she plummeted from the tree towards the ground. Eleanor watched her, placing her own hand over her mouth.

"She's falling!" Dax shouted. "You forgot what I said!"

But then, as Eleanor refocused her gaze, she saw Claire rotate her entire body in one swift motion so that her feet were now facing the ground and her tail upwards. Claire hit the ground with a thud and her legs took the impact from the fall. Her tail pointed upwards and her orange head slowly lowered. A moment passed, and then Claire turned her head back up at the tree to meet Eleanor's eyes.

"We cats were made for this sort of situation," she said. "I'm prepared to hit the ground hard when others drop me."

"I'm so sorry that I lost hold of you," Eleanor said. "That was an amazing landing, though."

Claire slowly closed her eyes and then opened them once more. "I guess you're right. Now it's your turn."

"If possible," Dax said, "I think it would be better if you came down more slowly. You don't need to fall!"

Eleanor smiled. "I think you are right, Dax."

No longer carrying a cat, Eleanor found climbing down to be much easier now. She took her time, though, testing each branch with a pull to make sure it could support her weight. The breeze was much more gentle now.

A few minutes later, she was nearly back to the ground. Turning her head to look down once more, she saw the black dog and orange cat seated together. Seeing them made her feel extremely happy.

"You're almost back!" Dax yelled.

"Dax…" Claire said, shaking her head.

He turned towards her. "What?"

"You don't need to shout. She's right in front of us."

Dax nodded his head and then looked at Eleanor again. "OK," he said at a volume just above a whisper. "Eleanor, you don't need to climb anymore. I think you can fall now."

"I'm glad to hear that," she answered. She let go of the branches and fell two meters down, landing on the soft forest floor.

Dax's eyes were bright. "That was amazing! It was incredible! Wasn't it, Claire?"

With a roll of her eyes, she said, "It was something. I'll give her that."

"Yes, it was something," he continued. "It was a lot of something! Eleanor, thank you so much for helping save my friend. I don't know what would have happened if I hadn't run into you."

Claire rose up and began to pace. "It was nice that you helped me out, so thanks for doing that. You might be a decent enough person. What are you doing out here in the woods, anyway?"

"Me?" Eleanor was caught off guard by the question.

Claire nodded slowly.

"I…I think I got a bit lost…"

"We already knew that."

"She got lost just like us. Isn't that neat?" Dax asked with a grin.

Claire continued pacing. "Not every question deserves an answer." She turned to face Eleanor. "But how did that happen? How did a tree-climbing hero like you get lost out here?"

"I…" she began with hesitation. "I was walking home in the woods behind my house, and I saw an owl, and I—"

"You saw the owl, too?" Dax asked.

"I did. I saw it, and I wanted to take a closer look at it."

"What happened next?" Claire asked.

Eleanor felt that it was impossible to explain the next part of her story.

"Did you jump into a cardboard box, too?" Dax asked.

Eleanor blushed slightly. "Yes, in fact that is what happened to me. How did you know?"

"Because he tricked me into following him into one," Claire answered.

21

"I just wanted the owl to be my friend. I like friends!" Dax exclaimed.

"True enough, and when I saw you climb into that box with the owl and you didn't come back out, who was foolish enough to go look for you inside?"

"You! You were foolish."

Claire shook her head again. "I told you that making new friends is a bad idea." She turned to look at Eleanor. "Not you, though. You saved my life, so that means I won't hate you as intensely as I normally would."

"That's good news for you," Dax said.

Unsure of whether she should smile or appear serious, Eleanor replied, "I was happy to help you, Claire. I also climbed into a cardboard box while following the owl. The flaps closed on me, and when I got back out, I was in the middle of a creek."

"Right!" Dax answered. "Now I remember. You were all wet. That was because you were in the creek. Creeks are full of water and wet."

Claire's eyes became small as she stared off in the distance. "Indeed," she began. "Creeks are not only full of water, but also wet. Thank you for that, Dax." Her head turned towards Eleanor. "So you were drenched in a creek after climbing out of a cardboard box, just like what happened to us. Poor thing. You must be awfully frightened to be out here, lost like this."

Eleanor looked at Dax and then back at Claire. "I was upset earlier, missing my home, but I feel better now. I am not afraid at all."

"She's brave," Dax said. "She is the brave tree-climber!"

Claire replied, "Well, it's good to know that you are never afraid of anything. It has certainly helped me so far."

"What about you?" Eleanor asked.

"What about me?"

"Dax said you are pets. Is that correct?"

Claire closed her eyes and nodded twice. "Yes, we are. Our owners are a young couple who live in a big house in the middle of a cul-de-sac."

"They're great!" Dax exclaimed, his tongue hanging out of his mouth.

"As for me," Claire continued, "I do not miss them at all. I would be perfectly happy to have new owners. The husband never wanted to play with Dax, and the wife never stopped trying to pet me."

"I like to play," Dax added. "I guess I wish he was around more. Sometimes it doesn't seem like he likes me."

Claire turned to look towards the mountainous slopes on the other side of a tree grove. "None of it matters now, as we are lost. Dax doesn't have his owners, and I don't have my bed."

"We're lost!" Dax exclaimed. "We don't know where we are! We are t—"

"What we are," Claire finished, "are two hopelessly lost pets."

The trees, standing tall and solemnly around them, felt menacing under the morning sky. A boulder nearby reflected the sunshine. The sounds of birdsong, with its different pitches and rhythms, rose in volume. Eleanor looked at the two pets, and then at the walls of trees behind them. She scratched the back side of her head.

"I understand what you two are saying," Eleanor began while folding her hands. "However, I think that maybe by working together we will be able to find our way out of this forest. Maybe if we travel together, you won't be as hopeless as you think!"

Claire and Dax looked at each other. Dax began to hop in the air. "Work together like a team! We can be a team!"

Claire once more bristled her whiskers. Faintly, Eleanor could see that she was smiling. "You know, I don't think that's a terrible idea. Though you are a human, you seem to be nicer than they usually are. You clearly have a lot of skills. Perhaps it would make more sense, then, for the three of us to find our way out of here."

"We can do this," Eleanor said, raising her voice slightly. "We can certainly find our way out of here, and I promise to be nice, nicer than any human you have ever known!"

"Well," Claire said, "I'm afraid that would not be saying very much."

"Let's go! Let's go!" Dax yelled, continuing to hop.

"Indeed," Claire added. "But where are we supposed to go?"

Eleanor looked up from the two pets. Behind them in the distance were the high slopes that led to the mountains. "It doesn't seem like we have much of a choice. That rock wall is too steep," she said. She then pointed her finger to the left, towards the wide trail. "Dax and I were walking along this earlier. I think that if we continue on it, we may move towards the ocean. I remember getting a view of it up in the tree. I am sure that if we head towards it, we are bound to find another box somewhere along the way. If it was through a box that we arrived here, then that must be the way to leave as well."

"Sounds good to me," Dax said.

"If you're sure…" Claire added.

"I am." Eleanor stood tall and put her hands at her side. "Shall we get started?"

3.
SEARCHING FOR A CERTAIN LILY PAD

Eleanor, Dax, and Claire moved briskly along the trail down a slope, observing the bright grass lining both sides of it. As she placed a hand to her forehead, Eleanor was able to see an area not far ahead where there were less trees, a clearing.

"I think if we continue along this way," Eleanor began, "we should soon reach an open space where we will be able to see more. It should help us better orient ourselves."

"Seeing more is better than less," Claire replied, "except when climbing tall trees is involved."

"I like to see, too!" Dax agreed. "I see things all the time."

"I wonder how big this forest is," Eleanor said. "Do you know?"

"Big enough to fill me with despair," Claire answered.

"It is much larger than the yard where I usually run around," Dax added.

Eleanor smiled as she brushed her brown hair out of her face. "I normally also spend a lot of time in my yard. My father always told me to stay near our house, as the forest is massive. I have never actually been to the end of it." She looked up at the tree canopies above. "I wonder how this place will compare to it."

On both sides of them were trees, like lampposts on a city street. Eleanor watched the leaves dangling from the pointed tree branches above. She then gazed down at her feet and could hear, faintly, the sound of her feet pressing against the soft forest floor.

They took a turn to the right and heard the sound of water flowing. Excited, Eleanor turned and took a few steps before realizing she was standing at the bank of a river. She looked down and saw the crystalline, light blue water splashing between two boulders, gently spraying white foam onto the sandy banks on both sides.

"Wonderful," she said.

She looked up to follow where the river traveled, seeing it turn to the left, to the right, and then back to the left once more. A little farther out, and she was able, if barely, to see that this very river was emptying itself into something enormous.

Claire's paws made no sound as she walked. She sounded bored as she said, "This river must eventually lead somewhere, correct?"

"It does," Eleanor answered. "In fact, it looks as though it empties into some sort of big pond up ahead. If we take a closer look we should be able to find a new river from there and follow it to the ocean just as planned."

"That's great thinking!" Dax exclaimed. "You are very smart, Eleanor."

"If one is simple, then everyone else must seem brilliant," Claire said under her breath.

Eleanor placed her hand under her chin. "Let's continue to follow this river and see where it goes,"

Walking parallel to it, hearing the soothing lapping of water, they continued at a swift pace. They followed each turn it took and eventually approached an edge.

Eleanor stood still. She looked down over the small precipice to see that, indeed, the river was emptying itself into a stunning pond. It was gigantic, much larger than the field at Eleanor's school where she played soccer with her friends. The water on the surface was perfectly still, shimmering with sunlight. The trees that lined the pond appeared different than the one Eleanor climbed only minutes ago. These were smaller and stood so closely to the water that it appeared as though they were drinking from it with their roots. On one side was a fallen log, resting peacefully. The sound of flies and buzzing bugs could be heard.

Eleanor stood still. "It's lovely," she began.

"Maybe it is," Claire said, "but we don't have time to stand here and admire it."

"Water!" Dax shouted as he sprinted towards it. A loud splash followed as droplets sprayed Eleanor's shoes. Claire jumped in alarm and dodged it. Standing with her furry tail pointed out, she hissed, "What do you think you're doing?!"

But Dax was too occupied splashing in the water to listen, his head appearing every few seconds only to then vanish into the blue.

Claire looked at Eleanor and her eyes became small. "Never underestimate how thoughtless others can and will be," she said.

"I'm sure we have a moment to spare for him to enjoy himself," Eleanor reasoned.

When Dax's head next appeared, his nose touched a green lily pad. Moving his head back quickly, his eyes glowed as he turned towards Eleanor and Claire. "What's this?"

"That's the carpet for the pond," Claire answered.

Dax tilted his head to the side. "Carpet?"

"Now, could it be?" a new voice called from not far off. Eleanor turned her head in the direction it came from.

27

"Who was that?" Claire asked.

"It wasn't me," Dax said.

Claire turned to look at him, her orange tail slowly swaying.

"I know it wasn't you. I know what your voice sounds like."

"I didn't say anything," Dax continued. "I am in the pond swimming."

"Now, now, you youngsters. Please don't go anywhere."

"I think I can see something," Eleanor said.

A little way up along the bank of the pond appeared a figure, only to then quickly vanish. This happened several more times. Next came a rhythmic chirping sound. Then, over a patch of thorns, leapt a frog who landed on the rocky sand, creating a plop sound. He possessed two small eyes which appeared dizzy, as though a moment ago they had been spinning. His folds of green skin were wrinkly, and his legs made a slight suctioning sound when he prepared to jump again. His eyes adjusted to see the travelers, and then he took another jump, soaring across the distance separating them. He landed several centimeters from Eleanor's left shoe.

The frog's eyes rolled in his head quickly until they were gazing at Eleanor. "Now, did you indeed find it, after all of this time?"

"Who are you?" Claire asked.

The frog jumped a meter into the air in a vertical line and this time landed facing Claire. "Me? Why, my name's Frippery. I am a professor here on this pond." He coughed loudly, and it sounded like a croak. "I am a foremost expert on lily pads, and I have reason to believe you located at long last my precious item."

Claire turned to look at Eleanor and then back at Frippery. "If I agree with you, will you leave us alone?"

"It's all right, Claire," Eleanor began. "Hello there, Frippery. My name is Eleanor." She beamed. "That black dog in the water is our friend Dax. It is wonderful to meet you here."

"Certainly, yes," Frippery answered.

"I like your pond!" Dax shouted, making another big splash.

Frippery shuffled his feet slightly as his eyes spun again. "Why, hello there, canine! It would seem that you three have stumbled onto our pond here, haven't you?"

"Yes, we have," Claire replied. "But I still don't understand what you are going on about. What is this item? What are you looking for?"

In a flash Frippery jumped onto the pond. He landed on the lily pad nearest Dax, producing a slight ripple in the water.

"How did you do that?" Dax asked, treading water with all four legs.

But it did not seem that Frippery was paying attention. Craning his head over the side of the lily pad, they could hear him muttering sounds under his breath. He then propped himself up on his front legs in order to inspect the surface of the lily pad closely. After several minutes, he jumped back onto the bank of the pond.

"No," he spoke. "That one is not it. This certainly only complicates my dilemma…"

"Dilemma?" Eleanor asked.

Frippery turned to look at her. "Yes, very much so. I suppose I should better explain myself."

"We wouldn't mind that," Claire replied, appearing bored.

"Yes, I will elaborate. You see, I am the leading expert on lily pads in this entire pond region. I maintain one of the most extensive collections of them to be found anywhere. I have large ones, small ones, light green ones, dark green ones, young ones, old ones, generic ones, and rare ones. If you were to suggest any type of lily pad to come into your mind, any at all, I can assure you that I possess it somewhere in my archives."

Claire was looking at Eleanor. "I think the only kind we would think to suggest would be the lily pad kind."

Frippery blinked twice. "You are joking, but please note that I am not. Far from it. Much of my life's work has centered around gathering these lily pads, these precious aquatic flowers, in order to glean the stories that they tell to the curious mind. Within each and every lily pad is contained all the romance, tragedy, and pathos that characterize an entire ecosystem. This is why I have devoted my life's work to assembling them. For five decades I worked as professor of Botanical and Pond Studies at Ribbit Amphibian College, right here on the eastern bank of this pond. It has truly been a joy and an honor to impart my knowledge and love of lily pads into the minds of our very finest young frogs."

"That does sound like it would be a very enjoyable and rewarding project," Eleanor replied. "This is a marvelous pond. However, we need to be getting on our way and cannot afford to be delayed here for too long."

A fly started buzzing near Eleanor's ear. She raised a hand to try and brush it away and then heard a single slurp sound as the bug disappeared. She did not understand what had happened until she looked down and saw that Frippery was chewing. As he swallowed, he sighed and said, "They used to taste much better here. It is a shame."

Eleanor laughed nervously. "Thank you, Frippery," she said.

"You are most welcome."

"So, as I was saying. We are hoping to continue on our way out of the woods."

Frippery was nodding thoughtfully.

"Do you know what the best way is to get out of here?" she continued.

"Ah, yes. Of course. Now I am following along with your explanation. Eleanor, was that your name?"

"Yes," she said with a smile.

"Yes, Eleanor. You see, if you are indeed seeking to traverse this pond, what you need to understand is that it can't be done at this time."

"What do you mean?" Claire spoke up with a sharp tone.

"Why, yes. I am happy to explicate." Frippery turned so that he was facing the pond. They all looked out to see the still pure blue water surrounded by narrow trees. "The outer edges of this pond, the trails that go around it, are thoroughly covered with dense walls of thorns. Significant backtracking is likely your best option. But if you do wish to continue in this direction, then you will need to cross the pond itself. Seeing as how you are all land-based creatures and not amphibious, I would not consider it safe or viable to attempt to make the swim."

"But I can swim," Dax replied. He left the water, walked towards the others, and proceeded to shake his coat off, spraying everyone else with water. Frippery didn't appear to notice this. He continued:

"I have no doubt that you, an exceptionally fit canine, might be able to swim the distance of this pond. But I must restate that doing so would not be advised. What you three need is to rethink your plan."

"That is unfortunate to hear," Eleanor said. "We were hoping to head towards the ocean. Are you sure there isn't any other way for us to get across?"

For the first time, Frippery appeared to smile as the edges of his mouth curled. His eyes spun a few times as he made a croaking sound. "Why, I am so very glad to hear you ask that, Miss Eleanor! That question brings me back to my original point. If you three are to traverse this pond, then you will need to aid me in finding my missing item."

"What is this item?" Claire asked, appearing impatient. "Are you still referring to a lily pad? Because I really don't see how finding a measly pond plant is going to enable a cat, a human, and a giant dog to make it across a pond."

Frippery continued to croak in amusement. Then he jumped out onto the water, landing on the lily pad again. "Trust me... Claire, was it?"

"That's me."

"Indeed. Yes, trust me, Claire. If we are able to find that which I have spent the past semester looking for, you three most definitely will cross this water. You see, I have been searching for a certain lily pad, one that I have only read of in my research tomes."

Claire raised a paw to her head to scratch it.

"Such a lily pad," Frippery continued, "has only been seen by a few frogs in all amphibian history. This very big lily pad —let us refer to it as the Sustaining Lily Pad—is able to carry the weight of anyone, any human or animal. Think of it as a boat of sorts. Yes, if we were able to find it, in addition to adding it to my own private archives, we would be able to use it to swiftly transport you across the pond towards the ocean. It would be a perfect plan, that is, if we were to succeed in finding it."

"So all we need to do is find something that has hardly ever been seen in all history?" Claire replied. "Sounds like a perfect plan."

"I am in full agreement," Frippery continued. His voice grew softer as he said, "I have spent so much time looking for it, so many fruitless afternoons hopping up and down this pond. How I would delight in studying it, recording its dimensions and sharing my findings with others! But where on this beautiful earth could it be?" He placed a webbed leg to his chin.

"Are you able to tell us where you have already looked?" Eleanor asked.

"A sensible question. I have searched every conceivable place. I have scanned the entire perimeter of the pond multiple times. I have scoured the center of the pond while traveling." He let loose a sigh. "I am afraid I can think of nowhere else to look."

"I see some more lily pads over there!" Dax began running along the bank of the pond towards a wall of thorns.

"I have already inspected that area, just as I said," Frippery muttered as he hopped in Dax's direction.

"Let's take a look," Eleanor added, walking after them.

Together they approached the wall of thorns. Eleanor turned her head upwards to look at the sky, more open now, a blue tapestry. She could feel the sharp chill of morning beginning to fade as the day unfolded. Next she looked out straight across the pond to the other side. She faintly saw the other sandbank, though from such a far away distance it blurred together. The water remained relatively still, though the occasional ebb and flow of gentle water could be seen, as though the pond decided to sigh every now and then. Realizing she was distracted, Eleanor turned around to look at Dax.

"I'm sure it's here!" he exclaimed, his paws covered in dirt.

Floating before him on the water were several dozen lily pads.

Frippery shook his head slowly. "None of these are it. Please believe me when I state that my review has been thorough."

"Why don't you check again?" Claire asked.

Frippery paused for a moment and then hopped on to one of the lily pads. He continued to look at it carefully, adjusting how he sat. Only seconds later, he jumped onto the one next to it and continued what he was doing. Hop after hop, jump after jump, Frippery continued in this way until he investigated each

33

of the lily pads individually. Eleanor, Dax, and Claire stood still watching him.

Finally, Frippery jumped back onto the sand. "As I said, none of these are the one that will assist you."

"That's unfortunate," Eleanor said.

Claire added, "At least we gave it a t—"

"Over there!" Dax shouted. He stuck his head out and pointed with his nose to the center of the pond.

Frippery said, "No, I—"

"I will take a look!" Dax continued. "We really gotta find this thing!"

He proceeded to swim deep into the water. He made a humongous splash with each stroke, which sounded like a crashing cymbal. Eleanor turned to look at Claire, smiling once more.

"I can't believe him sometimes," Claire said. "But then again, given what I know, maybe that isn't true."

Frippery made a croak sound as he cleared his throat. "Now, I'm not sure what it is you are hoping to find out there in the center of the pond, but I can assure you that no Sustaining Lily Pad is to be found out there. There simply is no possibility of it."

Just as quickly as Dax had disappeared, he returned. He gave himself a big shake and water droplets sprayed in every direction. In his mouth, he held a lily pad, which he dropped onto the sandy bank.

"Is this the one?" he asked.

Frippery lowered his head slightly to examine it. "It is not."

Claire said, "Dax, maybe w—"

But Dax was already sprinting back into the water again.

"He sure is determined to find it," Eleanor observed.

Again, Dax was back on land and shaking water off of himself. He dropped another lily pad from his mouth.

34

"What about this one?"

Frippery looked at it, turning it over slowly. "No, not this one, either."

"What a bummer!"

Claire smirked. "Playing fetch, but without us having to throw anything. I think I like this."

"You know, Dax," Eleanor began crouching down next to him. "Maybe we should let this go. Maybe Frippery is right about all this. I'm sure we can find another way to cross the pond."

Dax looked at her first, next at Frippery, and then ran back into the water, creating another gigantic splash of water. Just as he was out near a collection of floating lily pads, preparing to grab another, Claire called out:

"Give up all hope, Dax. You'll never find it!"

"Help! Someone... anyone!" a different voice called out.

Both Eleanor and Claire looked around to see who was crying out.

"Where did that voice come from?" Eleanor asked.

"Help!" the voice continued.

Frippery hopped towards the water's edge. His eyes appeared dizzy once more.

"I'm having trouble identifying the source of that distress cry," he said.

"Help!"

Eleanor, Claire, and Frippery looked at each other, unsure of what to do. Moments later, Dax appeared back on the sand-bank. This time, however, he did not have a lily pad in his mouth. Rather, on the top of his head sat a small, bright green frog. Much tinier than Frippery, he was shaking slightly.

Dax lowered his head to the ground so that the frog could be on the sand. Frippery hopped over towards him.

"Is that…ah, yes, it is you, Franklin. Are you all right? What seems to be the matter?"

Franklin looked up at him and began to speak quickly. "I'm so sorry, Professor. I was hopping around and went out too deep. I wanted to take a closer look at the lily pads on the other side of the pond. While I was hopping on them, one of my legs got tired, and then I tripped and fell into the water. My back left leg became so weak I couldn't swim at all." His eyes got big and he was breathing fast. "I'm so sorry. All I wanted to do was explore, but I ended up with a cramp and no way to swim anymore. But thank goodness, this dog—what was your name?"

"My name is Dax!"

"Yes, I am so lucky that Dax was out there swimming when I was. He heard me and came to ask me if I was all right. He's the one who brought me back to shore. Thank you so much, Dax! If you hadn't seen me, I would have sunk to the bottom of the deepest part of the pond and been stuck there for who knows how long!"

Dax closed his eyes and raised his head high. "I am happy to help you! You are my new friend."

Frippery's eyes moved from Dax to Franklin. "You mean to say that this dog was the one who rescued you?"

"Yes, it was him."

Looking at Eleanor and Claire with a slight smile, Frippery spoke, "Well, I must admit I am quite impressed by such a display of heroism. Franklin, you see, is one of my very brightest students." He hopped towards Dax. "Well done, canine!"

"Thanks!"

"You were very brave," Eleanor said.

"Yes," Claire added. "At least you found something noteworthy at last."

Dax broke out with a big smile. "Yes, I did find something!"

Franklin blinked a few times and moved his legs slightly. Then he made a croaking sound and took a few hops. "I think I will need to spend some time here on the bank before I make my way back across."

Frippery turned to look at him. "Franklin, have you come across a Sustaining Lily Pad, perchance?"

"I have not. Why do you ask?"

"Because I am attempting to help guide these three across our fair little pond."

"I see. No, unfortunately I have not come across any. I understand those to be rare. Is that correct, Professor?"

Frippery lowered his head slightly. "Indeed, it is, Franklin. You certainly have kept up on your reading assignments." He turned to look at Eleanor. "I really do apologize, Miss Eleanor. I have done all that I can. Without a Sustaining Lily Pad, there is no way for you three to cross the pond. It seems that sometimes, even when you gather all the lily pads in the world, you still can't make it to the other...wait a minute!" He hopped several times in excitement. There was a gleam in his eyes.

"What is it, Professor?" Eleanor asked.

Frippery hopped over to where Dax was. "Dax," he began. "I want you to swim out there and collect as many lily pads as you are able to. Don't stop, but rather keep on going until I say otherwise!"

"I can do that!" Dax cried. He then ran back into the pond.

"What's the idea now?" Claire asked.

"I have had a breakthrough. It is true that there are no Sustaining Lily Pads. This much is inarguable. But perhaps a different solution will lead us to the same outcome. Just watch and see!"

Claire crouched down and licked one of her paws.

"I look forward to seeing what you have planned," Eleanor said.

"As am I!" Frippery replied.

A moment later, Dax returned to the sandy bank, holding several lily pads in his mouth. His tail was also holding a lily pad. He let go of them and watched as they struck the sand one by one. "More?" he asked with his head tilted slightly.

Frippery nodded.

Another loud splashing sound followed. Up above, a few small, wispy clouds had formed. Rays from the sun struck several stones nearby, causing them to glow with a glittering radiance.

"Indeed," Frippery muttered softly to himself. "If I orient these pads in just the correct configuration..."

"I brought more," Dax said as he dropped them on the sand.

"Did you leave any remaining in the pond, Dax?" Claire asked.

"I did!"

Frippery moved his head one way and then another, as though counting them. "I estimate one more trip will be sufficient."

As Dax once more disappeared into the pond, Eleanor said, "We really do appreciate your help, Professor."

"Why, it is no trouble at all. It is my delight to assist. You see, you remind me a bit of my students, and what is a greater honor for a professor than to share his knowledge through teaching?"

"If teaching is what gets us across the pond," Claire said, "then sign me up for your class."

Dax dropped another load of lily pads at Frippery's feet. He then lowered his head, slid onto his belly, and fell asleep.

"Dax!" Claire shouted.

He made several erratic snoring sounds. "Good morning, Claire."

"I think," Frippery continued, "it is now time to assemble these pads in just the correct way so as to guarantee safe passage for us across this body of water."

"Let's do it!" Dax exclaimed.

"I was wondering if you might be able to tell us more about your plan," Eleanor said, placing her hand by her chin.

Frippery hopped over by the small mountain of lily pads. After surveying them for a moment, he turned back towards Eleanor. "As I mentioned earlier, though we lack the Sustaining Lily Pad, if we are to position all of these other ones in a precise way we may have a solution. I theorize that by doing so, we will be able to construct a vessel with the sufficient buoyancy to transport us."

"Huh?" Dax asked.

"Let's just get on with it," Claire said.

Frippery looked at her. "Thank you. Eleanor, will you please arrange all of the lily pads according to my instruction?"

"I can certainly do that," she said with a smile.

With considerable focus, Eleanor placed each of them as Frippery instructed, gradually forming one single circle. Dax again collapsed on the sand and slept deeply. Claire crouched down, licked her left paw, and proceeded to clean her fur behind her head. Occasionally, Eleanor would have to readjust the lily pads if Frippery was not fully satisfied with the placement. The sky above remained bright blue. She was delighted to look out and see the light shimmering on the water.

Eleanor placed the last one down. "How about this?" she asked.

Frippery hopped over and placed his head close against it, looking at it intently. "Yes, this should be effective." He then looked at Dax and Claire. "I believe we have done it."

Claire licked her left paw once more and then walked over to wake Dax up with a tap of her paw.

"Any treats for Dax?" he asked in delirium.

"No treats," Eleanor replied. "But the good news is we may have a way to get out of here."

"Oh, boy!" Dax called, his tail wagging quickly.

"Indeed," Frippery replied

"So, how does this work?" Claire asked.

"Yes, about that. Please follow me, Claire."

He hopped over to a collection of nearby pond weeds. Tall and light green, They grew out of the water, indifferent to the flies buzzing around them.

"What do you want me to do?" Claire asked.

Frippery turned towards her. "You have claws, yes?"

"Depends on if I am going to be asked to do something."

"I gather that you do." He pointed at the weeds with his head. "Please go ahead and use them to extract these weeds."

"'Extract?'"

"Erm," he cleared his throat with a croaking sound. "Please cut the weeds off with your claws."

"Is this really what I need to do to get home?" she muttered to herself. Then, one after another, she sliced the weeds with swift scratching motions.

"Very good," Frippery said. "Please keep going."

Claire continued cutting for several minutes, striking alternatively with her paws. Eventually, all the weeds were now in a small pile of strips before Frippery.

"Marvelous," he said.

Next, he summoned Eleanor over to pick up the weed strips and bring them to the lily pad platform.

"Now," Frippery continued, "the final step in our project is to use these weeds as a sort of rope to fasten and secure all of the lily pads in place. Eleanor, are you able to assist me with the tying?"

"Yes, I can do that," she answered.

She lowered herself down and, following Frippery's careful instructions, ran the weed strips across, wrapping them together tightly. She then tied the weeds together using the only knot she knew, the one she also used to tie her shoes. It did not take long before all the lily pads were fastened together, creating a single platform.

Frippery smiled. "Some may say that lily pads are not able to carry much, and this is generally true. Yet, when one pieces together a large grouping of them, and when one uses only the most supportive ones to be found anywhere in the Togetherwood, it is truly astonishing how strong a platform can be made. Why, you might even call it a boat!"

"I like boats!" Dax said. "Let's call it a boat."

"What is the Togetherwood?" Claire asked.

"Come again, Miss Claire?" Frippery answered.

"You mentioned that these are the best in the Togetherwood. Where is that? Where are we?"

Frippery's eyes became still. "Why, I am referring to our present location, to the ground we are standing on. This entire ecosystem, a complex network of rivers, an extensive shoreline, and a very dense forest. All of it together forms the Togetherwood. Where else could I be referring to?"

"It really is interesting to hear you explain this," Eleanor said.

Frippery blinked several times. "As much as I consider myself a curious mind, I really don't find anything remarkable about it. I am simply stating a fact about where we are. Regardless, we need not get carried away with tangents. I had been mentioning earlier the fact that we now have a boat to use."

"It just looks like a bunch of plants that got duct taped together," Claire said. "How will we even get it moving? It doesn't exactly have a sail attached to it, now does it?"

"Correct," Frippery answered. "This is why our star pupil Dax will need to keep swimming for us."

"Me?" he spoke with his ears pointed straight.

"Yes, Dax. You will swim with all of your might as you push against the boat, propelling us forward."

"I can do that!"

Frippery looked at Eleanor. "Will you please pick up this boat and place it in the water?"

She nodded and then slid it off the sand and into the water. She held it steadily while Frippery and Claire boarded it. When Eleanor finally got on, she felt the vessel move slightly, no doubt the result of holding so many passengers. Dax positioned himself behind the boat, ready to be its engine.

Frippery, beaming with a smile they had never seen, said, "Truly incredible! Let us make our way across!"

The motion of the boat was unsteady at first, swaying one way and then the other chaotically. But once they were away from the shore, it became quite steady. The deep blue water that flowed around them was darker now. All was quiet except for the sound of Dax kicking and panting. Eleanor reached her head over to see a series of splashes.

"Are you all right, Dax?"

"I am," he called between taking breaths. "I am all right. I like swimming!"

Claire, now rolled into a relaxed ball, said, "I like that you like swimming, Dax."

They continued crossing the pond in a tranquil mood. Eleanor, seated with her legs crossed, looked down at the dark green lily pads beneath her feet, which were supporting such a great amount of weight. So, she thought to herself, this place was called the Togetherwood. Why had she never heard of it in any of her classes at school? How was it connected to her hometown? The breeze blew her hair into her eyes. After she moved it out of the way, she realized she had forgotten her train of thought.

Frippery spoke suddenly, breaking the silence:

"Indeed. My life has been dedicated to research, exploration, and preparing the next generation to meet the world. But unfortunately, this year has not been easy for me, as I must prepare for retirement. As you by now know, I enjoy teaching and sharing my knowledge."

Eleanor, the only one listening, nodded solemnly without responding.

"It is not easy for me to consider the end of my career. My life has always been in the classroom. How can I ever consider a life without a class of pupils, a group of young minds eager to learn? Am I to spend my days simply hopping about, catching flies without a care? Such a life sounds horribly lacking." He turned his head to look at Eleanor. "I suppose this is why I have enjoyed assisting you three so much. As I look at my final semester of teaching, I am savoring each and every opportunity I get to teach others about the pond, the lily pads, the wonders of it all." He looked up at the blue sky. "Instructing you three today in how to create this boat has been such a very lovely joy for me."

Eleanor once more adjusted her hair. "We have certainly had a great time learning from you."

"In fact," he continued, "this day has taught me that success rewards the determined. Though Dax was unsure of the solution, he didn't give up."

"I will never give up!" Dax shouted from behind, gurgling water as he kicked.

"You three also taught me that, perhaps, I don't need a class of registered students in order to teach. Maybe I can teach after my retirement, even if it simply means helping someone cross the pond. After all, there is no limit to what lily pads can do."

"How can we thank you for your help?" Eleanor asked.

Frippery's eyes grew big with excitement. "The best way you can repay me is to never tire of learning."

Eleanor smiled. "We can do that."

"I suppose we can," Claire added.

At last, they approached the other sandy bank of the pond. Eleanor got off the boat as both Frippery and Claire jumped out of it. Dax slowly made his way around and promptly collapsed on the sand.

"Now I really need a nap," he said.

Frippery sat still. "I trust you will be able to proceed from here?"

"We should be ready," Eleanor answered. "You really have been very helpful in guiding us. Thanks again!"

"Yes, despite my intense doubts and reservations, you should be thanked," Claire said.

Beaming and making a small ribbit sound, Frippery replied, "I should be on my way, then. Safe travels to you all. Should you ever need anything else, I am never more than a hop from this pond!"

As he went away, Eleanor said, "Though that took us a bit of time, at least we made it across. Now we can continue on our way towards the ocean."

Claire looked at Dax, who was snoring loudly. "It may be true that we crossed the pond, but the fact is we don't have any idea where we are. Did you hear what he said? What is the Togetherwood?"

"Yes, that was strange," Eleanor said as her brows furrowed.

"One minute I'm taking a lovely cat nap, and the next I'm in a cardboard box, teleporting somewhere else completely."

For a moment, Dax snored even more loudly, which sounded like a plane passing by overhead.

"It is beautiful here, though, isn't it?" Eleanor answered with a smile as she gestured towards the pond behind them.

"Whatever it is, we need to get out of it. Who knows what will happen after the sun sets?"

"All we need to do is continue going. I know we will find another box on our way!"

"I insist we will never find a box again and that the cold, shadowy night is all that waits for us," Claire replied as she looked at her paws. "Whatever you say, though."

"I mean it," Eleanor replied as she walked over to Dax and lightly patted his head.

After making more bizarre noises, Dax opened his eyes. "What is it? Do you have a treat for me?"

"We are going to keep going," Eleanor said.

"Keep going? OK!"

He bolted away from them up the nearby path.

"Dax!" Eleanor called.

Dax skidded to a halt, his tail pointed. "Yeah?"

"I think it will be good for us to stay together."

"Oh, OK. That sounds like a good plan."

They walked along the path, which soon began to follow a strong river. It sprayed water droplets into the air as it deposited white foam on some round boulders.

"That is a good plan," Claire said to herself. "Now all we need is to know where we are."

4.
No Need to Sink in This River

Eleanor, Dax, and Claire traveled along the trail, tracing the curves of the river. The steady rushing sound of the water grew louder, as though it were another companion joining them. The trail had become less rough, the dirt more wet, the mud a darker shade of brown.

Claire's paws made no sound as she walked. "Dax," she began.

"Yeah?"

"What you did back there, getting all of those lily pads and helping that frog o—"

"I remember him! His name was Franklin."

"I'm sure it was. Anyway, it was great for you to do all of that, to be so unceasingly eager. However, I want to remind you not to overdo it."

"Huh?" he asked, appearing very confused.

"More than anything else, we want to get out of here. If you keep on being helpful and caring, at some point we might put ourselves in danger. Then no one will be happy."

"But Franklin was the one in danger! He needed our help. Right, Eleanor?"

Walking on Dax's other side, Eleanor paused for a moment and then answered, "We do want to be cautious, it is true." Then she turned to look at Claire. "But we also want to be brave and help others when we can. So, I suppose both of you are right."

"Hooray!" Dax cried.

"Don't expect me to help anyone," Claire grumbled.

Suddenly, they heard an unsettling sound. High-pitched and wailing, it was very loud. As Eleanor looked around, she was unable to locate where it was coming from.

"What on earth is that?" Claire sat still, covering her ears with her paws.

"I don't like it," Dax added.

Claire continued to search for the source of the noise. Then, all at once, there was no longer anything to be heard.

Dax sighed. Claire slowly placed her paws out of her ears.

"Well," she said, "At least that's over w—"

The agonized wailing resumed once more.

"Just as soon as I think I couldn't be more wretched," Claire continued. "Why won't it stop?"

"I wish I knew where it was coming from," Eleanor said. She turned her head quickly, looking up the trees, down at her feet, wincing as the sound grew even louder. Finally, having given up searching, she looked over at the river. Within the steady current of rushing water was a spot where many big bubbles were appearing and disappearing instantly. As she looked at it, she realized that the shrill sound was coming from it.

"I think that's it!" she shouted to the others while pointing her finger below.

All of the bubbles vanished as something broke the surface of the water. It was a light blue fish who stared at Eleanor with a troubled expression. A pause followed as no one spoke.

"Hello," Eleanor said, "Is t—"

"Don't bother me!" the fish shrieked in a high-pitched voice. "Can't anyone let a fish feel her sorrow in peace?" She turned away from the travelers and placed two fins beneath her eyes. She continued crying, her tears spraying as though out of a fountain.

Claire placed her paws in her ears once more and squinted her eyes. "I understand that being sad is difficult, but must she make these sounds?"

"It's really loud," Dax added.

Eleanor crouched down on her knees and looked up at the sky. Several more pockets of clouds were forming and drifting by. She then turned towards the fish, took a deep breath, and asked, "Is there anything we can do to help you?"

The fish slowly lowered her fins from her eyes and stopped sobbing. "Anything…to help?"

Eleanor nodded.

"Well, I…what's your name?"

"Me?" Eleanor pointed to herself.

"Yes, you. What's your name?"

She introduced herself along with Dax and Claire.

"OK," the fish answered, staring down at the water.

"What about you?" Eleanor continued. "What is your name?"

"Me? I….I…." She raised her fins towards her eyes. She breathed in and sniffled. Then she stared at Eleanor intently, neither blinking nor moving her head. She opened her mouth and whispered something inaudible under the sound of the river.

"What was that?" Eleanor asked with a smile.

"Freya," the fish repeated. "My name is Freya. But what's the point?"

"What do you mean?"

"What I mean is…what's the point? You can call me Freya, but does that mean you really know who I am? I don't even know who I am."

Eleanor's expression became puzzled. She turned towards Dax and Claire before saying, "It is wonderful to meet you, Freya. I was wondering if you might be able to tell us why it is that you feel so sad."

Freya sighed. "Do you really think you could possibly understand why I feel this way?"

"Maybe not completely. But I always like to listen."

"The reason I feel so much sadness is because I don't know where I went wrong."

"Did you make some sort of mistake?"

"Yes, I did. It was after I took a wrong turn. This river," she waved a fin to gesture behind her. "Is very, very long. All I was trying to do was make my way to the ocean, but I couldn't even do that right. This is the wrong way. I followed it all the way and ended up at a lake." She shook her head several times.

Eleanor said, "It's all right."

"How can it possibly be all right? I'll never find my way back! Now I will have to float here, lost forever."

"You could go ahead and take the correct way now," Claire suggested.

"It's true," Dax added.

"I just don't know what to do," Freya continued as though she hadn't heard her.

"Perhaps we should all work together, trace our way back up the river, and go in the right direction," Eleanor reasoned. "We are also trying to find the ocean. I am sure if we travel together, we can figure this out."

Freya slapped the water with her fin. "But what's the point? We're just…we're just going to mess up again."

It was then that Claire took a few steps forward, nearing the edge of the trail. "Hey, Freya," she said.

"What?"

Claire paused for a moment, as though deep in thought. Then she said, "I get it. Making a mistake is an unpleasant thing. It happens to everyone. I have made poor decisions and just wanted to roll up into a ball. In fact, I wouldn't mind doing that right now. I understand you may not want to try again. But would you at least be willing to help us?"

"Yeah!" Dax added, "Maybe afterward, we can all roll into a ball!"

Freya continued to stare at the water. "I suppose you three really do want to leave here. I...I guess I can help you."

"We really appreciate that you are willing," Eleanor said.

Freya nodded her head several times slowly. "I guess we should just get this over with already, then."

She turned around, lowered her head underwater, and swam upwards against the current.

"Where is she going so quickly?" Dax asked.

Freya broke the surface of the water a few meters up the river from them. She swam between two boulders and then suddenly came to a halt. Eleanor, Dax, and Claire made their way up the trail until they were next to her again.

"You sure are fast!" Dax exclaimed.

"Too fast for our own good," Claire added.

"It's true," Freya answered. "I am so fast that I always end up lost and alone," she sighed.

Eleanor placed her hand over her forehead, so she could better see up the river. In the distance she noticed a fork, a spot where the river split. Over there, the boulders were larger and the current raged more loudly. "We passed by that area earlier," she said.

"Makes sense," Claire said.

"That must be where I missed my turn," Freya said. "We need to go the other way at the fork."

"It's great that we were able to become oriented again so quickly," Eleanor said.

"Until I mess up again." Freya made a splash and disappeared into the water.

"Let's catch up to her!" Dax cried.

The sun was increasingly covering the trail with warm, bright rays as the morning wore on. The trail, wet from the river, reflected this sunshine with little glittering sprinkles of light like diamonds lining the path before them. Eleanor walked in front, her head turned studiously towards the river. Witnessing a line of bubbles shoot up against the current, she knew it was Freya swimming. Her jaw dropped in astonishment when the fish broke the surface of the water to leap over several enormous rocks. Freya swam gracefully and effortlessly, turning sharply, jumping, and diving, all in order to make her way up towards the fork. The trail of bubbles finally disappeared as Freya raised her head above the water, floating in one spot as she waited again for the others. It was a moment before Eleanor, Dax, and Claire caught up to her.

"Your swimming really is incredible, Freya," Eleanor said.

"So fast," Dax added.

"I suppose they're right," Claire muttered.

Freya turned around to look at them, and then lowered her head. "You keep saying that. I might be fast, but I never end up going anywhere. I always find a way to get lost."

"But we are on the right path now, aren't we?" Eleanor said with a bright smile.

"Let's go that other way," Dax said.

Freya raised her head, gazing at the fork in the river, the white spray of water misting up from the rocks. She disappeared beneath the water for a moment and then, with a massive splash, flew over several rocks, surfacing on the other side.

"Wow!" Dax exclaimed, his tail wagging quickly. "That was amazing!"

"But how does she expect us to follow her?" Claire asked.

"What do you mean?" Eleanor replied.

Claire sat still and gestured by tilting her head forward. "What I mean is how are we going to follow this fish when she is dancing around in the water, and we are stranded on land?"

Eleanor realized what she meant. In order to follow Freya along the new path, they would all need to cross the river. Hearing Freya sigh from not far off, Eleanor replied, "Surely there is something we can do." She walked towards the edge of the river and placed her hand in the water, delighted by its chill.

"Yeah!" Dax called. "We can get over there."

"You two are very inspiring," Claire said, "but do you have even the faintest inkling how we might get across this river?"

"I have an inkling!" Dax shouted. He sprinted off the edge of the trail, flinging his head forward and creating a spectacular splash. Eleanor and Claire watched as the water current pummeled him continuously. Unaffected, he sprinted up the side of one boulder and leapt off it, causing an even bigger splash. Freya was frozen in place, simply watching him.

"I can make it," he said as he used his front paws to climb the edge of the trail on the other side. With all of his strength, he pulled himself up. He suddenly lost his grip and fell back into the river. Eleanor heard Claire faintly cackle behind her. Once more, Dax pulled himself onto land, and with a burst of power he stood up. Victorious, he shook his entire fur coat, spraying droplets of water in every direction.

He smiled. "I did it."

"You did," Freya said, "but it doesn't matter. There's no way for the other two to make it over."

"She's right," Claire agreed.

Eleanor placed her hands on her sides. "I am certain there is a way for us to cross this river."

"What did you have in mind?" Claire asked while staring at her, her tail wagging slowly like a pendulum.

Eleanor frowned as she looked around. She walked away from the river, back towards the trees.

"Is she leaving us?" Freya asked. "Everyone always leaves me at some point," she sighed.

Claire, brow furrowed, watched as Eleanor suddenly appeared, holding two long, slender tree branches in each hand.

"And what are you planning to do with those?" Claire asked.

Eleanor tapped the branches together twice. "These must have fallen from one of those trees. With these, I can keep myself supported while I get across."

"It will never work," Freya said, still floating in the river.

Eleanor smiled once more. "You two just need to have a little more faith in things. Watch!" She stepped past Claire and approached the edge of the trail. The roar of the river was very audible, jets of blue water flowing powerfully over the rocks. On her left shoulder, she could feel a slight breeze.

"You can do it!" Dax called from the other side. "I did it, and now you can do it."

Carefully, she extended her hand to place the right branch into the river. She felt it scrape the rocky ground beneath the water's surface. After maneuvering and adjusting it for a moment, she was able to sense that the bottom of the branch was in a stable position. Then she made the same motion with her left hand, finding she could secure this branch much more quickly. She raised her head upwards and saw a rock resting in the water between her two outstretched arms. With sharp focus, she looked to see which part of the boulder was the most flat and then, feeling the wind pick up behind her, stepped out with her left foot. She felt it make contact with the rock. Both of her arms wobbled slightly as the branches tilted to help her maintain her balance. After her other foot was also safely on the rock, she giggled.

"It's working after all, isn't it?" she exclaimed.

The roar of the river was even more thunderous now, like a pair of lungs that breathed in without ever stopping. Droplets of water landed in Eleanor's head. She blinked several times and shook her head from side to side. Still holding the two tree branches tightly, she looked forward and saw several more boulders. Unsure of which one to trust with her feet, Eleanor paused for a moment.

"You should use this one," a voice called from the right.

Eleanor turned her head and saw Freya pointing with her fin at another rock which was close by.

"Are you sure?"

"Yes, I am. You will probably fall in, but at least this one is flat."

Why, Eleanor wondered, was her attitude so relentlessly negative? Why was she so mean to herself? It didn't make any sense to her. Her balance soon began to shift, and she was no longer able to wonder. She once more flung the two tree branches forward until they became secure with the rough ground beneath the river. Then, with another hop, she made her way onto the new rock.

"Thank you, Freya! I didn't fall after all."

"I guess I was wrong about that." She made a slight splash with her left fin.

A voice called from behind, "I know you're trying to not drown, but is there any chance we can hurry this up a little, please?"

"I'm almost there, Claire!" Eleanor answered.

She continued in this way, following guidance from Freya when necessary, until she arrived on the other side and stood next to Dax.

Claire's green eyes became small. "The thing about being a cat..." she suddenly jumped onto a rock. She instantly turned and jumped to the next one, and then the next one, until she was across the river and with the others. "...is that you know how to jump." She closed her eyes, clearly content.

"I guess you all made it over," Freya said. "I was a fool for thinking you couldn't do it. How could I have thought that?"

"There is no need to be too hard on yourself," Eleanor replied, noticing how upset she appeared. "All of us are wrong sometimes, but the good news is that we made it." She pointed with her right hand. "Should we continue now and follow this river?"

Freya nodded slowly and then continued swimming with the current. Eleanor, Dax, and Claire went along the trail which stretched ahead of them into the horizon. The sounds of birds chirping mixed with the many swaying tree branches. Every now and then Eleanor would turn to look down and see the line of bubbles indicating where Freya had swum.

Up ahead, nestled by the trail, was a patch of flowers which were white with small streaks of red. Eleanor stopped walking, leaned forward to pluck a flower stem, and breathed in through her nose deeply. She closed her eyes and smiled. Turning towards Dax, she said, "It really smells lovely."

"I want to smell," Dax replied.

"I'll pass," Claire added.

Holding another stem in her left hand, Eleanor lowered the flower down so that Dax's black, round nose pressed against it. For a moment, he sat still and said nothing.

"Well?" Claire asked.

Dax hopped in the air twice, water droplets still flying from his black fur. "What a nice smell! I really like the way they smell!"

"So you're saying they were passable, then?"

"I think he's saying more than that," Eleanor said, still smiling.

A splashing sound caused the three travelers to turn their heads back towards the river. Freya's snout floated just above the blue ripples. "Is something delaying you? You aren't leaving me, are you?"

"We're not," Claire answered. "We just needed to attend to something very important."

"It is important," Dax agreed. "These flowers smell unbelievable."

Freya lowered her head down towards the water. "Do they?"

Eleanor said, "They really are delightful. I apologize that we can't share it with you, with you being down in the water and all…"

"It's fine," Freya said. "I'm used to being left out. Don't worry about me."

"I know, I hate feeling that way," Claire said.

"You do?"

Claire nodded.

"Should we keep going?" Freya asked, looking at the water.

Traveling alongside the river, the air fresh and crisp, Eleanor smiled. To her left was a wall of trees, each one a thin trunk with crooked branches twisting in every direction. Across the river, there were gentle, sloping hills full of grass that shook with the wind. At the top of the hills were even more trees. Looking straight ahead, there seemed to be no end to either the river or the trail; only bends and twists in the water greeted her. Eleanor looked down at her feet and sighed as she started to wonder what her family was doing.

"Those flowers remind me of the ones in my father's garden," she said. "I can recall him having a patch of white ones that looked just like the ones we saw. Even though the flowers in our garden don't have any red streaks I really do think they look similar."

Dax was breathing rapidly like an engine, his tongue dangling. "That's pretty interesting. I wonder if they are the same flowers!"

"I don't think so," Eleanor replied.

"They're not the same," Claire said. "If the ones at your home look different, then they are different."

Eleanor raised her head up and walked with bigger steps. "The garden my father has at home is wonderful. He has plants and flowers of every color and type imaginable. I remember when I was younger, how he would have me pull weeds for him and explain to me everything he was growing."

Freya's head appeared above the water with a small splash. "Are you three still there?"

Eleanor didn't seem to hear her. "I really did treasure spending time in the garden. Of course, I also spent plenty of time running through it with my brother when we would chase each other."

"I didn't know you had a brother," Dax said. "That's awesome!"

Eleanor nodded. "He is four years older than me. Sometimes he will bother me, but I do think he is a good brother. His name is Edward."

"What is your brother like?"

Her face lit up. "He is kind, patient, maybe a bit of a troublemaker. But I know that he is-"

"WHY DID TODAY HAVE TO BE LIKE THIS?!"

Past the edge of the trail in the river came a loud wailing sound, which alternated with sobbing. Floating in place in the water, Freya wiped both her eyes with her fins as small streams of tears poured into the river. The travelers waited in silence. Eleanor felt astonished. What could be causing her to cry so suddenly? Just as soon as it seemed that she was at last composed, more sobbing would soon ensue.

Eleanor walked over towards the edge of the trail and crouched down on her knees. "Was it something I said? Did I —"

"I DIDN'T ASK FOR THIS!! I DIDN'T WANT IT TO BE THIS WAY!" she lowered her head and a sniffling sound followed.

Dax's ears slowly lowered down until they were flat. Eleanor looked back at the others, shrugging.

Claire, who had been licking her right paw and grooming her back, rose up off the ground, silently walked over to where Eleanor was crouched, and spoke with an even tone:

"You don't have to talk to us if you don't want to."

The sounds of crying ceased. The river itself, somehow, seemed more calm.

Claire sat down and then said, "We all know life can be difficult, you know."

Freya swam towards the cat, raising her head high above the current. She answered, "But how could you ever understand the things that have brought me such overwhelming sadness? Can you understand the unbearable burden of my soul?"

"Probably not."

"You can't?"

Claire lowered her tail and blinked several times. "You're a fish. I'm a cat. We are different, which seems pretty simple to me. If you want to talk to us, feel free to do so. These other two," she tilted her head to look at Eleanor and Dax briefly, "can be awfully…positive about things. But I can promise you

I won't try to brighten anything for you at all. So if you want to talk to us, it's up to you."

Freya raised her fin and wiped away some tears. "That's beautiful."

"Well?"

"Fine," Freya answered. "You might not know this, but I can be a very sorrowful fish."

"I think we knew that."

"Regardless, the reason I am even more sad today of all days is that one year ago on this very day my own brother Frederick was eaten by a wolf." Freya raised her fins and cried, though this time it was quieter and did not last as long before she continued. "Frederick and I were swimming in this very river when he was too close to the edge of the shore. I looked up and saw that dark gray fur. Oh, it just...IT JUST HURTS!"

"I'm sure it does," Claire said plainly.

Eleanor stepped forward. "I didn't mean to remind you of such a sad day. I was only remembering something that came from those flowers. I would like to apologize, Freya. You have been so very helpful to us, and I would never want to remind you of losing someone. Will you forgive me?"

Freya lowered her head and did not speak.

"...Freya?"

"Why is it that you get to have your brother, and yet I must live this way?" her voice was soft now. "We were two happy fish, swimming up and down this river, not concerned about anything. Now he's gone forever."

"I...um..." Eleanor found she had no words. Why did she have to feel guilty for having her brother?

"We don't have any good answers," Claire replied. "Difficult things happen, and that's just how it is."

Eleanor added, "But please know that we care about you."

"We're really lost," Dax said. "We are dealing with a difficult thing, too!"

For several seconds, no one spoke, and it felt as though the rushing currents of the river were louder than ever before. It sounded like a steady hush, a sigh from the forest.

"What do we do now?" Dax asked. The others gazed at him.

Freya looked up and away from the water. "I guess we need to keep going, don't we?"

"Are you sure you want to continue?" Eleanor asked.

"I think so."

Claire sat still. "You might not be able to change what happened a year ago, but I really hope you choose to help us."

"I don't want you to be lost here," Freya answered. "Well, let's continue, then."

The river was wider now, the current more forceful, a steady spray of white mist falling. There were more rocks and stones lining the riverbed, some round and smooth, others rough and jagged. Eleanor noticed that there was a wall of pebbles lining the bottom of the water, little stones that were dark blue, gray, and light turquoise. When she next looked back up, she saw something striking.

Before them, the river split evenly in two directions. Eleanor looked to the right, and saw the faint silhouette of mountains in the background, like the first streaks of paint on a canvas. To the left were fewer trees, the water flowing slightly downwards as though sinking into the earth. She stood motionless.

"Well," Claire began, "any ideas?"

Floating gently in the water, her head now poking out of the river, Freya answered, "You want to go to the ocean, right?"

They nodded.

"Whatever way you go will not really matter, since nothing really matters." She raised her fin to the left. "But the ocean will be this way."

"You are so very helpful," Eleanor beamed. She hoped that her compliments would for once be received.

"Anyone could do what I do," Freya replied. She made the turn and continued swimming.

Eleanor, Dax, and Claire proceeded along the path, noticing that the trees were becoming more sparse and the grass less green. Smiling, Eleanor turned to see a small orange tail sway through the air slowly next to a continuously wagging black tail.

Already, the travelers were faced with another fork in the river, this time with three different streams to choose from.

"What do you think?" Eleanor looked at Freya.

Freya looked at one stream and then another. "We need to take the middle one. You three should be able to hop over the water and follow the path over there. It isn't very wide."

Taking turns, Eleanor and Claire jumped over the stream. Dax simply ran into the water and plowed through to the other side. Together again, they followed Freya's instruction and continued onward.

Eleanor was beginning to worry that they had possibly made an incorrect selection of where to go. What if they should have turned right at the first fork in the stream? Trying to trust Freya, she did not have long to wonder about this before they were presented, once more, with a fork in the river. Shooting off in five separate directions, Dax said, "I like having lots of options!"

Claire sat still and placed a paw to the top of her head.

Eleanor laughed nervously. "Do you still know where to go, Freya?"

"I should." Freya's eyes squinted. "Yes, I do know which one to take. For once, maybe I won't mess something up. Where we need to go is t-"

At that moment, the travelers heard a howling sound from not far off. Haunted and anguished, the howl went on for several seconds and then vanished just as quickly as it appeared.

Eleanor scratched the back of her head. "Surely it i—"

"THAT'S IT!! I NEED TO LEAVE!" Freya shouted.

"I don't think we need to be afraid of anything," Dax said.

"It can't eat all of us," Claire added.

But Freya was swimming away in the opposite direction, each splash like a rock falling into the river, unleashing ripples. "FIRST IT CAME FOR MY BROTHER!! AND NOW, ONE YEAR LATER, IT'S GOING TO FINISH WHAT IT STARTED AND EAT ME TOO!"

Eleanor, Dax, and Claire looked around, but Freya was nowhere to be seen.

"She seems really scared," Dax said.

"Where did she go?" Eleanor asked.

"She went backwards, over there," Claire pointed with a paw. "I want to speak with her again."

They turned around and walked in the opposite direction of the flowing river. Eleanor, who normally walked in front, was surprised when she saw Claire trot quickly up ahead of her. Eleanor was wondering where, exactly, Freya had swum off to. How far backwards would the three of them need to walk in order to be reunited with her? Would they even find her?

Though faint at first, Eleanor, Dax, and Claire all began to notice a familiar sound. They continued to follow the path, hearing the wailing sound that could only indicate Freya was crying nearby.

"That must be her!" Dax exclaimed.

Eleanor folded her arms. "Is there anything we can do? She seems inconsolable. If only we could help."

"I wish she felt less sad," Dax said.

Now the sounds of weeping were so loud that Eleanor placed her hands in her ear. She stared at the river and saw Freya huddled beneath an overturned log.

"Freya," Claire called.

Still the weeping continued.

"Freya!" she shouted.

At once, she lowered her fins away from her eye. "Wh-what?"

"You told me about your past. I wanted to tell you a little about mine. OK?"

Freya nodded slightly.

"I don't remember very much about being a kitten, but I know I was born in my litter and my dad was nowhere to be found. It was me, my two sisters, and my mother. I have never met him."

"Your dad was gone? That's really sad."

"I was very sad, yes. At the time, we were living on the street, in a cul-de-sac. Not the one where Dax was."

"There are a lot of cul-de-sacs in the world," Dax explained.

Claire continued, "We all got along well enough. But that all changed when the coyote came through the neighborhood. I remember my mother mentioned that there was one on the prowl and that we should be careful. We thought we were being cautious enough, but we had no house to hide in, no owners to watch out for us. One evening when I returned from hunting moles...I..." She came to a halt again, looked at the dirt, and sniffed several times.

Dax ran over and wrapped her in a tight embrace. "I don't want you to feel sad, too!"

Freya floated silently in the water.

Claire thrust Dax away from her, and he landed on his back. "No need for that." She wiped her face with her paw several times. "When I came back to see my mother and the rest of the

64

family, they were nowhere to be seen. I can only assume what happened to them. I then spent a few days wandering. Soon I came across a certain house that always seemed to leave out a bowl of milk for me each evening. I visited the front porch of the house every day to enjoy the treat. Though I was alone and miserable, it did feel nice to think that maybe someone else cared about me."

"We do care about you," Dax said.

"I ended up being adopted by Dax's owners, and proceeded to live a quiet life of comfortable, leisurely boredom. Well, at least until I ended up here." She turned to look directly at Freya. "The reason I am telling you this is not to show you that I know how you feel. Rather, it is to let you know that it is possible to move past some of the horrific things that happen to us. I know you feel sad, Freya, but maybe there is something better waiting for you. Maybe there is no need to sink in this river. Will you help lead us out of here?"

A pause followed. Freya lifted her fins to her eyes to wipe them once more. The blue water of the river moved through her, but she floated perfectly still. "What happened to Frederick…I never knew how to recover from it." She looked at Claire. "But maybe, just maybe, you are right. You were able to be strong and keep going. Maybe I can, too!"

"You certainly can," Eleanor said with a smile.

Freya's head shook slightly. "He wouldn't want me to be like this. Frederick would want me to be enjoying my life. I may mess a lot of things up and be an emotional wreck, but I will give it a chance. I will help you leave here…for my brother."

"Wonderful," Eleanor replied. "Thank you!"

"Hooray!" Dax hopped in the air.

"I'm glad," Claire said.

With a speed and sense of resolution the others had never before seen, Freya charged down the river, jumping over rocks and logs, turning sharply as needed, creating countless splashes. The others ran with all their might to keep up, the sound of Dax's panting filling the air. Eleanor looked down at her feet as she ran to see dust collecting on her shoes. Only a few minutes later, they once more were at the point where the river split in five directions.

"Which way do we go?" Claire asked.

Surveying each choice intently, Freya whispered to herself, "Closed lake...closed lake...takes way too long...yes," she extended her fin. "This is the fastest way to the ocean."

The sound of a howl caused several perched birds nearby to fly off.

Freya shook slightly. She motioned with her fins as though preparing to swim off, but then she looked at the others, her eyes eventually resting on Claire's.

"We need to go this way," she said, pointing with a fin.

"I'm ready!" Dax proclaimed. He jumped off the path into the river and proceeded to flail his legs haphazardly.

Freya giggled.

"Perhaps not the most impressive stroke you've seen," Claire said.

Eleanor stared at the water intently. "Let's go ahead and follow him." She worked her way over and across the water to land on the new trail. Claire leapt over the water and joined her.

No longer afraid, Freya helped guide them at two more splits in the river. Later on, they followed the new tributary, which grew wider than they ever before had seen it. The water flowed freely, reflecting the blue sky and the bright sun above. Trees lined the sides of the river on both sides, standing over it as though protecting it.

Freya jumped out of the river and made a big splash as she struck the water once more. "I remember this spot. From now on, there will be no more forks in the river. It will be one direction until you reach the ocean."

"That is excellent news," Eleanor said. "We are close!"

Freya drifted over towards the river bank, surfacing next to Dax. "You three really helped me out. Thank you for showing me how to not be so scared. Thank you…for making Frederick happy."

"We are happy to do it," Eleanor replied. "Without your help, we never would have made it this far."

She turned towards Claire. "Thank you for telling me your story."

"You're welcome."

Freya gave a very small smile. "I need to go and visit my little sister. She lives on the next tributary over. I just hope she still wants to see me."

"Of course she does!" Dax shouted just before his head sank beneath the water.

Still smiling, Freya leapt into the air, made a splash, and disappeared from view.

When Dax reappeared, Eleanor said, "I really think you were wonderful, Claire, with how you spoke to Freya. She really listened to you!"

"Sometimes I meet others who make sense to me," she said, shrugging.

Eleanor smiled as she wiped droplets from her face. "I suppose all we need to do now is continue along this river to arrive at the ocean."

"That's great news," Dax replied as he surfaced. "We are moving so fast!"

"We are," she replied with a smile. "Let's keep going!"

Following the steady currents, Eleanor, Dax, and Claire continued on their way. Eleanor looked over at Claire. Indeed, she had been mistaken to assume that her snide remarks and astute observations meant she was uncaring. Eleanor felt a deep admiration for her, honored to be traveling with her and Dax.

5.
A Peace Treaty in the Estuary

After a while of traveling in silence, Eleanor looked up and was struck by how cold the air had become. She opened her mouth and thought she could taste salt on it. Dax now walked to her right and Claire on her left.

"I think we may be approaching the shore," she began.

"Not that it will help us in any way," Claire answered. "Whether I'm stuck in a tree or floating in the middle of the ocean, I'm still stranded in some place called the Togetherwood with no hope of ever being found."

"I like the ocean," Dax said. "I think it's great! I like to run out at the big waves and hit them."

"What happens after you hit the waves?" Claire asked.

Dax continued to pant, his tongue hanging out of his mouth as he thought. "That's when I get flipped upside down. I get water in my nose!"

"What about after that?"

"Then I go run back out and hit another wave," he answered. "I do it again! It's great!"

"I also like to swim," Eleanor said while brushing her hair out of her eyes. "I don't think we will have time to do more of that, though."

"Why not?"

"Because," Eleanor replied with a smile, "I think right now it is more important that we stay on land when we arrive at the beach. From there, we should be able to see where the next box is."

"Maybe there is a box underwater," Claire suggested. "I'm sure if he does enough somersaults in the crashing waves, he'll find it."

"I can find it!" Dax exclaimed.

Walking alongside the river, they approached the top of a slope where the grass swayed in the breeze. Eleanor placed her hand near her forehead and was delighted by what she saw below. The river, bending and twisting, eventually opened up and fed into the vast, open ocean. She felt awe as she gazed out at the sea gradually touching the sky, the different shades of blue coming together wonderfully. To her right, she saw that both Dax and Claire were seated.

"Wow," Dax said, his eyes big. "Water is a beautiful thing."

"It is a lovely estuary, isn't it?" Eleanor said.

"Huh?"

"I don't think he knows that word," Claire explained.

"Oh," Eleanor replied. "Sorry about that. I remember learning about estuaries in one of my books at school. They are in the area near where a river feeds into the ocean. There are usually multiple streams, and the entire system can be quite complex."

"That's great!" he exclaimed." I am so happy to be in a complex estuary."

Claire curled into a ball. "Water in the ocean, water in the river, none of it is going to help us get back home."

"Our next step will be to go down towards the sand. Then we will be able to t-"

"Look at that!" Dax exclaimed, hopping in the air several times while staring at the sky.

"Ugh, what is it now?" Claire asked.

"Look at it! Look at it!"

Her hand still at her forehead, Eleanor tilted her head up. The clear sky, occasionally obscured by clouds, seemed empty to her as she looked around.

"I don't think I see anything, Dax," she said. "Would you be able t-"

"Over there! They're flying so fast, like spaceships!"

"I don't care what it is," Claire said." I just want to keep going, without any distractions or excitement."

It was then that Eleanor was able to see it. Soaring through the sky, moving steadily, were thirteen ducks in a V-shaped formation. They flew fearlessly. Eleanor found herself especially captivated by the one flying in front all on his own. She wondered what it might feel like, to move through the sky at such a high speed and lead others.

"It looks to me like they are headed towards the river," she said. "I think they are lowering their altitude."

"Can we go see?" Dax pleaded. "Let's go see them!"

He sprinted off at once, jumping over the edge of the slope, rolling and sliding his way down near the riverbank.

"He always needs to do that, doesn't he?" Claire said while stretching her front legs.

"Perhaps if we go and join him," Eleanor reasoned, "we might find someone else who can help us."

The river felt even wider to Eleanor when they reunited with Dax down below. Looking out, she was struck by how the wind scraped against the top of the rippling currents.

"I don't think I see the ducks anywhere here," Eleanor said. "Perhaps we lost sight of them?"

"Over there!" Dax exclaimed while pointing his paw.

Several dozen meters away, marching in a single-file line, were the thirteen ducks. Each of them raised their left webbed foot at the exact same moment, and then in turn raised the right webbed foot. They were moving next to the river, quacking in a steady rhythm. As Eleanor looked more intently, she realized that the duck marching in front wore a hollowed-out wooden bowl on his head. Giving no notice at all, he came to a halt, turned around, and spoke with a booming, commanding voice:

"Bills up!"

"Our bills are up!" the others responded.

"Tails straight!" he continued.

"Our tails are straight, too!"

A pause followed, and then the leader said, "Wings loose."

The other ducks all spread their webbed feet out and flapped their wings, relaxed. Hoping to observe them more, Eleanor took several steps forward, hiding behind a rock. She watched as they spoke to one another. She found it marvelous how they were capable of showing such discipline and coordination. Just as she pulled herself back away from the rock, she heard a voice call out:

"An intruder, sir!"

"Where do you see it, Private?" the leader duck asked with a firm voice.

"Over there, Captain!" he pointed with a wing.

Eleanor did not have time to run or hide, for the next moment she looked up she saw the leader standing attentively in front of her. He placed his right wing to his helmet and saluted Eleanor.

"Who goes there?" he asked.

Fear and panic seized her as she felt her heart beating rapidly. She spent several seconds thinking of how to respond.

"We will save you, Eleanor!" Dax's voice called from nearby.

Running at full speed, he jumped over the leader, performed a chain of somersaults, and crashed into a nearby log.

"Maybe I will instead," Claire added, sauntering slowly towards them. "It seems like you have this under control, though, Dax."

Confused, the leader looked at Dax, Claire, and then finally at Eleanor. "I do not know who you are," he began, "but I need to know your loyalties. What brings you out here on duck soil?"

"We're loyal to Eleanor," Dax said, nodding at her.

Eleanor wiped sweat from her forehead. "I must apologize. We did not mean to intrude on duck soil. All we were hoping to do is pass through here on our way to the shore."

"Identify yourself."

Eleanor introduced herself and the others.

"Roger that," the duck replied. He stood up even more straight than before and made another salute. "You can refer to me as Captain David Drake. I am the head soldier of this unit."

"Did you hear that?" Dax asked. "He said he's a captain. That's incredible!"

Captain Drake made the slightest of nods. "Affirmative. I completed four tours in this estuary, leading up to Operation Riverbank Robbery. Now I lead this division."

"Can you give us a tour of the shore?" Claire asked.

"It sounds like you have an impressive history," Eleanor continued. "I'm sure you have had a lot of amazing experiences in your military service."

One of the other ducks was now standing next to Captain Drake. "Sir, are these civilians hostile?"

"Negative, Private. They are unarmed and show no sign of training or tactical knowledge."

"I think he's right," Dax said, his mouth hanging open as he panted.

"You can insult us as much as you want," Claire snapped, "but we need to keep moving." She turned towards Eleanor. "Right?"

"Yes," she replied. "I think we will keep going and not delay you in your operation."

But as she took a step past the boulder and towards the glassy water, several more troops appeared and formed a wall, blocking her.

"She's attempting to enter the battlefield, sir," one of them said.

Taking several steps towards her, Captain Drake said, "I understand that you three are civilians. Unfortunately, you cannot be authorized to pass through this checkpoint at this time."

"And why is that?" Claire asked, her tail slowly swaying.

Standing up straight, he replied, "In approaching the shore, you are attempting to enter a combat zone."

"Are we fighting someone?" Dax asked.

"The 2nd Duck Division is presently engaged in combat with a local outfit."

"Wow!"

Captain Drake waddled towards the river, placing his wings at his side in a formal display. "It has been a brutal campaign. For days now we have been clashing with a battalion of beavers on the other end of the estuary, commanded by a Brigadier Betty."

"It sounds like a serious situation," Eleanor said. "I'm sure it has been challenging for you."

"Affirmative. The past few days have seen us fight for several meters of territory only to need to give it back hours later. I have helped us carry out numerous air strikes."

"Why are you fighting them?" Claire asked.

Captain Drake tilted his head. "Did not copy that. Please repeat."

"Why are you leading a group of ducks to fight some beavers?"

"Do not show disrespect to a superior," one of the other troops proclaimed. "We do not question his orders."

"We are not intending to show disrespect," Eleanor reassured. "I think my friend was only trying to understand the situation, as she wonders if there might be a better way to work through a conflict than by fighting."

"I didn't care to hear your answer that much, really," Claire said to Captain Drake.

But he did not stop surveying the rest of the estuary. "The story of this war, of such a bitter conflict, is not one that can be quickly relayed. What I can say at this moment is that our enemy, a ruthless one, is plotting our defeat. Brigadier Betty knows no end to her cruelty, her longing for undue power. If we did not put up our resistance, the estuary would surely fall to the beavers before this coming sunset. Such a course of action cannot be allowed."

Another duck approached Captain Drake. "Sir, we have received the intelligence you were waiting for."

"On with it, Lieutenant."

His beak shook slightly. "As you know, we deployed a unit earlier this morning to approach the beaver headquarters by water and observe them."

"And?"

"It appears that Brigadier Betty and her soldiers have been adding to their stronghold."

"Are they building a dam?" Dax asked.

The two ducks turned to look at him. The lieutenant responded, "Yes, in civilian terms, it is a dam. Anyway, sir, our spy confirmed that the beaver headquarters has doubled in size since sunrise. At this rate, it will only be a matter of time before they secure that river, taking back another major section of the estuary."

"Unallowable!" Captain Drake declared, stomping the sandy riverbank. "Yet…very respectable." He turned to face the other troops and resumed speaking in a bold, intense voice. "Did you hear that, 2nd Duck Division? The beavers think they can gnaw off a few trees and take this water away from us. Now, are we going to let them do that?"

"No, sir!" they all cried at once.

"Are we going to migrate and fly south from here out of fear?"

"No, sir!"

"Well, then, what are we going to do?"

A pause followed as no one spoke.

Captain Drake shook his head to the side several times while looking at the ground. "A soldier with no plan is no one fit for my squad." He marched several steps towards the duck on the left end of the line and spoke to him. "What's your name, young fowl?"

"My name is Roy, sir."

"Very well. Now then, what are we going to do to stop the beavers from capturing the estuary, Roy?"

"I think we need to fly over the dam and ambush them, sir."

"What else?"

"Perhaps we could also engage them from the water as well."

"What else?"

Roy stood straight, his beady eyes unblinking.

"I think I know what else," Dax whispered to Claire.

"I'm sure you do," she whispered back. "Maybe you should join them, being the excellent flier that you are."

"I don't know how to fly."

"I really hope others aren't talking," Captain Drake announced, "because the last thing this division needs during a strategic crisis is socializing."

He waddled over to Dax and stood in front of him. "State your name, dog."

"Dax. My name is Dax!"

"Understood. Are you able to answer my question, Dax? Are you able to share with the other soldiers here what we are missing in our plan if we intend to storm the beaver fortress?"

Dax spun in a circle as though chasing his tail. "We need to run over there, real fast! Then we can-"

"I hope you will forgive our friend," Eleanor cut in. "I know he can be eager to share what he is thinking, but we don't want to participate in planning violence."

"But I do want to participate! I want to be a soldier!"

"Miss," Captain Drake said to Eleanor, "I certainly hope he joins us because your furry friend here might be a better tactician than all my other troops combined."

"I want to be a tactician!" Dax continued.

"They really will recruit anyone, won't they?" Claire said.

Captain Drake turned to face the others. "Let that be a lesson to the rest of you. We are going to take back this dam, striking on three fronts. You four over there," he pointed with a wing, "will take to the skies and provide us with aerial coverage. When you hear my quack, you will dive down. You four," he pointed with his other wing, "will operate on water. You will sail out towards the middle of the river. Again, when you hear my quack, approach the dam and monitor all escape routes. We cannot allow any of them to try to flee. The rest of us will move along this riverfront and board the dam on webbed foot... or paw or foot. Have I made the plan clear?"

"Yes, sir!"

"Bills up!"

"Our bills are up!"

"Tails straight!"

"Our tails are straight, too!"

Captain Drake stood still for a moment. He then raised a wing to his wooden helmet as a salute. "Quackity-quack!" he yelled.

"Quackity-quack!" the others echoed as they saluted.

Eleanor folded her hands. "Though we really are impressed by how organized you are, Claire and I will not be fighting. We hope no one is hurt."

Captain Drake turned to face her. "Roger that, Miss. I am confident that we all have the same hope. Now, then, let's just hope that the beavers don't force the situation to become too violent."

Eleanor watched as the row of ducks, moving in single file, approached the riverbank. One by one they jumped towards the water but immediately flapped their wings, propelling themselves until they ascended up into the sky. It was only seconds before they disappeared into the clear blue horizon. Eleanor saw, too, how the other group entered the dark blue water, their webbed feet disappearing as they hovered in the current. They then drifted off in the same direction as the airborne ducks. With Dax walking on her left side and Claire her right, Eleanor followed the row of troops marching several meters ahead. Captain Drake was in the front, taking each step decisively and with confidence.

"No one wants there to be war," he began, "but sometimes our enemy leaves us with no choice."

"Really?" Claire responded. "It sure seems to me like you enjoy what you're doing."

"The Togetherwood is a region that has always known conflict," he continued. "When I was a duckling, I saw how battle shaped my father into being the hero he was. As colonel, he saw multiple tours up and down this very estuary." He raised his bill slightly, as though looking over the edge of the river. "I know that without the efforts of our division no civilian anywhere will be safe or able to live a life of freedom. We are the only line of defense that can protect our fellow citizens from tyranny and brutality. Is that right, troops?"

"It is right!" the other marching soldiers exclaimed.

Eleanor walked with her hands at her sides. "It sounds like you have certainly made many sacrifices in service of others. Though I detest violence, I do think that deserves appreciation."

"Yeah," Dax added. "You ducks are really cool!"

"Your praise has no place in this," Captain Drake continued. "We are only fulfilling our duty to serve. Nothing more, and nothing less."

"Don't worry, I will be sure I don't give you any praise," Claire said.

"Brigadier Betty and I grew up here on this very river. Before we both enlisted, you would be correct to call us friends. However, once she was recruited and joined the beaver forces, I knew there was no way I would ever maintain cordial relations with her."

"Why is that?" Eleanor asked.

Marching steadily, Captain Drake paused for a moment before responding. "Betty believed that in serving their cause, she would be able to improve our fair estuary. But the efforts of our enemies could not be further from noble. Isn't that right, troops?"

"Yes, it is right!" they called.

"They have done nothing but spread their lies of being better than all other animals in the Togetherwood. They seek power not to serve, but in order to subjugate the rest of us. This is not something that the division can allow."

"It makes sense to me," Dax said.

Eleanor scratched her head. "I understand you are hoping to protect the estuary, and you even think the beavers are harmful. But I wonder if perhaps there is a misunderstanding in all of this. Maybe they are not quite as evil as it seems?"

Captain Drake stopped marching and turned to face her. "You would do well to not speak out of line, Miss. I don't know where you are receiving your intelligence, but it is false. Moreover, it threatens the morale of the division. Either you will desist, or you will run the full length of this river carrying a boulder in each hand." He stared at her without blinking. "Is that clear?"

Eleanor felt a bead of sweat on her forehead as she slowly nodded.

A nearby duck said, "Sir, we are approaching the enemy headquarters now."

"Very good, Lieutenant. Confirm its coordinates."

"Approximately fifty meters due west, sir."

"Roger." He turned his head to look towards the dam, a massive bundle of log strips lumped together in one spot. "Are you ready to take back our estuary?"

"We are ready!" they called.

"Will you fight until all of your feathers are ruffled?"

"We will, sir!"

"I don't have any feathers!" Dax called before turning to look at his tail. "I have fur."

Captain Drake nodded one time. "It is time for us to engage."

He tilted his head upward so that he was looking at the several troops flying in a circle around the dam. With great force he exclaimed, "Quack, quack, quackity-quack!"

Eleanor heard the ducks in the sky echo back the same sound.

To her right, she noticed the others floating on the river water quack in the same way.

How, she wondered, could the situation have come to this? Why was there a need to fight, and why did it appear impossible for there to be reconciliation? Though she felt discouraged by what she heard Captain Drake say she still held on to the hope for peace.

Immediately, the flying soldiers up above dove towards the dam, zooming towards it at an incredible speed. The ducks in the water swam towards it as well. Finally, the rest walking nearby on land repeated the quacking and sprinted off.

Captain Drake said, "An operation without the captain leading the charge is no operation at all." He ran off and followed the others.

Claire licked her paw and brushed it against the top of her head. "Let me know when this is over."

"We gotta go!" Dax cried. "Quacker-quackity!"

Eleanor looked at Claire with a puzzled expression. "I think I will follow after them. As I said earlier, I will not be fighting in any way."

"Me neither," Claire said.

"Will you walk with me?"

"If I have to. I don't want him to have all the fun," she said, nodding in Dax's direction.

The dam was a wall along the river comprising countless branches and sticks. Many of them poked out, pointing in every direction. What struck Eleanor most about the structure was how very sturdy it was, blocking the flow of the river. Whoever engineered it, she was sure, was an expert at their craft. With trepidation, she stepped onto it, feeling her foot hardly move at all against the bundle of sticks. She heard the sound of quacking not far off.

"We will take back the estuary!" a voice cried.

"We will! We will take it back and keep our bills straight!"

"I don't have a bill!" Dax called.

Loud splashing sounds followed. On both sides of the dam, the water swirled, and it was only when Eleanor looked up that she was able to see the cause. The ducks flying above were opening their webbed feet, dropping tree branches down. In the distance, she saw one of them landing on the riverbank, searching for a branch to grab as he prepared to fly up into the sky again.

The row of trotting ducks approached the center of the dam.

"We will seize the central hub! Quack!"

"They're here!" a new voice called.

Standing in the center of the dam were several beavers. Round and furry, their flat tails were gigantic.

"These fellas had the nerve to crash our housewarming party," one of them said, his two front teeth big and razor sharp.

"What do you reckon we ought to do?"

"I know!" His beady eyes gleamed. "Let's blow them away with our hospitality!"

They then turned around and proceeded to flap their tails rapidly. A billowing gust was created, and seconds later the ducks in front rose into the air and disappeared.

"Hold the line!" one of them yelled. "We need aquatic coverage."

On the side of the dam, several additional soldiers appeared, floating in a box-shaped formation.

"Fire away!" a voice rang out.

Instantly, they raised their bills and opened them slightly. Streams of water shot out, spraying meters ahead and hitting the beavers. Several of them shook and one fell into the water.

"You ain't the only ones who like water," one of them said. He dove beneath the river, surfaced, and sprayed water back at a duck.

On the dam, several beavers were still creating a breeze with their tails.

"It doesn't hurt me," Dax said. "That's weird."

"Is this the best you can do, 2nd Duck Division?" a familiar voice asked.

Captain David Drake marched towards the beavers. He began flapping his wings forcefully, creating his own breeze, and caused one of them to stumble. The others took a step back.

"This here is their big boss," one of them said.

"Really? I ain't trying to get blown away today."

"Now, lookee here, you," a voice spoke from nearby.

At once, Captain Drake stopped flapping his wings. Eleanor, Dax, and Claire turned and saw another beaver on the other side of the side of the dam. Bigger and rounder than the others, she also wore a wooden bowl as a helmet on her head. She stared at Captain Drake intensely, who returned it. It seemed to Eleanor as though they both knew something no one else did.

"The enemy commander has been sighted," Captain Drake spoke.

The other ducks in the area were shaking slightly.

"You were aware of this operation," he continued. "How was this the case?"

"Hush now," Brigadier Betty replied. "You ain't the only one running reconnaissance operations on this here river."

"Understood."

"Are they going to fight each other now?" Dax asked. "I hope we win!"

"I hope they both lose," Claire said. "Maybe then we can get on with our lives."

"Please stop!" Eleanor exclaimed. She took several steps forward until she was standing in between the two commanders. She held up her arms. "There is no need to be fighting. I know there may be a conflict between you, but there must be a way to move past it."

"Know your place, civilian," Captain Drake said. "You are speaking out of turn."

"You oughta listen to her, Drake," Brigadier Betty said. "She may well save you from an embarrassing loss. Right, troops?"

The sound of the other beavers' laughing filled the air.

Captain Drake flapped his left wing forcefully. "Do not intimidate my troops. We will retaliate if necessary."

Eleanor turned to face him. "I understand that you feel angry, but would you be willing to take a moment to explain to me how this all started?"

"Where to begin?" He shook his head dismissively. "Countless attacks, constant insults regarding our marching technique, and now here you are building a stronghold in the strategic center of the estuary."

"Listen here, you," Brigadier Betty replied. "That ain't the whole story. What about all the times you toss sticks at us, make a ruckus with your quacks, and violate the no-fly zone?"

"That zone was renegotiated. You are the one who violated-"

"What's that over there?" Dax asked, staring past the row of beavers.

"It ain't for him to know," one of them said.

Brigadier Betty took several steps closer, her tail flapping against the wood floor. "Come on now…what's wrong with the pup seeing this?" She turned her back to the others, and when she reappeared she held in her paws a bundle of bright-green grass. "This here ain't no secret. This is angel grass, seasoned with salt. It's one of our favorite snacks."

Dax turned towards Eleanor and back at Brigadier Betty. "Can I eat a little bit? It looks delicious!"

"Be cautious, Private," Captain Drake said. "It might be poisoned."

"What?" Brigadier Betty cried, wrinkles forming around her nose. "D'you think I feed my own troops poison?" She lowered herself down and looked at Dax. "What's your name, little pup?"

"My name is Dax," he said, holding his head high. "I am in the Duck Navy!"

"It's a division," Captain Drake corrected. "It's the second one."

"What happened to the first one?" Claire asked.

"Out of turn, civilian."

Brigadier Betty looked at the others and then back at Dax with a sweet smile. "I like you, Dax. You have a lot of energy. Go on, now, have a bit of some grass, fresh from the river."

"This can't be healthy," Claire began. "He really s-"

"Yum!" Dax exclaimed. "What tasty grass!" He spun in several circles as though chasing his tail.

"He really isn't much of a soldier, is he?" one of the ducks said to another.

Captain Drake turned to face his troops. "Now is the time to fall back. We will need to strategize for another day."

But as he turned around and raised his beak, he felt something bump against him repeatedly.

"Mr. General, sir!" Dax exclaimed.

"Captain," Claire corrected.

"Oh! I meant Captain!"

Turning around to face him, the leader asked, "What is it, Private?"

"You gotta try this angel grass from the enemy. It's delicious!"

Several ducks gasped in surprise

With a composed expression, Captain Drake said, "Do you understand at all what you are saying to me, Private?"

"I reckon he understands well enough," Brigadier Betty answered. "He was just enjoying one of our favorite treats."

"Understood. However, I will not be able to eat this. To partake would be to commit treason."

"But you gotta try it," Dax continued, hopping several times. "Treason is really yummy!"

A pause followed as no one spoke. Up above, the few patches of clouds slowly crawled across the horizon. As Eleanor looked at the ducks and then at the beavers, they all appeared tense.

Captain Drake slowly lowered his bill and scrutinized the grass as though it were a battle map. "The strategy must be adjusted," he said finally.

"Huh?" Dax asked while straightening his ears.

"After giving it thought, I will comply with your order, Private."

He took several steps towards the beavers, leaned down, and took a bite of angel grass. After he swallowed, he turned to look at Brigadier Betty and said, "I have confirmed that the enemy's food is delicious."

"Can you believe this?" a duck whispered to another.

Brigadier Betty took several steps towards him. "Well, now, you shoulda already have known that."

"Why do you say that?" Eleanor asked.

Captain Drake turned to face her. Standing still, saying nothing.

"You do remember, don't you?" Brigadier Betty asked.

"Affirmative, I do remember," he answered, now pacing around the dam. "It was back at the academy. You and I took numerous courses together: basic tactics, stealth operations, and codes to name a few. It happened when my own instructor humiliated me in front of our cohort. He told me that my marching was crooked and my aquatic-based combat pathetic. All of my fellow recruits laughed at me." He became still again. "Except for you, Brigadier. You were the one who invited me to join you for a snack."

"That was really nice of you!" Dax called.

"Affirmative," Captain Drake continued. "It was nice. And then when I joined you, I was presented with this very grass, seasoned much the same way. You listened attentively as I relayed my difficulties from training, and you also shared yours as well. In short, you were my friend."

"You can become friends again today as well," Eleanor said. "Do you remember what I said earlier? There is no need for violence." She turned to look towards Brigadier Betty. "I do not know what led to this conflict, but I do know that by coming together today, you two can live the way you did before."

"Well, I'll be!" Betty exclaimed. "I think she's gotta point, Drake. So, what do you say? Do you want a snack?" she asked while holding it towards him.

After taking another bite, Captain Drake turned towards his ducks. "Troops, I speak to you as your proud commander. We have skillfully executed many operations, served our citizens well, and traveled all over the region. Today, after many skirmishes and clashes with the beavers, we will resolve to draft a formal peace treaty with them."

"Really?" Eleanor asked in astonishment.

"Affirmative."

"Really?" Claire raised her eyebrows.

"Affirmative again." Captain Drake opened a wing to gesture towards the beavers. "Given new intelligence I have gathered on them, their delicious food and hospitable culture, it seems appropriate to reach an official, binding agreement on the dam construction." He looked at Brigadier Betty. "Are you willing to discuss terms in greater detail today?"

"Yes, indeed. I reckon it's time we returned things to how they used to be."

"You were able to end the war, Captain!" Dax called. "I have so much respect for you!"

"And we have great respect for you as a soldier," Captain Drake continued. "Effective this day, you are upgraded to Specialist."

"Specialist?" the other ducks echoed.

"Affirmative," he continued. "You are hereby Specialist of Snacks."

"Really?" Dax cried. "This is the best day of my life! I got to eat, and now I'm promoted!"

"Does that mean we can get out of here now?" Claire asked.

Captain Drake turned to face the water. "In accordance with our talks, I will plan to spend the rest of the afternoon with you, Brigadier, to draft a formal peace treaty. This river and estuary will return to a state of normalcy. A compromise will be found between the construction of dams while leaving the surrounding territory open for duck occupation."

"That sounds like a good deal to me," Brigadier Betty answered.

Captain Drake turned towards Eleanor. "I must thank you, Miss. You and your associates taught the 2nd Duck Division the power of renewed diplomacy." Wrinkles formed under his beady eyes. "It seems that there is more to this world than tactics and discipline alone."

Eleanor smiled. "We must thank you as well, Captain. You helped lead us along the river, closer to the estuary. It really was amazing to see you lead your troops towards peace!"

"Your kind word is appreciated." He looked towards the horizon of the river. "Tell me, Miss, where is your outfit headed?"

"We were heading towards the ocean. We hope to find our way back home from there."

"My troops oughta be able to help you find your way," Brigadier Betty said.

"Really?"

Several beavers walked forward until they were standing on the edge of the dam. Two of them picked up a wooden log and gnawed at it, their teeth moving as fast as a buzz saw. Seconds later, it was transformed into a small canoe. Two others walked forward with long sticks.

"It's a canoe!" Dax yelled.

After thanking the ducks and beavers one more time, Eleanor stood still and raised her hand in a salute. "Quackity-quack!" she proclaimed.

The others saluted back.

Eleanor sat in the canoe, holding the wooden branch. Claire sat next to her rolled in a ball, and Dax paced from one side to the other with his head hanging out of the canoe.

"I know that we are very close to the sea," Eleanor said. "It must be just around the next bend in the river. We will be out of this estuary soon!"

"Hooray!" Dax exclaimed.

"I hate water," Claire said.

Holding the wooden stick firmly in her hands, Eleanor began to paddle the canoe, turning around occasionally to see the ducks and beavers eating grass together, peace at last returned to the estuary.

6.
THE UNQUESTIONABLY BRAVE EXPLORER

Eleanor felt joy swell inside of her as they paddled the canoe towards the edge of the ocean. It now seemed as though the canoe was carrying them of its own accord, the currents of water brushing gracefully against the sides of the boat.

"I can see it!" she said while pointing.

Dax's head swiveled. "Where is it?"

"Over there."

Dax instantly jumped out of the canoe, making a splash in the water as he soon drifted away.

"He might be a duck after all," Claire said.

Eventually, paddling the canoe to the side of the river, Eleanor, climbed out of it and stood on the sandy earth. She placed her hand beneath her chin. "We are finally here, free from those high, sloping hills. As I mentioned before, I think that if we found ourselves here through mysterious cardboard boxes, then there must be more of them around here somewhere. It really is a big, open area, isn't it? If we continue searching, though, I am sure we will see one somewhere around here."

"I suppose that makes sense," Claire replied. "Let's just not get sucked in by the waves and drown like him."

Amidst the crashing waves, they heard Dax shout, "I love swimming!"

Eleanor and Claire nodded at each other and then ran out to call him back to shore. Once he shook himself dry, they walked along the beach, hoping desperately to see a box somewhere along the dry sand.

Eleanor, Dax, and Claire traveled not far from the sweeping tide, feeling the sharp cold of the waves cutting the air. The sounds of seagulls crying above echoed throughout the entire beach. Every now and then Eleanor felt bits of sand get caught in her shoes. She took each step thoughtfully, as though her shoes were heavy weights.

"I do miss my family," she said, looking at the sand. "My brother, I wish I was with him. I feel awful about how I treated him this morning."

"What did you do?" Dax asked.

Eleanor took a deep, audible breath. "This morning, on my way to go and play in the woods, I told him he needed to mind his own business. He was asking me where I was off to, what part of the woods and for how long. It is amazing to think of where I ended up!" She waved her arms to gesture at the waves. "Anyway, I was very annoyed by how he was asking me so many questions. He was making me feel like a little girl, like I had no idea what I was doing. I wanted him to understand that I can be independent, and so eventually I became so frustrated I yelled at him. I told him to leave me alone. When I put on my sneakers and opened the screen door, I remember how he came out and stood on the back deck. He was looking at me. I thought he was going to say something, but he didn't. He picked up a rock, threw it into the trees, and went back inside. I feel so horrible about it all. He didn't deserve for me to treat him that way."

"I'm sure he will get over it," Claire replied. "He was just being an overprotective big brother."

"Sorry about that, Eleanor," Dax added. "An older brother can be a great thing to have! It's nice having someone look out for you so you don't have to figure everything out alone. Right Claire?"

"Speak for yourself...."

"I remember that you two live in one house," Eleanor said. "Do you get along well?"

"Of course we do!" Dax cried.

"No, not really," Claire said.

"We are together a lot, since our owners don't spend much time with us."

Eleanor looked down at a spot between her feet. "I do get along with Edward very well. I really appreciate him. But today, I was unable to show him that, and now I feel guilty. I wish there was something I could do. I wish I was with him."

"We will get back to your home," Dax said, tail wagging. "We will get back, and then you can give Edward and your parents a big hug. Everyone will be so happy!"

"I know you're right," Eleanor replied as a slight smile formed. "This place, the Togetherwood, does seem very big."

"It's big enough that it can only be entered through a magic cardboard box," Claire answered. "So if you were hoping to give all those hugs, we should focus on moving faster."

There was a pause as Eleanor listened to the crashing waves. "It's all so very peculiar," she said finally. "Normally, I wake up each day, have breakfast with my parents, and then I go to school or play outside. Never did I think about how important these things are. But now, out here, it all seems so far away, like a dream."

"I like to have dreams," Dax said. "Yesterday, I had a dream that I could chase my tail and catch it!"

"What we need to do right now is keep going," Claire said. "While we're on the subject, do you have any idea of where we're planning to go on this beach?"

Eleanor shook her head. "My hope was that we would see a box very soon on that dry sand over there." She pointed to her right.

Both of Claire's ears perked up. She stopped walking, turned her head quickly, and said, "We need to stop."

"Why?" Dax asked.

"Quiet!" Claire answered with a sharp whisper. "I heard something. I'm not sure what it was, but I think we may be in danger."

"What could it be?" Eleanor asked.

"I'm not afraid!" Dax exclaimed, raising his head high. He took several steps forward along the sloping sand. There was a loud swooping sound and a gray blur. Dax fell over at once, his legs laying limp, groaning.

Eleanor brushed her hair out of her face as the breeze continued. "Dax? Are you all right?"

Claire jumped over Dax in one swift motion. She turned her face towards the sky. "I told you we're not safe here." She pointed with her paw.

High up above, flapping its massive wings menacingly, Eleanor saw a hawk. Without blinking its eyes, the bird was gazing at Dax as it prepared to dive down.

Once more, Claire jumped over Dax. She began to kick up sand with her back legs, creating a cloudy mist.

The hawk, now unable to see, soared downwards and tumbled into the sand. Eleanor hopped back when she saw the bird crash nearby. Next it stood up on its talons, focusing its gaze, its beak razor sharp like a sword. Its green eyes locked onto Claire, and it proceeded to squawk.

Dax was still laying in the sand, motionless. Eleanor turned to look at Claire, who said, "We need to get out of here." She scanned the shore for a place to hide. "Over there," she continued, pointing with her paw again. "We need to get over there fast or else we're gonna die slowly and with unending agony."

At that moment, Eleanor noticed something that might prove helpful. Far off, just before the horizon's edge, was a worn tree log. Eleanor was standing in place, frozen, but when she heard the flapping sound of the bird once more she started to run towards Dax. She slid down by him and felt the sand burn against her knees. "Dax, are you all right?"

Weakly, slowly, he opened his eyes to look at Eleanor. "I got cut. It really hurts." Eleanor looked at his belly and saw marks running alongside it. She placed her hand gently on his stomach and rubbed it.

"I liked it when my owners would pet me," Dax said.

Eleanor smiled. "I'm sure you did. But right now, we need to get going." The flapping sound grew louder still. "Follow me!"

She immediately stood up and sprinted across the thick, sloping sand towards the log. The blue sky above was broken by some patches of thick clouds, which became bigger with each passing minute. Running, breathing heavily, she turned her head around and was relieved to see Dax trotting towards her. When she looked up, she saw the hawk hovering above him, flapping its wings powerfully. Every time its wings flapped, an air current was created, a gust of wind that pelted against him.

"Dax!" Eleanor cried.

"I'm coming! Wow, I'm slow today!"

"Hurry up, you two!" Claire called from the log. "Even when a giant monster is relentlessly hunting us, you still take your time."

The hawk scanned the shore, finally pointing straight at Dax, who continued to move sluggishly.

Eleanor, still running, came to a halt. How, she wondered, could she help Dax move faster? Then she had an idea. She crouched down in the sand and picked up a rough, worn wooden branch. She stood up and hurled it towards the log with all her strength. As she ran, she heard Dax shout:

"Fetch! I will get it! I will retrieve the branch!"

The hawk, diving towards Dax, was far too slow to catch him. Though still clearly injured, he moved slightly faster as he approached the log. He grabbed the wooden branch in his mouth and then turned around. He began to trot towards Eleanor.

"I will give it back to you," he said.

Eleanor, running and pumping both her arms, felt the dense sand hardly move when her feet met it. Nearly out of breath, she laughed when she saw him approach her.

"You've got to be kidding me..." Claire called from the log.

Eleanor took the branch from him. The sound of flapping wings was still present behind her. Dax sat in the sand, staring at her joyfully.

"I'm happy to play fetch," she said, "but I really do not think now is the best time for it."

Dax didn't blink as he looked at her, then at the branch, and then at her again.

Still hearing the hawk, she raised the branch up above her head and said, "All right. I guess if you really want to, why not?" Again she tossed it and it soared over the log, disappearing. A cloud of sand formed when Dax went after it.

When Eleanor turned around, the hawk was nowhere to be seen. It was not until she looked up above that she saw the sun blotted out by a dark figure. With a piercing squawk, the hawk again dove towards Eleanor. She jumped, feeling the strain in her legs, and landed in the rough sand. Immediately, she pushed herself back up with her arms and continued to run, nearing the log at last. She used her hands against the jagged wood to propel herself up and over, landing on the other side. She wiped sweat from her forehead.

"Were you waiting for anything in particular?"

Eleanor tilted her head down and saw both Claire and Dax huddled together inside the log. Claire continued, "I think now would be an acceptable enough time to enter the log, don't you?"

Nodding, Eleanor got down onto her knees and slid inside. She had to tilt her head forward to ensure it didn't hit the wooden ceiling. Behind Claire and Dax, Eleanor was able to see the blurred edge of the beach and lines of trees behind it in the background. When she turned her head to look to the other side, she saw a faint blue backdrop, no doubt the edge of the ocean.

"What do we do now?" Dax asked.

"That is a good question," Eleanor replied.

Claire lowered her head between her orange paws and closed her eyes. "What we do," she said, "is wait. We take a cat nap. Well, I guess I can take a cat nap. You two can sit there and cower in terror." She slowly closed her eyes.

Dax smiled. "It was fun to play fetch."

Eleanor wrapped her arms around her knees. "I'm glad you enjoyed it." She then blinked several times quickly. "I just realized something. Do you hear that?"

"Hear what?" Claire asked, her eyes still closed.

"Actually, it's a matter of what can't be heard. I don't hear that bird flapping its wings. I think it gave up when it saw us hiding here. I think we are safe now!"

"Hooray!" Dax exclaimed.

"Finally..." Claire tilted her head down.

"What do we do now?" Dax asked. "Maybe I can go swimming again."

"I don't think we have time for that just now," Eleanor answered with a smile. She crawled through the log towards the end and slowly poked her head out. Then she made her way back into the center of the log. She took a deep breath. "I really don't know what we should do now. I suppose we could get out of here and keep walking along the beach," she paused and placed her hand at her chin, "but I don't know how far we will be able to go before we run into that hawk again."

"Or something worse," Claire added.

"I do not like sitting here," Dax said. "If we stay here, then nothing happens." He rolled onto his back and waved his paws towards the ceiling of the log. "This is boring!"

Eleanor stared at the wood, deep in thought. "I think we are all correct. I wish I knew what we should d-"

"What, ho! Who goes there within that lumber shelter?"

Eleanor, Dax, and Claire all looked at each other. Eleanor shuffled towards the edge of the log. As she stretched her neck out to take a closer look, she was startled by whom she saw.

Standing proudly on two feet, taller than anyone the travelers had met yet, was a badger. He was coated in thick, black fur and clutched a wooden oar in his right hand. A white stripe of fur ran across the middle of his head, separating his determined eyes. The badger stood still.

Eleanor motioned back into the log, but at once she heard the badger say, "Do you serve a righteous cause? Tell me the truth, and I assure you your fate will be all the better off."

Eleanor swallowed audibly. "Yes, we do."

The badger crouched down low, leaned towards Eleanor, and looked at her carefully. Then he stood up straight again and beat his own chest with his left paw, saying, "Now, I can see clearly that you lot are noble enough. I've no doubt that you are capable, seasoned travelers, who may well be of great use to me in my endeavors."

Claire slowly walked out of the log to sit next to Eleanor. "Who are you?"

The badger turned his entire body to face Claire and said, "Me? Who am I?"

"That was the question, yes."

Holding the wooden oar with both paws, the badger answered, "Why, I am Sir Bradley van Bardsley. I am the greatest explorer who ever ventured."

Claire rolled her eyes.

Eleanor introduced herself and the others.

Bradley stood even more straight, holding his head high. "A pleasure to meet you three. I am an unquestionably brave explorer."

"What does that mean?" Dax asked, his head poking out of the log.

Brow furrowed, Bradley answered, "What it means is that I am so brave that it simply cannot be questioned. I have traversed countless kingdoms, surveyed numerous domains, visiting many, many places. I have climbed the highest mountains, swam across the deepest seas, conquered the most untamed forests. There is no part of this Togetherwood that I have not seen."

"You have seen all of the Togetherwood?" Eleanor asked, feeling hopeful as she imagined a way back home.

Bradley pointed the wooden oar at the sky. "Yea, verily."

"Did you hear that?" Dax said. "Yay! Hooray!"

"I think he is speaking in a more refined way, Dax," Eleanor explained with a smile. "What he means is 'yes, I have.'"

"She speaks truthfully," Bradley said. "As I had been recounting... within this most excellent land, I have seen everything there is to see. I...." He lowered the stick and sighed. "Well, now that I think of it, I have not quite explored every area."

"What have you missed?"

Bradley reached a paw into the fur on his chest. He pulled out a piece of paper that had been folded several times. Unfolding it, the others were amazed to see a remarkably detailed picture of the Togetherwood and the surrounding areas.

"What's that?" Dax asked.

"This," Bradley said as he puffed out his chest, "is a map, and not just any map. On this sacred parchment, you will see a depiction of all the Togetherwood. Every brook, every tree, all of it is here, on this unassuming little piece of paper." He tapped his paw against a corner of the map. "I would be a lost and lonely badger if I hadn't one day found this paper while venturing in a distant land."

"It looks wonderful," Eleanor said. "May I take a closer look at it?"

Bradley handed it to her and she unfolded it. The details shown on the map were so intricate and numerous that it took Eleanor a moment just to gain a sense of what she was looking at. In the center was a forest, lovely and green. Leading out of this were several streams, weaving together in complex ways as they occasionally fed into ponds and lakes. Eleanor realized that these surely were the same rivers that she and her companions had followed Freya through until only recently. Sure enough, the rivers emptied into the ocean on the leftmost side of the map, right near one of many crease marks on the paper. As her eyes scanned across the map, she saw how the beach gradually led back into a dense forest, which was where "The Togetherwood" was written on the paper itself. Deeper still into the forest, moving further up the map, Eleanor saw a spot that contained a clearing with a single tree. Standing menacingly, its wood dark, the tree left an impression on Eleanor.

When she looked at the left side of the map again, it became clear to Eleanor what Bradley meant when he said that he had not, after all, explored every place there is to see.

Looking up, she said, "This part of the map isn't complete, is it?"

Bradley shook his head several times and said, "Sadly, no, it isn't. I have seen all that there is to see, and yet this place, this beach, has until now been uncharted. But that changes today!" He smacked his left paw against his chest.

"You're going to document this entire shore?" Claire asked.

"Surely and certainly."

"You mean," she turned her head slowly one way and then the other, "you're really going to explore this entire beach, and then draw all of it on that piece of paper, all by yourself?"

"Not only am I going to do it, but I will do it better than anyone before or after."

Claire groaned.

"I think it would be lots of fun to go with you, Mister Bradley," Dax said. "Count me in!"

"Now, now, that's Sir Bradley to you. My, you three are quite a handful, are you not?"

Eleanor folded her hands and let them rest by her waist. "You will need to excuse us," she said. "We have been lost and wandering for quite a while now." She looked at the map again. "We are hoping to find our way back home. We thought that if we made it to the beach, we might be able to locate a way back. Do you know of any cardboard boxes?" She placed her finger on the bottom left corner of the map, slowly moving it up across the unlabeled, blank portion of the map.

"Cardboard boxes?" Bradley echoed. "I know not of what you speak. And regrettably, I cannot say for certain what may be found here on this fair beach, seeing as how the blank portion of the map is much larger than I would like. For, you see, I long to live my life with a map that has no blank parts at all. None!" He raised his wooden oar again.

"Maybe there is a box somewhere around here," Claire said. "After all, there is so much blank space here. M—"

"Not for long!" Bradley declared. "Nothing will be uncharted when I am done here today."

Claire looked at Bradley and then continued, "Well, for now at least, there's plenty of unknown space here."

"You're right," Eleanor said. "I'm sure if we keep going north here along the shore, we will come across a box at some point."

"I wouldn't be too sure," Claire said.

Dax hopped several times. "If it's all blank, then that must mean there's more wooden oars to play fetch with, right?"

"Definitely not," Claire said.

"We may not know what resides in the center of this unknown, blank section of my map," Bradley continued. "But this we do know for certain: we will never know what there is to see if we stand here speculating, daydreaming, delaying." He held the wooden oar with both paws, and his eyes became intense. "If it is indeed a box you seek, then it is a box that you will encounter. I've never been more sure about anything in an entire lifetime of glorious exploration. We must make our way northward, to the ends of the earth."

"Or the map," Claire said.

"Or the map," Bradley echoed. "Yes, we must move through this hidden, secret hole on the map, entrusting our destinies to fate. We do this in hopes that you three will find your way out of this place. We will do it. We will be persistent, we will be strong, we will be brave!"

"We will!" Dax shouted. "I like this badger."

Smiling, Eleanor said, "It all sounds like a great plan. If we keep moving, it's only a matter of time before we find our way."

"I guess we should go," Claire agreed.

The four travelers marched across the sandy expanse. Sand flowed with the vigorous breeze, drifting towards the waves, only to later return to where it started. Like a lung exhaling, the sound of the ocean crashing against the shore was so loud that Eleanor felt like it was happening right next to her ears. At this point in the day, morning was shifting into afternoon, and as the sky filled with more clouds, the sun's rays frequently became hidden. Eleanor walked with Dax and Claire on both of her sides, as Bradley marched in front with purpose and resolve. He suddenly came to a halt and craned his head forward.

"What are you doing now?" Claire asked, annoyed.

Bradley turned around, and they saw that he was holding a small, muddy twig in his left paw. "What, do you three believe that this beach will go ahead and simply chart itself?" Eleanor noticed that the twig was wet, and that he was lightly brushing the map with it in order to fill it out.

"Are you drawing?" Dax asked.

Bradley looked up from the map. "Nay, I assure you I am doing no such thing." He reached out his arm, and they saw the twig more closely. "With this humble tool, I, Sir Bradley van Bardsley, will successfully trace every contour, every line of this beach area. No secret will remain after I am finished." He pointed with his paw at a log a few meters ahead of him. "Very well. What shall I call yonder landmark that I have discovered?"

"You didn't discover it," Claire said. "It was there before you saw it, and it will be there after we leave."

"I think you made an incredible discovery," Dax added with a grin.

Wrinkles appeared under Bradleys' eyes as he smiled. "Truly, without any doubt at all, this is an awesome discovery that I have made. I will call this log...Bradley's Newest Log. Yea, I think it is a fine name."

"I like it," Dax said.

"I agree that having a name for your discovery is good," Eleanor added while looking at Claire. "Perhaps we might like to continue walking now?"

"Eleanor is most correct." He swung the wooden oar, slicing the air in front of him. "Onward!" he bellowed.

They only walked perhaps fifty more meters before Bradley turned and approached the edge of the beach where the tide started. Claire sat still while Eleanor and Dax followed him.

Eleanor stared at the majestic waves, hearing a seagull squawk above, and then asked, "Did you discover something else, Bradley?"

The badger turned around, holding two shells in his hands. "These two shells," he began, "do not resemble any other shells that I, or any other explorer for that matter, have ever seen."

"What do you mean?"

"Such rough, pointed edges. Their beauty is untold! I will call them...Bradleys' Pretty New Shell and Bradley's Very New Shell."

"Which one is which?" Eleanor asked.

Bradley reached out his left paw. "This was the first one I picked up, and then this other one."

"I understand," she replied, scratching her head and smiling.

Bradley raised both his arms up, holding the two shells towards the sky. "I truly am an amazing explorer, full of skill, wisdom, and bravery! I am unquestionably brave!"

"Hello!" Claire called. "Don't get me wrong. I enjoy collecting shells, too. But shouldn't we keep going?"

Bradley said, "That one doesn't have the spark of adventure, now does she?"

"I don't think that is the case," Eleanor answered. "Claire is just eager to be home and not gone for too long."

"Don't worry about her," Dax said. "She's always like that."

Bradley placed the two shells into a pouch that was wrapped around his waist. "Very well. We may continue onward. But please know that world-class exploration is never in a hurry. You did know that, did you not?"

"We do now!" Dax exclaimed.

The squawking of seagulls echoed across the empty sea air. Waves crashed against the edge of the sand again and again, causing the water to momentarily spread deeper inland, only to quickly recede once more. Bradley marched, carrying his wooden oar, his chest puffed out. Eleanor, Dax, and Claire had to move quickly in order to not fall behind.

"Hopefully, we will find a box soon," Eleanor said, breathing quickly as she walked.

"We may," Claire added, "so long as we don't find any more shells."

"I think we have plenty of time," she said with a smile.

"Say what you will. As for myself, I'm growing a little tired of his performance. He doesn't care about us at all. I t—"

"What, ho!" Bradley held his left arm out to stop the others from moving further. "You three, stand still if you hope to survive."

Claire sat and scratched her right ear. "What are you talking a —"

"I said it once, and again shall I say it: if you are hoping to leave this beach alive, to voyage again tomorrow, you must stand still."

"Don't worry," Dax replied. "I won't move."

"Very good, most brave and trustworthy fellow," Bradley said.

"Is there something we need to look out for?" Eleanor asked.

Bradley did not turn his head back to look at her. "Do you see yonder log over there?"

They all nodded as he continued:

"Of what sort of heinous, menacing, evil creature there may be behind it, I cannot say for sure." He lifted the oar and struck the sandy earth with it. "Yet what I will say is that it stands no chance against the powers of a pure, righteous explorer such as myself."

"I don't hear or see anything," Claire said, still scratching her ear.

"This much may be true, but I assure you that being silent and invisible are qualities reserved for the most hostile of enemies."

"That's too bad. I guess we're all going to die on this lovely beach, then."

Bradley smacked his left paw against his chest. "Nay, we will leave here. After I slay this foul monster, we will finish charting this beach."

"Do you have a plan for what to do?" Eleanor asked.

"Do I have a plan for what to do?" At once, Bradley leapt into the air and cried, "Prepare for battle, you dark being! Your evil ends now as destiny unfolds!"

They heard him land in the sand behind the log and roll several times. Claire said, "He sure likes himself a lot, doesn't he?"

"He is very sincere," Eleanor said. "I think we are fortunate to have him leading us."

"He's a hero," Dax added, his eyes wide with amazement.

When they turned to look at the log again, they no longer heard anything.

"What happened to him?" Claire asked.

"I don't know," Eleanor said.

Dax sped off towards the log, shouting, "Bradley! Are you all right? I will save you!"

Claire sighed and Eleanor turned to look at the water.

Several seconds later, Eleanor said, "We should go and take a closer look to see what happened to them."

Claire lowered her head lower towards the soft sand. "But should we?"

Eleanor approached the log. A few steps later, she was able to see Dax lying on the ground near the log. Then she noticed Bradley seated next to him. Bradley was once more scribbling away at his map with the twig.

Eleanor smiled, relieved to see them all right. "Was there anything over here?"

Bradley lowered the twig. "Thankfully, there was not. Now that I have fully explored this space, I am truly able to confirm that there are no threats to be found." He raised up the map. "I am updating our guide. I am naming this log...Bradley's Safe and Secure Log."

"Of course you are," Claire said as she hopped on top of it.

"You did great," Dax said. "You were brave! I want to be like you!"

Bradley smiled. "Yea. It is understandable that you too wish to be so brave that it is simply unquestionable. To be as brave as me, as heroic, selfless, and strong, is no mean feat. But I can assure you that with time, you too can become just as capable as I—"

It was with a piercing scream that they saw the hawk swoop down, grab Bradley in its talons, and then fly away.

"It's back!" Eleanor yelled.

Already the hawk was far away, flapping its wings wildly. Between its talons, they could see Bradley's head. He called to them, "Worry not, dear friends. Evil always seeks the valiant. It will not be long before I trample this foe."

Eleanor turned to the others. "We must go and rescue him."

Claire sighed. "I can't stand him."

Dax sprinted after them, kicking up small clouds of sand. "Let him go, you stupid bird! I will bite you and rescue my friend!"

Eleanor looked at Claire. "I know you think he is self-aggrandizing, but I really do consider him to be sincere. Look at how he's inspired Dax!"

"I detest arrogance. I don't care what he says or does; there is nothing impressive about it."

"Regardless of anything else, he's in trouble and needs to be helped." With that, she started to run after Dax.

"Always needing to help others...what about us?" Claire muttered under her breath as she trotted along as well.

They ran alongside the sweeping ocean, breathing in the salty, cool air. When Eleanor looked left, she saw only the dark blue horizon. To her right she observed a wall of thin, tall grass, a boundary between the beach and the path leading back into the Togetherwood. She ran with all her might, feeling sweat form on her forehead, her chest aching as it filled with air. Desperately out of breath, she came to a halt and leaned forward, placing her hands on her knees. When she recovered and looked up, she saw Claire trot to her side.

"What do we do?" Eleanor asked, nearly out of breath.

Claire tilted her head slightly. "Not far up there is a hill. It looks like the hawk is standing on top of it with him."

"What about Dax?"

Claire's eyes gleamed. "That's who I was referring to. I don't see the badger. I'm sure the hawk ate him already."

"Did it really?"

"No," Claire looked at the sand. "Probably not, but I wish it did."

"Remember to be kind. Let's keep going."

The hush of the ocean was softer now, the breeze completely gone. Even more clouds were present in the sky than before. Eleanor and Claire moved slowly and carefully up the side of the hill. Once they were able to see the hawk, Eleanor became still and crouched down low, whispering to Claire to do the same. She focused her gaze and saw that the bird stood with its wings spread out. Before it lay both Dax and Bradley. While Dax lay still, Bradley was shaking slightly.

"If this creature devours me, my map will never be finished!" He called.

Claire said, "That thing is going to eat them, so what are we supposed to d-"

Without thinking, Eleanor ran towards the center of the hill. "Go away, you mean bird!"

It twisted its neck to turn towards her and flapped its wings.

"You came to save us!" Dax called.

Still cowering, Bradley muttered, "My map…such a thing of beauty…it must be finished."

"How were you planning to stop a giant bird with razor sharp talons?" Claire asked from behind.

Eleanor stood still with both her fists clenched. She felt her heart beating in her head. Now that she saw how gigantic and frightening the hawk was up close, she turned back towards Claire and considered running away. But when she saw her friends lying on the ground, one of them shaking in terror, she knew she needed to save them. What could she do? She looked at her feet for anything useful. There was another squawking sound and she ducked out of instinct. Feeling the rush of air as the hawk soared just above her head, Eleanor noticed a rock nearby. She grabbed it, turned towards the bird, and tossed it at its beak. Though it was knocked back slightly, it did not seem to be in any way hurt. It moved again towards Dax and Bradley. It was then that she noticed that he still held his wooden oar, though he appeared too terrified to do anything with it. Eleanor kicked the sand at her feet and created a cloud in the air. A breeze moved the sandy mist through the air towards the hawk, momentarily blinding it. Eleanor ran towards Bradley and grabbed the wooden oar.

"Take it," he said. "Please save me from this cruel fate."

She lifted the wooden oar and realized it was much heavier than she imagined. When she looked at the bird again, she knew it was preparing to dive at her. As it lunged towards her, Eleanor swung the wooden oar with all the strength she had, hitting it in the front of the head. The impact of the strike caused the hawk to fall to the sand. It stood up, moving its beak dizzily. With a flap of its wings, it rose back into the air. It stared at Eleanor with a piercing gaze. Then, with another forceful flap of its wings, it flew away, leaving the beach at last.

As Bradley slowly rolled over onto his back, Dax began hopping in the air. "That was great! You did great!"

Wearing a worn smile, Eleanor approached Bradley and handed him the wooden oar. "I am returning this to you."

Rising up, he lifted the wooden oar and then dropped it suddenly. "I...I was a fool. So very foolish was I! I spoke grandly of courage, of strength, of goodness. Yet, in an hour of such need, a moment of crisis for my new-found friends...I..." He lowered his head. "I failed you all."

Claire said, "Perhaps y—"

"Unworthy! That is what I am, and there is no other word, no other name that I am to be called." He looked intently at Eleanor while holding the wooden oar. "You must take this."

"It sure is neat," Dax said. "You're lucky, Eleanor!"

She held it for a moment. Then with a smile, she placed it back in Bradley's hands once more. "I appreciate you offering it to me, but I can't accept this, Sir Bradley."

"And why not?"

"Because there is no way I could ever have been brave if I hadn't met you first. Any bravery I have came from your example!"

Bradley's brow became furrowed. "But how could I be brave?"

"That is a good question, isn't it?" Claire asked.

"Don't you remember what you said to us?" Eleanor continued. "You're so brave, it simply can't be questioned."

Bradley stood up and leaned back, raising both his paws, pointing the wooden oar towards the sky. "Yes! That is the truth!" He raised his left paw and tightened it. "Unquestionably brave!"

They walked down the hill and continued along the sandy path of the beach. Eventually, Bradley came to a halt and looked at his map with a renewed intensity.

"What is it?" Claire asked.

Turning the paper upside-down, and then back right-side-up again, Bradley answered, "We are back in the realm of what has been charted."

"Huh?" Dax asked.

"What I mean to say is that we are now approaching lands that have been explored before. If I continue this way, there are no more shells or logs for me to christen. It is of no benefit to me to leave this realm."

"What are we supposed to do, then?" Claire asked. "We didn't see any stupid boxes."

"That is true," Eleanor agreed while looking at Bradley. "Have you seen any cardboard boxes anywhere in all your travels? Are there any on the map?"

"Nay, I know not of what you speak. What is cardboard?"

"This is bad," Claire said.

Eleanor, feeling anxious, forced herself to smile as she said, "I am sure if we keep wandering we will find a way back home. Now that we made it to the beach, we are free to go in any direction." She turned towards the wall of tall grass she had noticed earlier. "Perhaps we might go that way?"

"I'm happy to go anywhere," Dax said.

Bradley bowed. "I must thank you three, for your company, your encouragement, and your incredible bravery. If you must continue onwards, then we will be separating here. There is much exploration here on the beach still needing to be done!"

"We have appreciated all your help," Eleanor said. "We wish you success as you complete your map."

"I suppose you were all right enough," Claire added.

Dax bowed towards Bradley. "I really liked exploring with you. You're a hero!"

"Nay," Bradley answered. "You are the true heroes, all of you! Farewell, and take care!"

Bradley waved and marched towards the water with his wooden oar, soon disappearing.

Eleanor, Dax, and Claire kept walking. Eleanor raised her hand to her forehead and squinted. "It is unfortunate that we didn't find any boxes out here."

"I knew we were doomed," Claire said, looking between her paws.

A serene breeze blew towards the ocean, rustling the tall grass near where they stood. Eleanor admired the grass, light green, delicate and yet sturdy.

"Look up in the sky!" Dax shouted.

Eleanor and Claire looked up and saw an owl flying towards them. Light brown, with feathers that rustled in the air, he became bigger and bigger until he landed on a rock nearby. He stared at them with a solemn, still expression.

"It's the owl!" Eleanor's face lit up. "This owl is the whole reason I became lost in the Togetherwood to begin with." She took several steps towards him.

"What's he doing out here by the beach, anyway?" Claire asked. "It doesn't seem very fitting."

The owl turned his head left, then right, and then left once more. "Return," he finally said.

"Return?" Eleanor asked. "Where?"

"Return…the forest…"

"I don't get it," Dax said.

"We were thinking of returning to the forest," Eleanor replied. "Is there somewhere we need to go?"

"Loneliest Hollow," the owl said.

"What?" Claire asked. "This bird is not much of a talker."

"You are saying you want us to go to a place called the Loneliest Hollow?" Eleanor asked, unsure of where that was.

"Why would we want to go there? Doesn't sound very appealing if you ask me," Claire said.

"I thought we wanted to go home," Dax added.

"That's right," Eleanor said. She turned to face the owl. "Sir," she began, "we did not want to go deeper into the Togetherwood. What we really hope for is to go home."

The owl closed his eyes. "Correct," he said.

"I am very confused," Dax said.

The owl turned to face the walls of tall grass and nodded at them. "Forward."

"Are you sure?" Eleanor asked.

The owl nodded quickly.

Eleanor asked, "I only have one more question. What is your name?"

There was a pause, and then he replied, "Octavious."

"It is lovely to meet you," Eleanor said. "This is Dax and Claire."

Octavious nodded and began flapping his wings. Again he turned towards the tall grass. "Loneliest Hollow…little time. Continue…help others…receive help…box."

He flew off at once and disappeared into the sky.

"It sounds like that's where we need to go," Eleanor said. "There must be a cardboard box there."

"What if that owl is wrong?" Claire asked.

"I'm sure he's right!" Dax exclaimed. "Let's go!"

Eleanor, Dax, and Claire looked at each other for a moment and then proceeded through the tall grass and along the path. Eleanor tried to reassure herself that the owl was guiding them correctly, but as she looked at the tall trees in the distance, wondering what might be awaiting them, she felt her confidence waver.

7.
AN INTERLUDE IN THE TALL GRASS

Eleanor, Dax, and Claire walked along the path, moving back inland and towards the forest.

"The grass is getting very tall here," Dax said. "It's hiding the ocean from us!"

"It certainly is tall, Dax," Eleanor agreed. "If I was playing hide-and-go-seek, I would be delighted to come across a place like this."

"Is that your favorite game?"

Eleanor smiled. "Yes, I think so. My friends and I all enjoyed playing it outside. Sometimes, we would play in the evening after the sun had already set, and it became cold."

"That sounds fun!"

"If I can concentrate, I can remember the feeling of hiding on the side of James' shed, waiting for him to find me. I can recall the feeling of the crisp air in September or October, waiting. One time while hiding I was left wondering whether James already found everyone else. I ended up waiting for a very long time that night."

"That sounds awful," Claire said.

"It did feel unpleasant," Eleanor continued. "I started to wonder if everyone else had gone home already to warm up without telling me."

"What did you do?" Dax asked.

"After enough time passed, I left my hiding place and wandered out to the middle of our neighborhood street to look for my friends. I shivered while standing under a streetlight, afraid they all were gone. When I called his name out, James showed up on the other side of the street behind our neighbor's house. Then, one by one, my other friends also appeared from their hiding places."

"They didn't leave after all!" Dax said.

"No, they did not."

"Why are you telling us about this?" Claire asked.

Eleanor placed her hand to her chin. "I'm not sure. What I like about the story is it shows that we are not always as lost as we might think."

"Sure, go ahead and say that," Claire said, "but none of this seems right. You had this plan for us to walk to the water and then find a box. Now, after talking to one owl, we're going back into the forest. Do we even know where we're going?"

"It may seem strange," Eleanor replied as she moved her hair out of her eyes in the breeze, "but I have a feeling that this is the right way for us to go."

"Oh, do you? And why is that?"

"As I said earlier, that owl was what caused me to get lost here in the first place. I think he knows something."

"How is that supposed to reassure me? Getting lost is the exact opposite of what I want to do." She turned her head around. "It was so much more pleasant and peaceful back there at the shore. We should have stayed there."

"I don't like it when we disagree like this," Dax said. "We should be united."

"To be united," Claire replied, "is to all share common sense, which would mean that we don't get distracted by antisocial birds."

Eleanor shrugged. "We spent plenty of time at the beach. I think it makes sense to continue along this path. There is no need to feel discouraged," she said with a smile.

"I'll feel better when I'm sleeping on my blue cushion," Claire replied.

They took a slight turn to the right as the bright-green grass became taller on both sides, gradually enclosing them. Beneath their feet, the path changed from sand to soft dirt. Blue sky mixed with gray clouds above. From behind, they heard the sound of the sighing ocean become a faint whisper.

Eleanor turned to look at the others while walking. "This is certainly not the end. It's true that we had our first plan, of making it to the sea. But we did not find what we were looking for. I think now we are on our way to where we need to be, we just have not arrived there yet. We can think of this like an interlude."

"An interlude!" Dax said with a grin. "I like interludes."

"Do you even know what that is?" Claire asked sharply.

"No," Dax answered while his tail wagged. "But I like how it sounds!"

Eleanor explained, "An interlude is something small that connects two bigger things. I remember when my father pointed one out in the music on his favorite record."

"It connects things? Like a bridge?" Dax asked.

Eleanor smiled. "Yes, like a bridge."

"None of that is going to help us," Claire said.

"I think it will. All we need to do is trust where we are going."

Claire stopped walking at once. She lowered her head to look at the dirty path. She tilted her head to the side.

"What is it, Claire?"

"Don't you remember what I told Freya? I had things happen to me, finding my whole family gone and being forced to wander with nowhere to go, that don't make me want to trust where I'm going. I can't know for certain that this will turn out all right for us." She didn't raise her head as she spoke. "Is that something you can understand?"

"I do think that makes sense," she replied. Remembering Claire's story from earlier, how she connected with Freya and inspired her, Eleanor felt amazed and impressed all over again. "Though you did experience some tragic events, you were able to use it all for good when you spoke with her. That certainly is valuable," she said with a smile.

"I suppose so," Claire answered. "Sometimes it is easier to tell others what we ourselves need to hear."

"You're strong, Claire!" Dax exclaimed.

"It's true," Eleanor agreed.

Claire did not seem to have heard what they said. "Hopefully, now that you have listened to my tale, you can understand why I do not take well to being told to trust in where I'm going."

"I think that is understandable," Eleanor replied simply.

Claire sighed. "I just wish we knew where we were going."

"Remember what I said earlier? We are passing between two parts of our trip. Before, we were on one section, and soon we will be on to the next one. Right now, we are just finishing up this in-between part, the interlude."

"I think everything will turn out great," Dax said. "We will keep walking and then escape from here!"

Eleanor beamed. "That's the spirit, Dax!"

They were now approaching the entrance of the forest, still blanketed on both sides by tall grass. Up ahead, past the looming trees with their twisting branches, Eleanor thought she saw something overgrown. She turned to look at Claire. What did it feel like, she wondered, to live with such painful memories? She had no answer. She felt deep admiration for Claire, but if she were to tell her so, would she believe it?

8.
REDEMPTION IN THE THORNY THICKET

There was a rustling sound that came from not far off. Eleanor, walking in front, tried to ignore it. However, she was finding that with each step she felt more and more uneasy. The rustling was now so loud that she felt certain an ambush was coming.

Turning to face Dax and Claire, she said, "Do you hear that?"

"It's very loud," Dax answered. "Do you think we are in danger?"

"If we are," Claire answered, "at least then I will be proven right."

"I don't think we need to worry," Eleanor replied, speaking to herself just as much as to the others.

Then, just as suddenly as the bushes began to rustle, they ceased altogether. All was silent with the exception of Dax's panting. Eleanor became aware of how the forest was gradually becoming dimmer and darker with each step.

"That was strange," she said. "I must say I am glad it stopped, though."

"Look at those!" Dax exclaimed, pointing his paw ahead. "Those look prickly!"

A few dozen meters ahead, down a gentle slope, was a wall of thorns, a thicket. Swirling and dark maroon, each and every part of the thicket was razor sharp. Eleanor saw that the path before them led straight into it. She wondered how they were to continue along.

Claire curled up in a ball and closed her eyes. "I guess we're stuck again. Might as well get some rest before we disappear forever."

"We're not stuck," Dax said. "There's gotta be a way to keep going. There's just gotta!"

Eleanor folded her hand into a fist and rested it beneath her chin. "I'm sure you are right, Dax. But as hard as I try, I really can't think of anything we can do."

At that moment, they heard a voice cry out, "Is anyone there?!"

The ears of both Claire and Dax perked up. Eleanor turned to face where she heard the voice and realized that it was coming from within the thorns. She took a step towards the thicket, listening closely. Again a voice called out:

"Hello?!"

Standing right next to the thicket, Eleanor placed a hand on a prickly branch, careful that she did not place her fingers over any thorns. She moved it slowly and was able, just barely, to see a dark gray figure huddled a few meters deeper inside, trapped as though in a room with sharp walls.

"Are you all right?" she called into the thorns.

The figure scurried and turned to face her. Eleanor saw two dark, beady eyes staring back at her. She realized that it was a raccoon.

"Hello?" Eleanor asked again.

The raccoon spoke with a deep, gravelly voice, "Well, I sure got myself in deep, didn't I?"

Eleanor moved the branch slightly again. "Do you need help?" she asked.

"What, do you think I'm on vacation in here?"

122

"He needs help!" Dax called from behind.

Eleanor nodded to him and then spoke to the raccoon once more, saying, "We would like to help you out of there, but what can we do?"

"What can you do?" The raccoon repeated. "There's always a way out of a jam. You just need to get a little creative."

Looking around, Eleanor noticed a tree standing a few meters away on a slope, with branches that looked particularly sturdy. She pointed at it and asked, "Should we…"

The raccoon nodded once, causing Eleanor to stop speaking.

Dax trotted up the slope and sat at the base of the tree. Eleanor hopped up to join him and grabbed a bough that hung close to the ground.

"What will we do?" Dax asked. "Will we play fetch?"

"We can play fetch," Claire answered. "Maybe Eleanor could toss that thing right into the thorns for you."

Eleanor pulled the tree limb closer to herself. "I don't think now is the time to play a game." She was pulling on it with all her might. There was a sudden loud snapping sound. She looked at the others while holding up a long, sturdy stick. "I think this will work," she said finally.

The raccoon was silent as they approached him. Eleanor held the bough with both hands and proceeded to smash the thorns with it. It was not long before she was breathing heavily, able to feel sweat forming again on her forehead. She paused for a moment to recover.

"There's a path now!" Dax yelled.

True enough, the first meter of thorns were now squashed to the forest floor, leaving Eleanor able to take two steps towards the raccoon.

"C'mon, kid," the raccoon called. "You gotta get me outta here…"

Claire licked her paw and groomed herself. "I have full faith in you, Eleanor."

After several more minutes of intense, repetitive whacking with the branch, Eleanor was standing next to the raccoon. She raised the stick again, but stopped when she saw him shuffle and then move towards her. He quickly crawled over towards Claire and Dax. He raised his nose into the air and took in a deep breath. "Freedom...it never smelled so good."

Dax, too, raised his head towards the sky and sniffed loudly. "It does smell good! It really does!"

Eleanor surveyed the raccoon. Her parents always used to warn her to be careful when coming home at night, to keep an eye out for this very creature. Her father told her that raccoons were monsters and to be careful. But as she looked at the one before her, she thought to herself that he didn't seem dangerous. She saw the dark gray fur along his coat, the white fur on his eyebrows and near his nose, creating the impression that he was wearing a mask. Looking a little more closely into his eyes, she thought he appeared tired.

Eleanor introduced herself and the others.

The raccoon's head was completely still. His whiskers bristled as he chuckled to himself.

"What is it?" Eleanor asked.

He reached out with his paw and removed a thorn from his tail. "So, you help someone out of a tough spot...and what? You're supposed to be pals now?"

"I was just i—"

"Nah, save it, kid." He took several steps away.

"Where do you think you're going?" Claire's voice rang out.

The raccoon turned slowly and gazed at her. "You're Claire, is that right?"

"If it has to be."

"Look here, cat," he said, taking a few steps back towards them. "I guess I'm grateful to you three clowns for the favor, but don't think I need anything else. This world is a rough and cruel place, don't I know it. This world," he waved a paw with sharp claws towards the thorns, "is a place that can give you a hug one second and then stab you the next. It can kill you without a second thought. No, I don't need your company."

"We didn't rescue you, so you could tell us your philosophy. What we need is your help in getting through here."

"Through where?"

Claire tilted her head towards the thicket.

The raccoon gave another small chuckle. "What…you want to go through there? Is that it?"

Claire didn't answer.

Laughing, the raccoon continued, "Didn't you see me just now, huddled over like a prisoner in a cell? C'mon. No way. There ain't no way anybody can get through there."

"But we can do anything when we work together. Isn't that right?" Dax cried, his tail wagging quickly.

"Do anything?" He waved his paw through the air. "You make me laugh, pup. The best thing anyone can hope for out here is to stay alive and stay free. That's what I've always done."

"Especially when you were surrounded by four walls of thorns and cowering over?" Claire asked.

The raccoon's eyes squinted as he kept taking steps. He was practically pacing in a circle now. "OK, kitty. Good one. So, I ended up a little stuck. There's a story behind that, you oughta know."

"I'm sure there is. I remember the ending of the story, which is the part where Eleanor helped you get out."

Eleanor scratched the back of her head. "Please, you don't need to feel any need to continue onward with us."

"Really? Then I won't, then."

"But it would be very nice to travel with you and maybe learn about this area here. It would be a treasure."

There was a bright gleam in the raccoon's eyes. He stopped pacing, turned towards Eleanor, and said, "Hold up, little miss. I just thought of something. Maybe…maybe we can arrive at a…you know, a deal."

"A deal?"

He nodded. "As much as I enjoy the lonely road of life, I do gotta admit I have something I have been needing help with."

"What's the thing you need help with?" Dax asked. "We can do anything!"

The raccoon scratched his back. "Thing is, I'm not really at liberty to go into the details about it all at this precise moment." He pointed towards a tree a few dozen meters away that stood close to the thicket. "You see that?"

They nodded.

"OK. So, I have a…a little errand that I need to take care of at the top of that tree there. Can you three help me with it?"

"What is the errand?" Claire asked.

"Sheesh. You three are nosy, aren't you?"

"We don't mean to be nosy," Eleanor said. "I think my two friends were just a little curious, that's all. I must say that I am as well!"

"Well, that's fine. That's dandy. What you need to know is that I would like for you three to join me in climbing up that tree."

"You are lucky," Dax said. "Eleanor is the greatest tree climber who ever lived."

The raccoon smiled, showing sharp teeth along the edges of his mouth. "I like being lucky." He turned to face Eleanor. "So that's where we are. If you three can help me with my errand, then I think…I think I can make it turn out good for you as well."

"What does that mean?" Claire asked.

"It means that I can help you get across this thorny thicket."

"Didn't you say there was no way through it?"

"I, uh… let's just say I misspoke earlier."

Eleanor's face became a rose-red. "That sounds like a wonderful deal! Thank you…what is your name, anyhow?"

"Me? Ryder's the name. I'm just nature's last fallen hero."

"Pleasure to meet you," Claire answered. "Hopefully, we don't fall out of the tree. At least it looks a little easier to climb than the one I got stuck in earlier."

It was only when they stood at the base of the tree that Eleanor realized it was very tall. She craned her neck to look up, the branches spreading outward like the hooks of an open umbrella. Feeling tension in her shoulders, she turned to see Dax smiling.

"I know you all will do an excellent job when you climb the tree," he said. "I am bad at it."

"And boy am I glad to hear you say that," Ryder said.

"Why?" His ears perked up.

"Because," he turned his head one way and then the other. "Someone needs to stay here and stand watch."

"What on earth are you talking about?" Claire asked.

"What…you think I just scale a tree like this one here in broad daylight without someone watching my back?"

"I can watch your back!" Dax exclaimed. "If you turn around, I can begin to watch it."

Ryder looked puzzled. "I'm not picking up what you're putting down, pup. Look here, the three of us are gonna climb this tree all the way to the tippy top. What we need you to do is to keep an eye out to make sure there's no trouble down here."

"Were you planning on there being trouble?" Claire asked.

Ryder hit the palm of his paw against his forehead. "No, no, no! I'm planning for the opposite of that, for there to be no trouble. OK? So, pup, just keep an eye out. If you see or hear anything out of the ordinary, anything suspicious or hazardous, you need to holler to us real loud and let us know. Once we get up higher in this tree…let's just say we ain't gonna be as attentive to what's going on down here."

"I can do that," Dax answered. He sat down and struck the ground with his two front paws. "I will defend this spot. I am a guard dog!"

Eleanor took a step towards the tree. "I think we are all on the same page. Did you want to lead the way, Ryder?"

"Nah, let's have the cat lead us."

"Eleanor is a better climber," Claire said plainly.

"Alrighty then. Can you lead us then, kid?"

"I can," Eleanor smiled. She placed both of her hands on the branches and felt at once a chilling breeze. Seeking to leave her nerves behind, she lifted herself up, placed her feet on a low branch, and proceeded to climb.

"Well, I'll be…the kid can climb," Ryder said.

Claire jumped onto a bough. "I told you."

With Dax walking in circles around the tree again and again, the others slowly made their way up towards the clouds. Eleanor was reminded of climbing earlier in the day when she rescued Claire. As her hands gripped each bough, she noticed that the texture of the wood was familiar to her touch. Resolved to not look up or down, she reached out one hand and then another. She could hear the sound of heavy breathing just below her:

"Too old…I'm just too old for this," Ryder groaned.

Claire focused closely on each branch before she jumped to it. The sounds of her claws scraping against the wood as she scrambled could be easily heard. "As long as we don't have to get down, I'll be fine."

Already, Eleanor was able to see the bigger area, the whole of the Togetherwood spread out before her eyes, unfolding just like Bradley's map. When she turned her gaze left, she saw, just barely, the tips of the green grass where they walked not long ago. She looked onward towards the edge of the ocean. The sea, which not long ago felt so wild with its big splashing waves, appeared calm and still from high up in the tree. Turning her head, Eleanor saw the thorny thicket and then beyond it a light green meadow, a clearing. Past that, she saw more dense collections of trees with no end in sight. For a moment, she stopped climbing and wondered where the Loneliest Hollow might be within all the forest, how reaching it might finally lead her home. She did not have long to ponder this before she felt something bump against her.

"Hey! You asleep there, kid?" Ryder placed a paw against his head.

"No," she replied. "Sorry about that."

"Well, fine then. Let's keep it moving."

Claire jumped onto a tree limb just above Ryder's head. "Speaking of sleep," she began, "aren't you supposed to not be out during the daytime? Isn't that a raccoon thing?"

He shook his head. "That's a common misconception. We come out all the time during the day."

Claire blinked several times as her tail swayed. "But is that really true? I don't think I've ever seen one of your kind around when the rest of us are out."

"We like to do our business during nighttime, sure. But, you know, the simple truth is…look, kitty, why are you making me explain myself? You should know I've had a very difficult day and now all I want to do is get back to my den."

Eleanor used both of her arms to pull herself up onto a new branch. "We were not trying to bother you, Ryder. I think Claire was just curious."

"Yes, I'm curious," Claire added, "I am just overwhelmed with curiosity. So overwhelmed, in fact, I am concerned that it's going to just knock me off of this tree."

"You're the one who asked to begin with," Ryder snapped, still breathing heavily as he climbed. "Sheesh. As far as my story goes...let's just say I've had a very colorful career. I've done all sorts of jobs. Trading, investing, cutting deals...I've had some tough breaks along the way. I'm a lonely raccoon trying to pave his own way in this brutal little world of ours."

Eleanor wiped sweat from her forehead and noticed her heart beating. "It sounds like you have experienced a lot. We just want you to know that we really appreciate you offering to help us out with your deal."

"He hasn't done anything for us yet," Claire muttered.

Eleanor, having gained the courage to look down, lowered her head and was able to see a black dot circling the tree repeatedly. "It looks like Dax is keeping a look-out for us."

"That may be," Ryder began before coming to a complete halt. "But..." he raised a paw. "You two...don't move."

Claire's claws scratched against the tree wood. "Why do-"

"Don't speak, either."

Eleanor held the nearest branch firmly with both her hands.

For a moment, there was silence. Eleanor felt more aware of the branch she was standing on, how it swayed gently as the breeze picked up. As she looked around at the distant trees, she realized how small she was in the scheme of the vast Togetherwood.

Ryder finally said, "Now, I don't want you two to be alarmed or anything," he pointed up with his paw, "but up there... they're posted."

"What's posted?" Claire asked.

"Guards."

"There are guards up here?" Eleanor asked. "I don't see any-one." At that moment, they heard a rustling sound. Out of the corner of her eyes, she saw a blur. It was then that she knew what Ryder was referring to. "Are you talking about those squirrels?"

"Yep."

"What do you think we should do?"

"I, for one, think it's time we went back down," Claire said. "We accomplished absolutely nothing by climbing up here and wasted everyone's time. Thanks again."

"We can't go back down," Ryder answered as if speaking to no one.

"And why not?"

"We just can't, not after getting this far."

"Were we getting close to something?" Eleanor asked.

"You bet we were," his whiskers bristled. "We're so close...I can smell it." He quickly turned his head to face them. "Re-member the deal, you two. If you want me to show you how to get through that little thorny thicket down there, then we are gonna see this through."

"See what through?" Claire asked, clearly annoyed.

"I don't have time to explain all the details right now. What I need from you two is to help me in getting around those squir-rels up there. I need you to trust me."

"We trust you, Ryder," Eleanor said. "If you tell us what we need to do, we will do it."

Claire sighed.

Ryder nodded. "OK. So, here's what we're gonna do. You see that up there?" he pointed towards the top of the tree with an outstretched paw.

"Yes."

"We need to get up there. Thing is, we can't let those guards see us. If we're spotted, then the whole thing's blown. By the looks of it, there are only three of them on patrol. If you look carefully, you can see them climb up one branch, and then drop down. They're guarding it close, alright."

"What are they guarding?" Claire asked.

"Can't say right now. Unless we start moving, they're gonna catch us in no time. Are you listening, kitty?"

"Only if it allows me to live to be reunited with the ground again at some point."

"Always with the attitude. Here's what we need you to do." He pointed in a slightly different direction, still higher into the tree. "You need to climb that way. You gotta climb fast, but don't make any sounds to draw attention to yourself."

"Don't worry, no one ever notices me anyway."

"Get going!" Ryder whispered loudly, startling the others.

Claire jumped up to a nearby bough, scrambling with her paws to stabilize herself. The wind blew against her bright orange fur. She turned her head to look and see where the squirrels were.

"Don't wait around all day!" Ryder whispered once more.

Claire refocused her gaze and continued to jump from one branch to another. Eleanor tried to not feel nervous as she saw how much each branch shook when she landed on it.

"What about me?" she asked.

"I think the cat will manage. You and I are going to finish what we started. Let's climb to the top."

"All right."

"What are you waiting for? You go first."

Upon looking down, she noticed just how high up they were. She swallowed, reached up, and pulled herself higher still. She climbed without speaking, trusting that Ryder was just behind her. While moving, she turned to look and see Claire, now a ways off, hopping from one level to another. She felt the twisted edge of a branch scrape against her knee. No other tree in all the Togetherwood, she decided, could compare in height with this one. A paw tapped against her back.

"Freeze, kid."

Motionless, she turned her head to look up and saw that a squirrel was climbing down several branches, moving closer. Eleanor's chest became tight, and she felt as though she couldn't breathe.

"Just wait…" Ryder whispered so softly that Eleanor nearly missed it. "…keep going, little buddy….just keep going… that's it…"

The squirrel, moving swiftly, was now climbing downward on the other side of the tree and disappearing from view.

Ryder wiped his forehead with his paw. "That's a lot closer than what I'm comfortable with. Keep going."

Still feeling nervous, Eleanor grabbed on to a nearby tree limb. What, exactly, were they doing here? In particular, she was struck by Ryder's ambiguity, having revealed so few details about their situation. Why was this the case? She could not shake the feeling that she had been sent on a questionable errand, that something about it was not right. The chilling breeze blew against her face. Despite how afraid she felt, she continued to follow Ryder's instructions.

"Uh-oh," Ryder whispered.

"What is it?"

He pointed down. "They caught her."

Eleanor saw one squirrel, and then another, approach Claire. At first, she appeared calm, but when the squirrels proceeded to toss nuts at her, she cried out:

"Fine! I'll leave! I didn't want to be up here, anyway."

The two squirrels pelted Claire with nuts repeatedly. Eleanor saw her lose her grip and nearly fall several times as the nuts hit her head. Still, the squirrels continued to follow her.

"It's a terrible feeling," Ryder remarked. "It really hurts." Eleanor saw a twinkle in his eyes when he next said, "But you know what that means, right? Now there's only one more guard up here. C'mon!" He gave her a gentle push.

"Why are the squirrels doing this?" she asked.

"Doing what?"

"Guarding this tree and throwing nuts at us."

Breathing heavily again, Ryder said after a moment, "Animals can be territorial. This here is their place, their domain. That's why we need to hurry."

"I understand. I don't think I can, though."

"Why? We're almost there."

"Because," Eleanor brushed her hair out of her eyes. "Claire is my friend and I care about her."

"Having friends isn't gonna help anyone right now," he answered. "What we need to do is finish the job."

"I understand. But you will need to continue on your own."

"What are you talking about?"

She was already reaching out her arms and starting to climb down. "I need to go and find her. I need to help her."

Ryder turned his head down and back up several times. "But...kid, we're so close...we're..."

No longer able to hear him, Eleanor felt more at ease as she looked intently for Claire. Beneath her feet were countless layers of branches, the ground and Dax barely visible. She was concerned that she couldn't see her. By using her arms to make any adjustments needed, she was able to slide down much faster than when she had been climbing. She did not spend much more time descending before she heard a familiar voice:

"I didn't want to be up here to begin with! Can I just go now?"

Huddled on a branch that stretched out farther than the others, Claire sat shivering in the breeze. Standing between her and the trunk of the tree were the two squirrels, clutching nuts as big as a rock. Eleanor, knowing that the squirrels hadn't yet detected her, wrapped her arms around the trunk of the tree to secure herself. She looked down at the very long branch and contemplated her next step.

Knowing that simply sitting and waiting wouldn't help anyone, Eleanor moved her legs swiftly and placed her feet down on a bough, at first without applying all of her weight. She was hoping to make sure that it could support her. She then held on to a tree limb just above her head, looked at the squirrels, and spoke:

"Hello there. I am not wishing to harm anyone at all. I believe this cat here, my friend, was preparing to leave the tree with me."

The squirrel standing in front turned his head back and stared at Eleanor with a stern, intense expression. "This cat here is an intruder, violating multiple sections of Squirrel Code."

Eleanor felt the wind pick up. She held the branch above her head more tightly than before. "I am not familiar with your code, but I must say that both of us apologize for going against it. Would it be all right if we just left now?"

The other squirrel raised his tiny hands in the air, ready to fling the nut. "Negative. This breach is unacceptable. It cannot remain unpunished." He hurled the nut toward Eleanor, who ducked at once and heard it slice through the air.

"Claire!" Eleanor shouted. "We need to escape!"

She saw an orange blur and realized that Claire had jumped towards the trunk of the tree. More nuts were flying through the air, aimed at them, hitting the tree and different nearby branches.

"I would be happy to do so," Claire called, now several meters below.

Eleanor maneuvered downward to the best of her ability, fearing that a nut would strike her at any moment. Her feet slid off the bough edges as she lowered her legs down to the next one, as though she was falling down a staircase. Leaves shook and shuffled with each branch she grabbed.

"I think we will be able to make it all the way down soon," Eleanor said. Suddenly, out of nowhere, she felt an intense ache in the back of her head. She placed her right hand against her temple and realized that a nut finally hit her. When she turned around, she saw a squirrel, several meters above, aiming a nut and preparing to throw it.

"Do you really think now is a great time to be staring at your attacker?" Claire asked. "I, for one, am going to get off this sick, stupid tree." As she jumped down to a branch below, she became still. "Eleanor?"

"Yes, what is it?"

"I don't think we are going to be able to leave this tree."

"Why not?"

Claire pointed down with an outstretched paw, her fur ruffled by the slight breeze.

Placing a hand to her forehead to focus her gaze, Eleanor saw at once what Claire was referring to. Down below on the ground was a mob of squirrels all raising up nuts to throw. Dax was gone.

"Are they going to climb up and attack us, too?" Claire asked Eleanor.

"I don't think so. It looks like they are waiting." She took a deep breath and realized her heart was racing. "I think they have trapped us. They are waiting until they get us."

Another nut collided with her left arm. She felt overwhelming pain and began to fear that she would no longer be able to climb. There was a shuffling sound from above. She looked up and saw a squirrel perched on the branch, its small beady eyes unblinking. "All intrusions must be put to an end. You are trespassers, and the time has come to be held accountable."

Eleanor placed both of her hands on the sides of her head and spoke with a shaky voice:

"We don't want to hurt anyone! What do we do, Claire?"

"Enough of your banter," the squirrel said, lifting the nut above his head. "The time for justice is now."

"Is it really the time for justice?" a familiar, deep and gravelly voice called from above.

"Who's that?" Claire asked, looking up.

Standing on a bough several meters above, smirking, was Ryder. Eleanor noticed that his right arm was cradling something shiny against his body.

"It's you!" she called.

The squirrel lowered the nut slightly. "An additional perpetrator," he said.

"Yeah…" Ryder said as he hopped down to a lower branch. "You can go ahead and call me that. Look here, squirrels, you can get as mad at me as you want, but leave these two out of it. I was just tricking them into helping me carry out a job. They didn't do anything to you."

"What are you holding, Ryder?" Eleanor asked.

"Oh, this?" he held the shining object in his right paw and raised it up. "This? This….is none other than t-"

"The golden acorn," the squirrel said. "The intruder has stolen it. He must be neutralized at all costs."

"Yeah, yeah, yeah…I hear you, little guy." He grabbed the tree limb above his head with his left paw and shook it. "I got your precious treasure after all. I almost wished it had been harder."

"He must be destroyed," the squirrel raised his bushy tail and prepared to toss the nut. "The acorn must be saved."

"You wanna save it? Go ahead and go get it."

With that, he threw the golden acorn as hard as he could from the tree. Soaring across the sky, every squirrel jumped slightly at the sight of the gleaming, shining acorn disappearing from view.

"It must be recovered at all costs," the squirrel said. He sprinted down the tree and joined the mob of squirrels in chasing after it, disappearing into a distant grove of trees. Within seconds, all the squirrels vanished.

"What do you two say we get out of here?" Ryder asked. He grabbed one branch and then another, making his way back down towards the ground.

"I would prefer to never be away from the ground for this long again the rest of my life," Claire said. "Let me help you," she said to Eleanor, nodding towards her injured arm. Claire proceeded to jump from one branch to another, showing Eleanor the easiest way to climb back down with her better arm. "Thank goodness this one is easy for me to climb."

"Thank you," she said.

Claire shrugged. "I remember when you helped me in a tree."

Eleanor was overjoyed when her feet pressed against the soft forest floor. She turned towards Claire and said, "That was harrowing."

"It was," Claire agreed.

"Unbelievable job," Ryder said. "Boy oh boy, I should retire one of these days...you know, settle down."

"Stealing is never good," Eleanor said. "I hope this is a lesson for you, Ryder. We would not have joined you if you had been honest about that from the beginning. Right, Claire?"

Claire shrugged. "The squirrels were jerks. I didn't mind making them upset."

"You're not wrong, kid," Ryder said.

Eleanor looked around. "Where is Dax?"

There was a silence that followed after she spoke. Then, Eleanor realized that she could hear the faint sound of panting. "Is that him?" she asked.

Ryder stepped past Eleanor. "Did they lock him up, too? I tell you…those squirrels are twisted."

"What are you talking about?" Claire asked.

Ryder pointed back towards the thorny thicket. Eleanor and Claire both walked towards it and saw Dax, enclosed by thorns, his ears low.

"Did I do something wrong?" he asked.

Ryder waved a paw dismissively. "You didn't do anything, pup. Let me help break you out." He walked over towards a wooden stick, came back to the thicket, and proceeded to smash the thorns with it, creating a path out. "They love to use these wooden sticks to create an opening in the thorns. Then they toss their victims inside." He winked at Eleanor. "I saw a master criminal do this earlier," he said to her.

Dax emerged from the thorns. "I'm finally free! There are so many things I can do with this freedom!"

"So they put you in there, too, didn't they?" Eleanor said.

"They did, and it was terrible!" He lowered his head slightly. "I remember when I was in a cage last time…"

"Last time?" Eleanor asked. "When was that?"

"I was in a shelter place. There were a lot of other dogs there, and some of them were mean. Every day, I waited for someone to adopt me. I watched some other dogs get owners really fast. I felt alone!"

"Oh, Dax…"

"I wanted to have a home. I ended up watching a lot of humans meet me and then go away."

"I am so sorry to hear that. Is that where you lived before you met Claire?"

"That's right! I was so sad back then in the shelter. I guess sitting here behind these thorns all by myself reminded me a lot of those days. I don't like feeling that way!"

"Spending too much time locked up will do stuff to you," Ryder acknowledged. "It's no good."

"That's why I always try to be happy and excited," Dax said. "Life is better that way!"

"I didn't know that part of your story," Eleanor said. "You must have experienced a lot of rejection, having your hopes dashed like that."

"That's OK!" Dax shouted with a grin. "Now you're here with me."

"We couldn't keep going without you," Claire said. "Who else would spray water on me, shout in my ear, or protect me as a guard dog?"

"No one! I'm the guard dog!"

"That's right," Eleanor said with a smile. She looked at him, imagining him sitting in a shelter with no one to play fetch with, no one to pet him or pat his belly. Why wouldn't anyone want to adopt him?

In the silence that followed, Ryder nodded several times. "At least we're all back together again and in one piece. You know, I'm a pretty nice guy. The trouble with me, though, is I love stealing stuff. Don't know why, but I always have." He turned and pointed at the tree. "My whole life I've wanted to get the golden acorn. They say it's the greatest treasure the Togetherwood has to offer. Never could, though. The security of the place was always too tight. So, when I saw you three...I guess

I thought I had a chance to pull off one of the greatest heists of my career."

"Stealing is certainly wrong," Eleanor answered. "But if you wanted the golden acorn so badly, why did you toss it like that?"

"Seems like a huge waste of everyone's time," Claire added.

"Why?" he turned to face them. "Because...you know...I've always liked to steal, but I realized something new today. It was when I was up there with you two. You," he pointed at Eleanor. "When I was so close to the treasure, all you were concerned about was your kitty friend here. You were actually ready to risk it all just to help her out. I've never lived that way. I've always just looked out for myself." He slumped his head slightly. "I don't like getting all sentimental and such, but I guess when I saw your care and concern...it just made me realize that maybe there's more to life than just swiping things. So, I went ahead and gave the squirrels their gold back."

"You are a very nice raccoon," Dax said.

"What, me? Nah, pup. I've got nothing on you three. I always told myself I wanted to get rich and be the greatest criminal in the history of this here thicket. Maybe, though, I was wrong." He turned and looked towards the thorns longingly. "Maybe I was just looking to be redeemed, to find something better to live for...you know, to start caring for others the way you three do."

"That's very touching, Ryder," Eleanor said.

"Sure it is. So, here's what I'm going to do for you. A deal's a deal. You held up your end of the bargain, so now it's my turn." He walked over towards a nearby rock, and slid it to the side. He reached down towards the ground, and when he stood up, he was holding an axe. "It's always good to know how to use something sharp. To think that the squirrels caught me on a day when I wasn't carrying this..." He proceeded to chop the tree again and again, breathing heavily from exertion. A few moments later, the tree began to wobble.

"You wanna do the honors, pup?"

"Honors? I like honors," Dax said.

"Then get over here."

Dax walked over to where Ryder stood. Ryder pointed at the tree and whispered something in Dax's ear.

Dax shouted, "One…two…three!"

He pressed against the tree with his front paws. The tree fell towards the thorny thicket with a single, smooth motion. It landed on the thorns and bounced up several times, finally becoming still.

"How is this supposed to help us?" Claire complained.

"How?" Ryder called. "This here is a bridge for you three. Just be sure you keep your balance when you cross it. Trust me, this axe has gotten me out of more than a couple jams."

Eleanor, Dax, and Claire climbed up onto the fallen tree. Eleanor said, "We really must thank you for your help."

"I should be thanking you three. Thanks to you, I wanna be good from now on. I wanna start helping others out." He raised a paw in the air. "Thanks a bunch!"

Waving, the travelers crossed the thicket on the log, amazed at how easy the walk was.

"He may have made some mistakes, but it seems like he is turning a new leaf," Eleanor said.

"I liked him," Dax added.

"Always nice to accompany a criminal in theft," Claire said.

"I wonder where we will go next," Eleanor said. They stepped off the bridge, passed through a wall of trees, and saw before them a sprawling, spacious meadow. The grass was bright green. "I recall seeing this when we were up in the tree. I know we are going to find our way!"

"I wonder what we'll see next," Dax cried.

"I don't," Claire replied.

They left behind the thorny thicket once and for all as they prepared to face whatever came next.

9.
THREE POWERFUL FLOWERS

Dax raised his nose into the air, breathed in deeply, and then exhaled. "I like the smell of this place."

"What does it smell like?" Eleanor asked.

Moving away from the tall trees, they were now approaching a clearing and staring into the center of a lush meadow. The grass, brighter than ever before, rustled gently with the breeze. The ground beneath their feet gradually rose and then dipped down in a series of gigantic, magnificent slopes.

He stared at the blades of grass near his paws as he walked. "I don't know. It kinda makes me think of when we found that flower with Freya!"

Eleanor halted, raised her arm out, and pointed in the distance. "There it is! That must be what you are smelling, Dax."

Spread before them was a field of daisies. Each flower, a white circle with a yellow center, was lovely to behold. While Dax sprinted off into the center of the field, Eleanor crouched down on her knees, picked up a daisy, and twirled the stem, watching it rotate like a propeller.

"This really is delightful," she said, smiling.

Claire looked at the blooming display and then back at Eleanor. "It's OK."

"Don't you like flowers like these?"

"Not as much as him."

They looked up and saw several daisies soar into the air and drift back to the ground. Speeding through was Dax. "They are pretty!" he shouted. "They are very pretty flowers."

"They are," Eleanor agreed. She sat down and crossed her legs. For the first time in quite a long while, she felt fully at ease. She surveyed the rest of the meadow, noting that it was very big indeed. The bright-green grass reflected the sunlight above with its glow. Beyond the grass, in the distance, were lines of trees, no doubt leading deeper back into the Togetherwood. Eleanor knew they needed to continue going on their way, yet she treasured having a moment to sit and simply enjoy being in such a beautiful place.

"My father loves to garden," she said, still twisting the daisy stem in her hand. "In the summer, he grows so many different flowers."

"Does he have this kind?" Dax asked.

"Yes, he always has plenty of daisies. He will also grow roses, tulips, and even marigolds."

"That's amazing!" Dax exclaimed.

"If I close my eyes, I can see what the garden in the front of our home looks like." She sighed.

"What's wrong?" Dax asked.

"Can't you see she wants to be home with her family?" Claire asked.

"I didn't see that."

Eleanor dropped the daisy and said, "It's all right. I know we are on our way."

"I want to keep playing in these flowers," Dax said. "I want to squish them all down and make a path!"

"What you mean is that you like destroying nature," Claire replied. "Can't you just sit here like us?"

"Sit here? That sounds boring! Goodbye!" He dashed off, the sound of heavy panting and rustling plants following.

Claire rolled her eyes. "We really shouldn't waste too much time. I don't care what that owl said. We're going the wrong way."

"I don't think so. I think we are getting closer to where we need to be." Eleanor looked up at the sky, light blue with few clouds.

Claire licked her front paw and started to groom herself. "I guess this is a nice place," she finally said.

"The sun is out, which is wonderful."

"Something about it does seem strange, though."

"What do you mean?" Eleanor asked with curiosity.

"It seems really still and quiet. It feels silent to me. It isn't right."

"Silent? Can't you hear the sound of Dax running around in the field?"

Claire's eyes darted to her right. "No. In fact, I can't hear that."

Eleanor sat up. "Where did he go?" She raised a hand to her forehand to block out the sunlight and gazed out across the meadow. There was no sign of anyone or anything, no matter which way looked. Just as Claire had said, the meadow was silent.

"So," Claire said, "not only are we lost in a beautiful little field of flowers, but now we have lost the only companion stupid enough to enjoy running around in circles with his tongue hanging out of his mouth. Things really are splendid, aren't they?"

Eleanor raised out a hand as if to quiet Claire.

"What?"

"I am trying to listen."

"Listen to what?"

"There is no need for hopelessness," a voice called from behind.

Eleanor and Claire turned around and saw a deer. She stood, not far away, her legs long and narrow, her fur tan. The deer's eyes were small and dark. She looked at Eleanor and then Claire, standing frozen in place. On the right side of her head, nestled near her ear, was an orange flower.

"Who is she?" Claire asked.

The deer walked slowly towards them, placing each hoof in front of the other gracefully. She stood several meters away, perfectly still. Then she crouched down, as if she were bowing, and finally raised her head up to look at them once more.

"If we surrender ourselves to that which is, then there is no need for fear," she said to them.

Eleanor pointed and said, "I like the flower you have on your ear. That is a beautiful color."

The deer replied, "All colors, if we look deeply, reveal beauty."

"Sure thing," Claire said. "Was there anything we could help you with? Because we really need to find our friend right now."

"Your friend will be found. All is as it should be, and as it will be."

Eleanor scratched the back of her head. "Would you be willing to explain what you are saying to us a little more? I apologize, but I think we both are having trouble understanding. Also, what is your name?"

"My name is Delilah. The truth which I want to share with you is this: each of us has a journey to take, and now my path has crossed yours. Yes, your friend is gone. Now is the time that we reunite with him. Together, we can find him, for together we can do anything."

"It is nice to meet you, Delilah," Eleanor responded. She introduced herself and Claire.

Delilah gave a slight, quick nod, and then stared at Claire intently. "In you I sense much sorrow, much darkness."

"Sounds about right."

"You were saying you can help us find Dax," Eleanor continued. "Did you see him at all when he was running around in the flowers? Do you know where he went?"

"I did not see him running. I do not know where he went."

"Then how are you going to help us?" Claire asked impatiently.

Delilah turned to survey the meadow. A slight breeze brushed against her fur. The sun, beaming from high above, was now even brighter as its rays cascaded down. "There are three flowers," she said.

"What?"

Delilah turned to face Claire. "In this meadow are many flowers, each one beautiful in its own way. But there are three flowers, three powerful flowers, which are hidden. If we collect each of them, then your friend will reappear."

Claire rolled up into a ball on the ground and shut her eyes.

Eleanor crouched down low next to her. "Are you all right?" she whispered.

"Me? I'm fine. I think I've just been transported to another planet."

"I know she is…eclectic, but she seems very wise. I think she can help us."

"Help us? You think she can help us? She's saying that if we dance around with flowers in our hair that Dax will magically fall out of the sky. She has no idea what she's talking about."

"Claire, I know this sounds strange, but I believe she can help us. I just feel very at ease with her. Besides, if we look for these flowers together, that should allow us to see more of the meadow. It can't hurt our situation, can it?"

"It can hurt our ability to be connected to reality."

"I would like to have her join us in our search."

Claire did not reply at first, but instead continued to sit in a ball. She eventually raised her head slowly upward, opened her eyes, and said, "OK, Delilah. If we need to find you your flowers, then we better get going."

Delilah said, "Now that we have harmonized our paths, it is time for stillness to pass to movement." She trotted off towards the center of the meadow.

"Wait for us!" Eleanor called. She found it incredible how fast Delilah ran. It was as though she were gliding, hovering just above the flowers as she moved. Eleanor and Claire both followed along as fast as they were able. The day felt even warmer when running.

To Eleanor's left were several patches of flowers, in bunches of blue, purple, red, and even yellow. They changed colors with each step she took. In the distance was the edge of the forest, a series of gigantic trees.

"Where exactly were you planning to lead us?" Claire asked, breathing heavily from the exertion of running.

Delilah came to a halt. She moved her head one way and then turned it quickly again. "Such a matter is not of my own doing," she said. "It is not us who control the flowers. No, they lead us."

"Of course they do," Claire sighed.

"Perhaps we might be able to stop here and catch our breaths," Eleanor said, leaning over with her hands on her knees.

Delilah remained completely motionless.

Eleanor savored the moment to recover. She felt the ache in her chest disappear and her breaths become slower and deeper. She brushed her hair out of her eyes. When she looked at Delilah again, she realized that the deer still had not moved.

"Delilah?"

There was a pause, and then suddenly Delilah jumped in the air, landing on the meadow ground with all four legs at once. She turned her head downward. "Here," she said simply.

"Here what?" Claire asked.

Her eyes focused on the ground, Delilah said, "Our first flower is within reach. It is close, closer than we know. It could not be closer."

"I think it could be closer."

"That is great news," Eleanor answered. "Do you know where it is, Delilah?"

"This patch will point the way," she answered.

Eleanor turned her head towards the ground and saw a collection of small flowers as white as the moon.

"I am sure you are right. Am I missing something?"

"To move towards the flower we seek is to walk away from these flowers. Distance yourself from the patch."

Eleanor took several steps backwards to the light yellow meadow grass. Claire yawned as she followed in turn.

Delilah, Eleanor, and Claire stood in a line next to the white patch. The flowers, swaying with the light breeze, appeared indifferent to the travelers. Claire continued to sigh. Eleanor soon noticed one of the flowers in the middle of the patch change color from white to red. The others immediately touching it then also became the same color. Over the course of the next few seconds, many more flowers transformed from white to red until a distinct picture was created.

"I see it," Eleanor said. "The red flowers have become an arrow!"

"Yes, the arrow is now here," Delilah answered. "If we only follow it, then we will take the necessary route."

"This is so bizarre," Claire said. "I guess we should follow it, though."

Delilah sped away from the patch, moving in the direction of the red arrow. Within seconds, she was fading away in the horizon.

Eleanor beamed as she trotted after the deer. "That definitely was impressive."

"How did she know that would happen?" Claire asked.

"I don't know. But maybe she really will be able to help us find Dax."

They continued to run along the rolling meadow and soon saw Delilah standing, again, next to a patch of white flowers. When they joined her, she said, "One patch begets another."

"What are you talking about?" Claire asked.

"We must be silent if we wish for the next arrow to appear."

"She's right," Eleanor added. "Let's just go ahead and wait patiently."

"She's right?"

Like before, the flowers in the middle of the patch changed color. Beginning in the middle and then spreading outward, the flowers transformed until another arrow appeared, this one as blue as the light sky above.

"It really is amazing!" Eleanor exclaimed.

Delilah turned her head at once in the direction it pointed. "We need to continue." She dashed off, disappearing again into the blur of colorful flowers.

Having now adjusted to the rapid stopping and sprinting, Eleanor and Claire did not hesitate to follow her. Even as she struggled with fatigue, Eleanor enjoyed the fresh air against her face. She looked ahead and saw rows of sharp grass. In the distance, Delilah once more stood perfectly still.

When Eleanor and Claire reached her, they saw yet another patch of white flowers.

"Well, what now?" Claire asked. "Is this arrow purple?"

"I really am curious to see where this leads," Eleanor added.

Delilah said, "No more beacons will guide us. We have arrived."

"We have?"

After staring at the sky for a brief moment, Delilah motioned towards the center of the flower patch. Lowering her head, she touched a single flower with her nose. At once, it flew into the air, slowly drifting downwards until it landed on Eleanor's head next to her left ear.

"You truly are discovering a new essence," Delilah said to her.

Giggling, Eleanor turned towards Claire. "What do you think?"

"Are you getting sucked into all of this nonsense, too?"

Eleanor placed a hand next to her head and felt the flower. "I do like it. It feels nice."

"But how is this going to bring back Dax?" Claire asked. "Am I the only one who seems to care about the question that really matters?"

Delilah took several steps towards her. "Full of anger, tortured by sorrow. This is how we know that you have not learned to truly see: you still wallow as a prisoner of suffering."

"None of that's necessarily wrong," Claire replied. "I just don't see what any of this has to do with finding our friend."

Eleanor crouched down low and pet Claire on her head. "Let's keep giving her a chance. I must say I like where this is going. Aren't these flowers beautiful?" She turned to look towards Delilah. "Where do we go next? You did say there were two other flowers to find, correct?"

"Yes." Delilah turned her head in a new direction. "Within the heart of the meadow lies the greatest treasure, one that we carry with us everywhere we go."

"All right," Claire grumbled. "Let's just keep going then, shall we?"

"If you do not mind me asking," Eleanor spoke, "how is it that you know the way to go?"

"Knowledge is available to all who simply ask," Delilah replied. She ran off.

"Let's follow her!" Eleanor cried.

As she ran through the meadow, Eleanor noticed the gentle slopes of the ground beneath her shoes. She was completely surrounded by patches of bright flowers. Some of them were enormous and close by, while others remained far off in the distance and seemingly small. The afternoon was growing warmer still. As she took a deep breath through her nose, she found the many scents of the meadow to be delightful.

Delilah, running only a moment ago, now stood still. Eleanor and Claire caught up and stood on both sides of her. The three of them surveyed a patch of purple flowers, bigger than any other they had yet seen. As she turned her head, she was amazed by just how many flowers there were, for it seemed as though there was no end to them. She turned towards Delilah and asked, "What do we do now?"

There was a pause, and then Delilah answered, "To be different is not wrong."

"What?" Claire asked.

"To be unique, to stand out," Delilah continued, "is to be a source of power. For this is how we will know what we seek: it will be different from all the others."

Eleanor placed a hand to her chin. Suddenly, she exclaimed, "I think I understand! Delilah, are you saying that we need to find the flower that is different than all the other ones?"

"Yes."

"How are we supposed to do that?" Claire asked. "There are a million of these purple things. How could we ever find it? There's no way."

"If there is belief, there is possibility."

"Let's give it a try," Eleanor said with a smile. She walked towards the patch, raised her hand to her forehead, and began to scan for a flower that wasn't purple.

Sighing, Claire followed from behind.

Eleanor walked confidently, but each time she looked around it seemed that she had not moved at all. Everywhere she looked, all the flowers were purple. With each passing second, she knew that Dax could be even more lost. Where was he? All was quiet except for the rustling sounds caused by the wind.

When she turned to her right, she saw Delilah run off.

"Where are you going?" she asked.

At once, Delilah stopped. She faced Eleanor and said, "Intuition speaks softly. I sense that it lies over this way."

Claire's nose and whiskers brushed against the purple blooms. "This is pointless. You're right, Delilah. There is possibility. Possibility that Eleanor and I are stupid enough to believe you know where you're taking us."

Delilah walked towards her. Bending her knees slightly, she lowered her head down towards Claire and said, "There is no need to despair."

"Maybe she is right," Eleanor added, placing her hand to her forehead and squinting her eyes. "I know it seems like this patch will never end, but maybe we are close to finding it!"

Delilah smiled slightly. "She is on the path towards discovery."

Claire sat still and raised her head up. "You two can say whatever you want. The problem is that even if finding a special flower would help us, there's no way to see it. I can look in any direction, and all I see is purple." She sighed.

Once more, Delilah lowered her head down to be close to Claire. "Rise up and climb onto my back," she said.

"What?"

Delilah shook her head slightly. "To see with an enhanced vision, you will need to ascend to a higher place."

"I think she wants you to ride her," Eleanor explained. "Then, maybe you will be able to see better when she stands up."

"Yes," Delilah replied.

Claire's eyes squinted slightly. For a moment, she looked as though she was ready to sleep. She then hopped aboard Delilah, who raised herself back up. Claire meowed nervously while maintaining her balance.

Eleanor giggled again as she looked at them. "You really are high up. How does the world look from up there?"

Claire's eyes were bigger than Eleanor had ever seen them. "I don't know about this."

"There is nothing to fear. No harm will befall you," Delilah said.

"Do you see anything different?" Eleanor asked.

"Everything looks purple," Claire answered. "All the flowers are the same color."

Suddenly, Delilah began to walk, causing Claire to scramble to stay in her position.

"You could have given me a little warning, you know," she grumbled.

"As we move, we will better see what this world has to offer us."

"So long as it isn't offering me a fall."

"Just think of it as being fun!" Eleanor said. She walked next to Delilah, deeper still into the patch.

"Close, careful focus will yield the reward," Delilah said.

"I am trying to focus…" Claire began, looking all around the patch with her head raised high. "It all looks the same. Everywhere I stare, I just see dumb purple flowers."

"You must gaze more deeply."

"I am gazing! I'm gazing, focusing, looking, and whatever other word you want to use. But as I keep telling you, all I see are…"

"Are you all right?" Eleanor asked.

"You are in silence," Delilah added.

A small grin formed on Claire's face. She looked at Eleanor and then said, "I think I might see a flower in this patch that isn't purple."

"Where is it?" Eleanor asked excitedly.

Claire pointed with her left paw. "It's over there. Delilah, keep it moving."

"Yes."

They continued through the sea of purple petals until they reached it, a single yellow flower resting peacefully. Claire leapt off Delilah's back and made a soft landing. She raised her head close towards the prize, reaching a paw towards it. The yellow petals bounced up into the sky and disappeared from view for a moment. Then, just like the white flower from before, it twirled and spun through the air downwards, finally landing on the side of Claire's right ear.

She moved her head rapidly from side to side. The petals did not slide off.

"A natural fit," Delilah remarked. "You, too, have encountered a new essence."

Eleanor looked at Claire while pointing at the white flower in her own hair. "They really are lovely, aren't they?"

"Whatever you say," Claire replied. She turned towards Delilah. "Did you say there's only one more of these we need to find?"

"Yes. Upon finding the final hidden flower, it is then that you will be reunited with your lost friend."

"What do we need to do next?" Eleanor asked.

"Follow me." She walked off, leaving behind the purple flower patch.

They followed her. "Have you always lived here in the meadow, Delilah?" Eleanor asked.

"Yes."

"Do you have other friends here? Are there others you like to look for flowers with?"

"No."

Claire said, "This place seems awfully quiet."

"That's true," Eleanor added. "I don't think we have met anyone else here since we arrived."

Delilah looked towards the blue sky. "From the meadow I came. To the meadow I will one day return. Within solitude itself, I am complete. For this alone I seek: to experience pure transcendence."

"You've got to be kidding me..." Claire muttered.

Delilah gestured with her head at the flower on Eleanor's head and Claire's as well. "These treasures you possess are powerful. In time, this power will return your friend to us. In time, all things will unfold."

"They really are pretty," Eleanor said. "I must admit, I wish I had ended up with the yellow one."

"Pretty flowers are fine," Claire began, "I just hope we find Dax soon."

"I'm sure we will," Eleanor beamed.

Delilah continued to walk at a brisk pace. "You will be reunited. Yet, you must remember that you complete yourselves on your own, just as you are."

"Could you repeat that?" Eleanor asked.

The flowers surrounding Delilah suddenly seemed to be very still. "To be complete by yourself, as you are, this is transcendence."

"You mean to be alone?"

"Not to be alone, but to be complete. Though I am a master, never would I expect such of others."

"I may not like others very much," Claire said, "but even I would never want to be by myself all the time. That sounds horrible."

"We must not be understanding what she is explaining to us," Eleanor reasoned. "Delilah, you are so wise. Will you please help us find our friend? We really need to find him and continue on our way."

"It is true, we will find him," Delilah replied. "But my wisdom remains: do not forget that you are complete on your own."

"That doesn't seem wise at all," Claire muttered to herself.

At that moment, a sharp breeze blew through where they stood. On both sides of Eleanor, she saw flowers soar into the air and slowly drift down towards the meadow ground. Red, blue, purple, orange, every color imaginable, they fell wonderfully towards the earth like pieces of a broken rainbow.

Eleanor looked up at the display, at the dozens of falling petals, and placed her hands over her mouth.

"Yet we must not wait," Delilah continued. "Once they all land on the grass, it is then that we will be lost with no place to go for eternity." She ran after the falling flowers, which now were moving away. Like streams of rain falling from a cloud blown by the wind, the petals were drifting away.

Eleanor looked at Claire without saying a word, and then they both followed after Delilah, moving through the tunnel of petals. She continually brushed colorful blooms off her forehead. It was very difficult, nearly impossible, to see in front of her feet, for they were everywhere. But trusting that she would not fall, she ran after Delilah as speedily as she was able.

"I hate to admit it," Claire said. "But it is a beautiful view."

"I think we need to hurry," Eleanor replied. "We don't want to lose her, do we?"

They continued to run as fast as they could, the views of the meadow hidden now behind the falling petals. The colorful streams soared with the wind each time it picked up. Eleanor felt that she was losing her breath. She came to a halt, bent her knees, and leaned forward again, breathing heavily.

"Where did you go?" Claire asked. She then saw Eleanor and walked towards her.

"I'm sorry. I don't know what has gotten into me. I guess I am feeling tired all of a sudden."

"I know what you mean."

Eleanor blinked several times. "But we can't just sit. Dax is missing, and now we don't know where Delilah went, either."

"More importantly, we're supposed to find some hollow before we fade away in the unending, brutal darkness of nightfall."

"I just hope Dax is all right."

"I'm sure he's fine. He's probably rolling around in the flowers somewhere, slobbering all over."

Eleanor felt the warmth of the sun on her head. She wiped the sweat off of her forehead. "Do you see Delilah anywhere?"

"I don't."

"What are we to do, then?"

"We might as well give up. A nap might be nice."

Eleanor crouched down low next to the flowers, picking up a blue one. She looked at it, tossed it to the ground, and then began to cry.

Under the bright sun, sitting in a field of colorful petals, Eleanor sobbed into her hands. All the frustration of wandering for so long, the sadness of being away from her family, the fear of never making it home, crashed over her like a tidal wave. She felt warm tears on her cheeks. For a moment, she really didn't believe that there was anything, anything at all in the whole world, that could help her feel better. It felt as though there was nothing that could lift the heavy weight crushing her heart. She felt completely alone until she sensed something furry against her knees.

Brushing against her gently was Claire, who weaved around her as her tail swayed. Eleanor lowered her hands to see her friend showing her that she was not alone. Wiping more tears from her eyes, Eleanor placed her hands on the meadow grass and looked up at the blue sky.

Claire did not say anything. Rather, she continued to comfort her. Eleanor now felt that everything was lighter, that maybe somehow, someway, it was possible for things to become right again.

"Thank you," she said while wiping the last tears. "You are a great friend."

"I may not normally like people," Claire said," but I admit I do care about you. Though it can bother me immensely at times, you do remind me to see the brighter side of things. So now I'm going to try and return the favor."

"I suppose those are the kindest words I could expect from you. Thank you!" she beamed. She hopped onto her feet at once. "We must keep going. The only question is where?"

Claire's tail stopped moving. "Do you see that over there?"

Behind Eleanor was a swirl of flower petals, spinning in circles like a small cyclone.

"I don't know what that is," she answered, "but maybe Delilah is over there. Let's take a closer look."

They walked across the meadow, passing rows of orange and green flowers, until they were close to the peculiar sight. Confused, Eleanor looked to the right and noticed that there was an edge, a cliff that overlooked a deep ditch below.

Eleanor walked close to it, careful not to fall. Deep down, at the bottom, Delilah sat still and slumped over.

"She fell so far down..."

"Of course she did," Claire replied.

Eleanor's eyes became wide. "But how could that happen? The flowers...the wise things she said...was she...?"

"She was wrong. Maybe she said some sagely things, but she thought she could do everything on her own. Look at what happened to her."

"I think I was blinded for a moment. We need to help her now." She craned her head to look down the ditch. "Are you all right?"

There was no response.

"Delilah, can you hear me?" she continued.

The deer's head moved slowly, facing the top of the pit to meet Eleanor's gaze.

"Lamentable," Delilah began. "A fall from transcendence, into oblivion."

"What happened?" Claire asked.

"Pursuing the storm of petals yielded only pain. For this is the end that accompanied my chase: a deep descent."

"Do you need help?" Eleanor asked.

"What help can meet my needs? I am complete. I am my own."

"What you are is stuck in a hole in the ground," Claire said.

Eleanor scanned the meadow, looking for anything they might be able to use to help Delilah. Not far off, resting between patches of flowers, was a lone tree. She walked towards it and saw that it had many branches of different sizes and shapes.

"This might be able to help us," she said as she grabbed a particularly sturdy branch.

It required much of her strength, but Eleanor was able to bend it enough that she finally could snap it off the tree. She returned to the edge of the pit, looked at Claire briefly, and then reached down into the dark with the branch. "I think if you grab on to this, we will be able to pull you back up."

"If I am lifted, it only reveals how terrible the fall," Delilah answered.

"What?" Claire asked in confusion.

Eleanor lowered the branch for a moment. "We see that you experienced an unfortunate accident. Both Claire and I are happy to help you."

Delilah stared at the wall of the pit. "Your intentions flow with compassion. Yet, completeness must be maintained. I must be true to myself."

Eleanor extended the branch towards her once more. "We know that everyone needs help now and then. Maybe, after we lift you up, you can keep that in mind so that you can help us when we experience our own fall."

"Any fall is weakness, the poison of transcendence."

"I don't really know what that means," Eleanor continued, "but I do know that bad things happen sometimes, and we all need the support of others."

"You should really just do us a favor and grab on to the stick," Claire added.

Delilah closed her eyes. She was motionless for a moment, and then she looked at them with a radiant smile. "Within one instance...pure insight! When we all are one, it is then that we transcend!" She bit the wood with her teeth and wrapped her hooves around both sides of it.

Using all of her strength, Eleanor was able to slowly lift Delilah up and out of the hole in the ground. As Delilah shook dirt out of her head, Eleanor noticed something in the grass near the edge.

"Isn't that flower beautiful?" she asked. She walked over and picked it up, delighted by its pink color. "I do not know why, but I find this one to be especially lovely."

Delilah's eyes became big. "At last what has been lost is found."

"What do you mean?"

Delilah pointed with a hoof at the pink petals. "We have found the third powerful flower. The journey is complete. One end begets a new beginning."

"A new beginning?" Clare echoed.

Delilah nodded. "The next step that awaits us is to place this where it belongs."

"Where does it belong?" Eleanor asked.

"Wow! Such a beautiful flower!" a voice called from behind.

Standing before them, grinning as his black fur moved with the breeze, was Dax.

"Where on earth did you come from?" Claire asked in disbelief.

He took several steps towards them. "I saw such pretty flowers. They were everywhere! I had to go run and look at them."

Eleanor placed her right hand on her hip. "Well, you certainly did scare us when we were unable to find you. We're glad you are back now!" she smiled.

"Me too!"

"But where did you go?" Claire asked. "How did you find us? Why are you here now?"

"Powerful flowers," Delilah said.

Claire turned to face her. "What did you say?"

"Three hidden flowers that are not ordinary. They are powerful flowers capable of transforming all, of channeling dream into reality."

"Why did I even ask?" Claire sighed.

"I want to wear the pink one!" Dax cried. "I want to wear a flower, just like everyone else." He moved towards Eleanor, who placed it behind his left ear. She and Claire stifled a giggle when they saw him grin at them.

"I bet I look great," Dax said. "I bet I look smart and impressive with my new flower. We are all wearing them!"

"They really have been remarkable," Eleanor replied. "Delilah, we must thank you for journeying alongside us. Though you experienced some difficulty along the way, you did teach us the value of seeing the meadow as a magical, transcendent place."

"I still would be curious to see what would have happened if we had just skipped the flower hunt and waited around for Dax to show up," Claire said. "There's no way to know now."

"It is only by faith that you may see," Delilah answered. She then shook her head slightly, as though she was being splashed with cold water. "Yet, what seemed true to me is now deception. From you three, I have learned something profound: true strength and wisdom does not come from following nature in solitude. No, neither does completeness. Instead, it is in friendship and care that we encounter something transcendent. No longer do I need to be alone, living in this way." She closed her eyes and made a small smile. "My eyes have been opened to a new power, the power of community, of being complete...with others."

Dax's ears lowered slightly. "What does that mean? My head hurts."

"What it means," Eleanor began, "is that..."

She did not finish speaking, as when she turned her head to look for Delilah, she realized that she was gone, vanished like a flower petal in the wind.

"She's nowhere to be seen," Claire said.

Eleanor smiled. "She disappeared just as mysteriously as she appeared. What it means is that we can continue on our way now." She pointed across several patches of flowers, towards a wall of trees marking the edge of the meadow. "I believe if we go that way, we will get closer to the Loneliest Hollow."

"Let's go!" Dax shouted.

"I know that we are going to discover what we need to find there. All we need to do is keep going!"

Eleanor, Dax, and Claire walked through the meadow, towards the edge of towering trees not far off.

"I feel embarrassed," Eleanor began. "How was I foolish enough to believe that these flowers had special powers? While we were in the meadow, Delilah struck me as an incredibly wise teacher."

"I guess she was convincing," Claire said. "It's not like she was all wrong. After all, Dax did show up right after we found the third flower. That's the part I still can't explain."

Panting and trotting quickly, Dax said, "As long as I have this flower in my ear, I know I'm ready to take on anything!"

10.
THE CUB WHO LEFT HIS CAVE

Eleanor, Dax, and Claire passed under an arch of creeping trees as though they were entering a building. Having become so accustomed to the blue sky, Eleanor was startled by how the view above her became a little darker. When she focused her ears, she was able to notice the sounds of leaves fluttering and grass shaking with the breeze.

"We must be getting closer now," she said to the others.

"We are!" Dax exclaimed. "With each step we take, we are closer to our goal."

"I know it may seem peculiar, but I really do believe we can trust that owl. If we keep going this way, it will only be a matter of time before we find a cardboard box and return home."

"But how?" Claire asked. "How do we know a box is waiting for us?"

"Because there is one!" Dax cried.

Claire lowered her head and looked at the dirty path. "Sometimes I wish I didn't think things through, too."

"The great thing about our situation," Eleanor began, "the thing to take comfort in, is that we have each other."

"What do you mean?"

Eleanor smiled and gestured with an arm towards Dax. "We have been through so many adventures, all in one day, but we have navigated them together, the three of us! I know that when we work together, it is only a matter of time before we succeed."

"It's true!" Dax added. "If I was alone, that would be OK. If I was just with you, Claire, that would be good. But when all three of us are together…well…hmm…that's GREAT!"

Claire jolted slightly when she heard this.

Eleanor scratched her head as she raised her foot over a thick tree root crossing the path. "I was thinking about this back in the meadow, back when you were gone, Dax."

"What were you thinking about?" Dax asked.

"Well, after you disappeared, we were really upset. We felt frightened and sad because we did not know where you were. Isn't that right, Claire?"

Claire looked up at the dark canopy of trees. "Oh, yes. We were so upset, so frightened, so sad. It was unbearable. I really still haven't recovered from it."

"I am sorry to hear that you are sad," Dax said. "I hope you feel better soon! I'm here!"

"Hopefully, a hawk will pick me up and fly over the ocean with me before I get any sadder."

Eleanor turned to look at Claire and then at Dax. "What I meant to say is that I think we three have a very special bond. Both Ryder and Delilah seemed to underestimate the value of having something like our friendship. I think it is a good thing to remember. Also, I don't want to imagine us being separated from each other again."

"Where is he? Oh, where is he? My sweetie, my little Caleb!" a voice called from behind two trees.

Claire sighed. "Ugh…what now?"

Dax sat still, his tail lowering towards the ground. "I think we need to stop," he said.

"Why is that?" Eleanor asked.

"There is a bear behind those trees," he said. "I'm a guard dog, remember? The guard dog always sees the bear first."

"Does the guard dog get eaten first as well?" Claire asked.

"I don't think we will get eaten," Eleanor whispered, sounding nervous. "But I do think we need to get away from here."

"How were you planning on us doing that?"

"I bet I could take him," Dax said. "I can jump at him and bite him, and then he will be defeated!"

At the moment, the trees shook slightly and they heard a loud thumping sound. Eleanor and the others saw two dark brown, furry paws reach out to bend the trees to the side. Frozen, terrified, full of panic, they tilted their heads up to see a fully grown bear.

Eleanor's mouth was wide open, her eyes still.

"I can take him....I still can...maybe I can," Dax whispered.

The bear looked down at them and spoke:

"Oh dear, oh dear! Oh, what will I ever do?"

Eleanor, Dax, and Claire did not speak.

The bear raised a paw to wave at the travelers. "Are you three all right? You look like you missed lunch."

"I am a little hungry," Dax said. "Wait... you're a girl bear!"

Eleanor, realizing the bear was not dangerous but concerned, asked, "I think we should be the ones asking you if everything is all right. You seem very upset, and if we could help, we certainly would like to!"

"Would we?" Claire asked.

"I think we can help," Dax said, "but can we eat something, too?"

The bear slowly took in a deep breath. "It just brings me so much relief to hear you say that. You three are sweethearts, I can tell already."

"My name is Eleanor," she said as she introduced the others. "May we ask you what your name is?"

The bear smiled slightly, her cheeks turning red. "My name is Beth Anne."

Eleanor also smiled. "It is wonderful to meet you. Can you tell us what it is that is upsetting you?"

Beth Anne stood up slightly. "Oh, it's just…it's just so terrible…it's jus-"

"— Just what?" Claire interrupted.

Beth Anne did not reply at first, but instead gazed at Claire. "You remind me of him, in fact."

"Of who?" Dax asked.

"Terrible," Beth Anne whispered to herself.

"It sounds like whatever happened to you has been very difficult," Eleanor said with her hands folded. "Do you think you might be able to tell us a few more details about it?"

Beth Anne raised her head into the air and lowered it numerous times, shaking it as though in great pain. "My son," she said at last. "Caleb, my cub…he's gone! He left his cave!"

"Where did he go?" Dax asked.

"Why, I don't know." She shook her head several times. "He and I were having another argument, and oh dear have we been having so many of those recently. I said things I wish I had not said, and now he is gone!"

"That's terrible! He needs his mother!"

"It's OK," Eleanor said, placing a hand on Beth Anne's shoulder. "I am sure it's scary to not know where he is, but I am also convinced he can't be too far from here."

Beth Ann grabbed Eleanor's hand and held it in her paw. "Oh, why, you certainly just are such a little sweetheart. Do you think you might be able to help me to find my little cutie-pie Caleb?"

Claire made a sound as if to clear her throat. Eleanor whispered in her ear, "It is good to help others. Don't you agree, Claire?"

She sighed.

"We can help you find him!" Dax shouted. He raised his nose high into the air and began making a loud sniffing sound. "I know what bears smell like, and I will follow his trail until we locate him."

Beth Anne suddenly looked less sad. "You three are such dears. I just haven't had that good a sense of smell since I got sick last week. You really want to help me?"

"Of course!" Dax's tail was wagging forcefully.

"Where do you think we ought to look?" she asked, staring at a nearby tree.

Dax was still sniffing the ground. He suddenly lowered his head, spun around in a circle, and pointed towards a distant grove of trees with his head. "The scent is this way!"

Eleanor, Claire, and Beth Anne walked along the forest floor, stopping occasionally when Dax came to a halt to resume sniffing.

"It certainly is nice to be back in the forest, under the cover of trees," Eleanor said. "It really is pleasant."

"It would be much nicer to be back at home," Claire said.

"Yes," she agreed, "but we must keep going along the path we are on, going one step at a time."

"Have you three found yourselves lost out here, exposed to all the elements?" Beth Anne asked, her voice full of concern.

"We are," Eleanor replied, "but we will not be for long!"

"Oh dear, it really is frightful to think that so many youngsters are stranded. First my Caleb, and now you three!"

"I don't think of it as being lost, but rather that we are on our way," she answered, speaking to herself as much as to the others.

"This place, the Togetherwood, it is just going to the dogs more and more every day."

Dax stopped sniffing and turned his head around. "Huh?"

"Oh! Nothing, dear!"

The sniffing continued.

Beth Anne, who made slight thuds each time her big paws hit the ground, sighed. "I just hope my cubbie-wubbie Caleb is all right. He's so delicate! He's like a little flower. It was only the other day that I held him in my paws outside our first cave."

"I am sure he will be just fine," Eleanor said, smiling.

Claire, walking next to Eleanor, said, "Of course he is. All he wanted to do was go outside and get away from her." She nodded towards Beth Anne. "I think that makes perfect sense."

"Oh dear...oh dear...." Beth Anne muttered.

Eleanor kept her eyes on Dax, who was off ahead, following the trace of Caleb. She found herself continually looking up above, at the majestic and jagged tree branches. If she turned her head any way, there truly was no end to the trees, the brown and maroon trunks and the dark spaces between them. The ground beneath her feet was soft, a rolling slant of dirt and grass that kept going, unfolding like a giant carpet. When Eleanor looked at Beth Anne and noticed how concerned she was, how she kept muttering to herself, Eleanor thought of her own parents. She wondered if her mother or father were at all worried about her, whether they were desperate to know why she had not yet returned home. Surely, she thought to herself, they must be in great distress. Thinking of this made Eleanor sad, as she wished she could comfort them, letting them know that she was on her way home as fast as she could go. Moreover, she also felt guilty, realizing that it was because she had gotten lost that they were experiencing such agony. Why had she climbed into the box to get close to the owl? Why hadn't she listened to her father and taken the correct path?

"Why are you so quiet?" Claire asked her.

"Oh," Eleanor stumbled as she nearly tripped over a branch on the ground. "I was just daydreaming."

"Unless you know how to make your dreams come true, you probably shouldn't bother. Besides, it looks like our faithful friend up here has gotten us even more lost than ever before."

"What do you mean?"

At that moment, Eleanor looked up and saw Dax, crouching still.

"What is it, Dax?" she asked. She then realized that he was no longer moving because he was standing at the edge of a cliff.

"I followed the scent, and it led me here," he said.

Eleanor looked past Dax and surveyed a lake down below, its water as blue as a crystal.

"I guess he's just lost and gone," Claire said with a yawn.

"Aren't you going to tell me where my son went off to, sir?" Beth Anne asked.

Dax stared at the water. "I think he jumped off of here and went for a swim."

Beth Anne craned her neck to look down as well. "But…he would never…I expressly told him…"

"What did you tell him?" Eleanor asked.

"I told him that he was prohibited from jumping off this cliff into the lake. It is much too dangerous. I do know some of his friends, other cubs with careless parents, have always been try-ing to get him to join them in leaping into danger. But he knows what his mother bear told him. He certainly didn't jump from here."

Dax sniffed at the ground once more and then looked at Beth Anne. "I know this is his scent. He must have jumped!"

Beth Anne stood up straight, her fur bristling. "Sir, I must say that I appreciate your assistance, but it now will no longer be necessary. I know some bears may raise their cubs to be reckless and irresponsible, but Caleb is no such bear. He was raised better than that. If you are suggesting that Caleb, my cubby-wubbie, would disobey his mother, then I must tell you I will need to look for him on my own."

With that, she swiftly turned around and walked back into the depths of the forest.

Claire rolled into a ball. "She did seem pretty appreciative, didn't she?"

"It is unfortunate," Eleanor replied. "Wherever Caleb is, I hope she is able to find him."

"I knew that helping others was a waste of time."

Dax noticed a sloping trail to their right, which gradually led down to meet the edge of the lake. "I just know he was here earlier. He was here, and then he jumped into the lake!"

"Whatever you say."

"I think we should go down there! If he disobeyed her instructions, we can go find him and then bring him back to her!"

"Down that winding trail over there to the lake?" Eleanor asked.

Dax nodded. "If we go to the lake, we can find him!"

"Maybe he doesn't want to be found," Claire said.

"No," Dax answered. "He wants to be found!" He sprinted over to the trail and made his way down, circling around the cliff, until he disappeared from view. Seconds later, they heard the sound of water splashing.

Claire gazed at her two front paws. "We don't have time for this. We need to get to this stupid hollow."

"Don't you remember what Octavious said? We need to help others and let them help us. Those were his instructions."

"Why should we care what some dumb bird tells us?"

Eleanor smiled. "Because they are good instructions." She took the trail down, following where Dax had gone.

"Ugh, humans…" Claire muttered as she followed her.

Down below, the clear water gently lapped against the edge of the grass. As Eleanor stood, she observed something that was black and bobbing up and down.

"What's that?" Claire asked when she appeared.

"I think I know what it is. Actually, I meant to say I know who it is."

Droplets of water flew through the air as they heard a familiar voice shout:

"I found him! He is here and I found him!"

Dax swam towards them until he arrived at the edge of the lake.

"Did you find who I think you found?" Eleanor asked as she crouched down to be at his level.

Nodding his head up and down vigorously, Dax replied, "The cub. I found him! His name is Caleb."

"Where is he, then?" Claire asked, also crouched down low, her paws vanished.

Dax turned his head left and right, spraying more droplets of water. "He's over there!"

"Where?"

"Wait a minute," Eleanor said as she took a closer look. "I think I see him now!"

Sure enough, out in the deep center of the water, there were several brown bears swimming. If she listened closely, Eleanor could hear the sounds of laughter and loud talking.

"Are you sure it's him? Did you talk to him?"

Dax nodded.

"Did you tell him his mommy wants him to go home and have a snacky-snack and nap time?" Claire asked.

"I didn't tell him that," Dax answered, looking puzzled.

"What did he say to you?" Eleanor asked.

Dax continued paddling his legs more forcefully, creating small waves. "He told me to leave him alone."

"Why did he say that?"

"I don't know. I don't get it. Moms are great!" Dax exclaimed.

Eleanor looked at the water, at how it shone and reflected the sunlight above in a beautiful way, like a mirror of the sky. "Beth Anne is awfully concerned about him. Maybe we should all try to talk to him again."

"She has no reason to be concerned," Claire said. "Look at him. He's out for a swim, having a merry time."

"That may be, but his mother doesn't know that. She is very worried about him, and we need to help her."

"Do you want me to go swim over to him again?" Dax asked. "I can do that. I am an excellent swimmer!"

"I think that would be wise, Dax," Eleanor replied. "Would you go talk to him and ask him to come over to us?"

"OK!" There was an explosive splash sound and then Dax was gone.

For the next several seconds, he was nowhere to be seen. Then, suddenly, Dax broke the surface of the water as he swam like his life depended on it. The sound of panting filled the entire lake area.

Eleanor saw that the bears in the distance noticed Dax swimming towards them once again. On the other side of the bears, further along the water, was the sheer wall of the cliff. Worn and old, it appeared ancient, as though it had witnessed many years of history and many different animals eager to swim. Dax soon arrived where the bears were floating. He could be heard speaking, followed by the bears responding. A pause followed.

"I'm sure those bears just want our furry friend to leave them alone," Claire said.

"Perhaps, but perhaps not." Eleanor then pointed. "Look!"

Dax was now swimming back towards them, followed by the three bears.

"It worked!" Eleanor exclaimed.

Still paddling his legs frantically, Dax said, "Eleanor and Claire, this is Caleb!" He turned to look at the other two bears. "What are your names again?"

"Trey," one of them said sullenly.

"Right! Trey! What about you?" he asked the other bear.

There was a faint mumbling sound.

"I didn't quite hear what you said," Eleanor said, brushing her hair back with her hand. "Could you repeat that?"

They heard a slightly louder mumbling sound.

"He doesn't like to talk to humans very much," Caleb said. "Actually, he doesn't like to talk to anyone, really."

"Charming," Claire said.

"Look, is there something we can help you with? Because we were kinda busy having an awesome time over there."

Caleb was much smaller than Beth Anne, but his fur was the same shade of dark brown. His fur on top of his head swirled up stylishly. His paws were small, and he looked at the travelers intently.

"What were you doing?" Eleanor asked.

Caleb pointed at the cliff. "What were we doing? Duh! We were jumping off that totally insane cliff into the water."

"It was unreal," Trey added.

"Your mother is very worried about you," Eleanor said. "Did you know that?"

"My mom? Who cares! She's so annoying, always getting upset about me, never letting me have any fun."

"Your mom is not annoying," Dax said. "Your mom is great!"

"I know you might be frustrated that she doesn't let you do things," Eleanor continued, "but your mother really cares about you. She wants you to be happy and also safe. I am sure she would be really glad to know where you are."

Caleb turned towards his friends. "You hear that, boys? This human is saying my mom wants me to be happy."

Trey and the other bear laughed obnoxiously.

"Who cares if she's worried?" Caleb said. "All we want to do is be extreme and have fun. You can tell her I will come home when I want to."

"Probably not the most thoughtful way to respond to having a supportive parent," Claire muttered.

Caleb swam towards the travelers. "Did you say something, cat? Do you know who you're talking to? I'm Caleb, the coolest cub anywhere. No one tells me how to live my life."

Eleanor placed her hand on her chin. "I suppose if you don't want to go see your mother, there is nothing we can do," she said, "but we can at least go and tell her where you are." She walked back towards the slope running up the side of the cliff.

"You wanna tell my mom? That's fine, go ahead. Go tell her."

"Do you wanna jump again?" Trey asked.

"Of course, I want to go again! What do you say, Spike?"

The other bear mumbled in approval.

The three bears climbed out of the water and scampered up the trail towards the top of the cliff.

Dax also got out and immediately shook himself, spraying water everywhere.

Claire jumped at the feeling of water. "Can't you give a little advance warning before you do that?"

"Oh," he replied. "By the way, I'm shaking!"

Claire sighed.

"Well," Eleanor began. "I think we should go back up and find Beth Anne. We can let her know that her son was down here by the lake, and that he is all right."

"That is a great idea," Dax said.

"Then can we move on?" Claire asked.

"All we can do is our part," Eleanor finished.

They made their way slowly back up, feeling the grass rustle with every few steps. Eleanor was able to hear the faint sound of the bears talking and snickering at the top. As they climbed up the slope, she looked up over the edge of the distant trees, thinking about how endless the Togetherwood truly felt. She folded her arms, feeling cold.

"Are you all right?" Dax asked, his ears perked up and alert. "You look horrified. Are there ghosts around?"

"Me? I...I am fine." She closed her eyes, breathed in deeply, and exhaled loudly. "You don't need to worry about me."

"Well, we won't, then," Claire said.

"What about them?" Dax pointed towards a massive rock in the clearing where the bears stood.

Eleanor looked and saw a cougar, its fur the color of dust, moving slowly and silently towards the bears. Caleb, Trey, and Spike were trembling, their mouths wide open and their paws raised in the air.

"I think they have had better days," Claire said.

Unsure of what to do, the three travelers became still.

"We need to not move," Eleanor said.

"We need to leave," Claire said.

"We," Dax began as he crouched down, planting his paws firmly in the ground, "need to fight it!"

"Have you lost your mind?" Claire said. "I mean, I knew you were dim and reckless, but somehow you have bested yourself. Have you seen that thing? It will eat you in seconds." She remained still, her tail hovering. "I suppose if you want a quick death, it isn't a terrible way to go, though."

Eleanor, despite her fear, was feeling bold. She clenched her fists and said, "No one is going to die."

"What makes you so sure?"

Before she could respond, Eleanor saw the cougar prowl towards the bears, closing the distance between them with each step. The bears backed up until they were pressed against the big rock. There was a gleam in the cougar's eye as its claws appeared.

Then Eleanor heard the loudest sound she had ever heard in all her life. A roar, so powerful and deafening that it made the birds leave their tree branches, filled the entire Togetherwood. Both Claire and Dax started from surprise. They wanted to look to see where it was coming from, but they had no idea where to turn because it seemed to be everywhere.

Claire closed her ears as though they were flaps and said, "What...in the world...is..."

"Look over there!" Dax shouted, pointing with his head.

To the right of the three bears, still roaring, was Beth Anne. Her legs were spaced apart, and her head was raised towards the sky. The few clouds above were drifting away quickly, as though they too were terrified of her. Now close by, she lowered her head, crouched down, and faced the cougar, breathing heavily. It did not move at first, but rather stared back at her intently. It turned to look at the three bears who were standing in place. Then, just as quickly as it had appeared, the cougar vanished, sprinting off until it was gone behind a line of trees in the distance.

Trey and Spike both slumped down. Caleb trotted up to his mother and felt her embrace as she wrapped him in a tight hug.

"So worried...you told me nothing about where you were going...you didn't even clean up your side of the cave," she said. "Oh, heavens. I'm just so glad I found you, my little cubbie-wubbie."

Caleb let go of her hug. He did not speak, but he did appear as though he had something to say.

"Are you just going to stand there?" Claire asked.

Caleb sat down and made a slight thud sound. "I was so stupid, Mom. All I wanted to do was be cool. I wanted to do some awesome, super-sweet jumps off the cliff with my friends, but I ended up getting us in danger. It's all my fault!"

Trey took a slight step forward. "Uh, Mrs. Caleb's Mom, we weren't trying to get him in any trouble. We just wanted to have a good time." He turned towards Spike and then continued, "I guess we're sorry about almost getting eaten and everything...if we have to be."

Spike made a solemn mumbling sound.

Beth Ann looked up at the clouds and wrapped both Trey and Spike in another tight hug. "To think that you two, such fine little cubs, could have been eaten by that cat!"

"We're not all that bad," Claire answered in defense. "Most of us only *think* about eating others."

"I suppose you're right," Beth Anne continued, "Still, the thought of you three being gobbled up by a predator... why, it makes my heart just faint!"

"You were really brave to face that cougar!" Dax called. "I want to be brave like you."

Smiling, Beth Anne replied, "Never underestimate the power of a mother bear's love for her cub!"

"Wow!" Dax said as he faced the others. "They are lucky to have her."

"They certainly are," Eleanor said. "We are just glad that everyone is all right, Beth Anne. I am sure Caleb and his friends will be safer and more responsible the next time they go out. Is that right?"

The three cubs nodded.

Beth Anne frowned. "But what I just can't understand is why you would go out like this, jumping off of cliffs, not telling your mother where you went. Why would you bring her such distress?"

Caleb ran a paw through the fur on top of his head. "I didn't want to worry you, Mom. I just got sick of you always hugging me, telling me I was your sweetie, never giving me a chance to go on a real adventure. I'm a big bear now. Didn't you know? Don't you remember how I said that next winter I'm going to go find my own cave to hibernate in? So, when you always treat me like a little cub, it just kinda bugs me. It makes me want to go out and prove myself."

Beth Anne lunged towards Caleb to squeeze him in another hug. "I was thoughtless, inconsiderate. How could I treat my little cub like such a…"

"He isn't a little cub," Claire muttered.

"Could you repeat that, dear?" Beth Anne asked.

Eleanor folded her hands and let them rest. "I think maybe there is a better way to look at this situation. Beth Anne, it sounds like Caleb would really appreciate it if you gave him more independence. Is that something you might be able to do?"

Beth Anne nodded.

Next, Eleanor turned towards Caleb. "And it also sounds like Beth Anne would appreciate it if you told her where you were going, that you practice more safety skills. Is that something you might also be able to do?"

"Safety skills?" Caleb echoed.

"Maybe less jumping off cliffs," Claire explained.

Caleb folded his paws. "But how am I supposed to live an extreme life, then?"

Trey placed a paw on his shoulder. "Caleb, buddy, there's nothing more extreme than the way your mom loves you."

"You know what? I kinda think you're right!"

Eleanor and Dax both smiled.

Beth Anne turned to face them. "I really must thank you for your help with searching for my cub and also getting through to him. Is there any way I can repay you?"

"Perhaps you could assist us with something," Eleanor answered. "We are searching for the Loneliest Hollow. Do you know where it is from here?"

At this, Beth Anne and the three cubs became quiet.

"What's the big deal?" Dax asked.

"Awesome! This dog is the real deal!" Caleb called.

His mother scowled at him. "Are you really sure that you want to go there? *That place* is the fastest way to never see your parents again!"

"Why is that?" Eleanor asked, curious.

Beth Anne sighed. "Oh dear, I really don't know how to go about explaining, it being such a sad story and all."

"Can we go get some of those red berries again, Mom?" Caleb asked, pulling lightly at her fur. "You know, like last week?"

"If you head that way, I am sure you will wish you hadn't," she told Eleanor quickly. "However, if you are really determined, and I see that you three are, then I can show you where to go." She took several steps towards a particularly tall tree, its trunk round and its bark rough. "If you head in this direction, you ought to find a path that will take you where you want to go. But, please, be safe!" She looked at Caleb. "Of course we can find those berries. Anything for my little cutie!"

"Thank you for directing us," Eleanor replied. Dax and Claire then joined her next to the tree.

"Catch ya later!" Caleb called to them.

"You'll have to jump with us next time," Trey added.

A mumbling sound followed.

"Thanks again, you three little sweethearts," Beth Anne said. As she walked away with the cubs, her smile disappeared. "Re-

ally a shame what happened to him such a long time ago..."
she said under her breath.

Before the travelers were trees that were taller than any they
had encountered. The canopy above was darker as well.

"Do you think we're close?" Dax asked.

"I do," Eleanor answered. "I'm sure we will arrive at our
destination very soon."

"Those cubs sure were fun!"

"Yes, they were. I do think it is understandable to want to go
out on adventures. That is, after all, what happened to me when
I was playing in the woods behind my house."

Claire took a turn to avoid a jagged tree branch blocking her
way. "I'm guessing your mother isn't going to show up, make a
big roar, and save us, is she?"

"If she knew where I was, I'm sure she would do anything
needed to help."

"I just wish our owners were that excited about us," Dax
said. He looked at Claire. "Do you think they miss us?"

"Not as much as they should."

For the next few minutes of walking, there was silence, and
Eleanor's mind wandered once more. Did she really love her
parents? If she did, then surely she wouldn't have caused them
such worry and distress. Overcome with regret, she looked up
at the dark brown trail before them, slowly becoming more difficult to see under the dense tree canopy above. She resolved
that whenever she returned home, she, like Caleb, would give
her mother a big hug and never take her for granted again.

11.
IT'S A JUNGLE THING

Eleanor heard a low rumble sound. She turned to look at Dax, trotting next to her and grinning, and realized that his stomach was growling.

Patting her own belly, she said, "I think I am getting hungry, too. We have been walking for quite a while, haven't we?"

"We've been out here wandering in circles for hours," Claire said. "Usually by this time of the day, Dax has had at least six meals."

"I like to eat," Dax added. "Eating is a great activity."

Eleanor felt another rumbling in her stomach. "It really would be nice to be able to have something to eat."

"It would," Claire said, "but there's nothing here. Take a look for yourself."

Sure enough, there was nothing in sight to eat. On both sides of the trail they walked were trees, menacing, tall, and dark, seeming to possess their own secrets. Their branches pointed at the blue sky like hands with fingers. With the exception of their walking and Dax's panting, there was nothing else to be heard, the quietness lingering in the air.

"I suppose you are right," she told Claire. "I am sure, though, that if we keep going, we will find something to eat. I bet we will have lunch just before we find the Loneliest Hollow, and that will be just before we return home."

"I remember what the bear Beth Anne said," Dax began. "She mentioned that there was a sad story there that had to do with someone."

"None of that matters," Claire said. "We're going to die before we even find out."

"I don't believe you," Eleanor said with a smile. "I am sure we are getting close to where we need to be. I know we had some difficult experiences earlier, but I really think we are through all of that now. I don't think we will have any more surprises to deal w-"

She didn't finish what she was saying, but rather stood still, her mouth open slightly.

"What is it?" Dax asked while hopping in the air, bumping into Eleanor.

Pointing with her finger, Eleanor asked, "Is that what I think it is?"

"Our demise?" Claire asked.

"No. Over there...I think I see...can it really be true? But how?"

In front of them was a small slope that led to a clearing. There was a circle of trees, and in the center of them, asleep on the forest floor, was a gorilla. Gigantic and black, his belly rose and fell with each breath he took, his snoring loud.

Claire tilted her head a little bit to the side. "But that doesn't make any sense. He is not native to this habitat."

"He looks very strong," Dax said. "Can we be his friend?"

Eleanor raised out a hand as though to stop him. "I think it would be best if we retrace our steps and consider a different path."

"Why? He looks nice!"

At that moment, the gorilla rolled over onto his side. Eleanor saw his face, his long arms stretched out on the dirt. Though he was still asleep, he appeared to be waking up.

"Let's turn around," she said.

But as they turned their backs on him, they heard several thud sounds. Eleanor looked over her shoulder and saw that the gorilla was now standing. He placed a hand on his stomach and scratched it. After blinking several times, he looked at the travelers intently, yawned, and then said:

"Wait a moment... where am I again?"

"Let's keep going," Claire whispered.

"We're in the Togetherwood place!" Dax called.

"Togetherwood place..." the gorilla repeated. "...that's in the jungle, right?"

"No," Claire said in a flat tone, her tail swaying.

"Huh," the gorilla said. He placed his hand under his chin and nodded twice. "...but how did I end up here, then?"

"I think we are all a bit confused about that," Eleanor answered nervously. "What is your name?"

"My name is Gregory."

Eleanor introduced herself and the others.

"It's great to meet you three. I am trying to remember how I got here."

"We would be very curious to know that as well," Claire said.

He scratched his head. "Hmm..."

"Do you remember what you did this morning?" Eleanor asked.

"Hmm...I think I do remember. I was in the jungle. I was taking a nap and relaxing, just taking it easy. Then I went for a walk. Then I got really tired, so I decided to take another nap. Now I'm talking to you three. Do you understand what I'm saying?"

"I understand!" Dax answered.

"I really don't," Claire said.

"I think that helps a little bit," Eleanor replied. "We are also lost. We are trying to find our way out of here. Maybe you are in the same situation."

"What do you mean?"

"Maybe you are also lost."

"Why am I lost? This is where I live."

Claire turned towards Eleanor and gestured to take a few steps away from Gregory. "This individual is obviously neither in touch with reality nor interested in it," she told her. "We should just keep moving forward."

"I agree that we should keep going," Eleanor said, "but I am not so sure that he is out of touch."

"He thinks he's in the jungle."

Eleanor placed her hand at her chin and nodded. "I am sure if we travel with him, we will come to learn that he has a story that explains who he is."

Claire sighed. "Eleanor, must you always see the best in others and like them?"

"Yes, I must," she smiled and nodded.

"I sure am hungry," Gregory said in the distance. He was now standing on top of a rock, rubbing his belly slowly with a big, black hand.

"The three of us are hungry, too," Dax said. "We have so much in common!"

"No, we don't," Claire said, glaring at him.

Eleanor took several steps towards Gregory and kicked over a fallen tree branch. "Do you want to travel with us? We were hoping to find something to eat as well. It really is merrier to go together."

Gregory hopped off the rock, stood up straight, and began to beat his chest with tight fists. For a moment, he struck himself rapidly with an intense energy, as though beating a drum. Then, just as suddenly, he stood still. He blinked several times.

"That was unbelievable!" Dax exclaimed. "How did you do that?"

Gregory shrugged. "It's a jungle thing." He turned to look behind where he stood. "Do you think there are any bananas over that way?" he asked.

"Yes, they're right next to the mangos," Claire replied.

"Huh?"

Eleanor placed a hand on Claire's neck and gently pulled. "What she meant to say is she certainly hopes so!"

Gregory lowered his giant fists to the forest floor and nodded. "That's great to hear. I'm so hungry. I would really enjoy a couple dozen bananas!"

"Perhaps we should follow this path, then. Will you lead us, Gregory?"

"Yes, I can do that. There's nothing in this jungle that scares me."

"Did you hear that?" Dax asked while his tail wagged. "This guy is amazing!"

Having left the clearing, they walked in a straight line, moving past more rows of sinister trees. With each step, Gregory made a thud sound as his hands collided with the ground. Occasionally, Eleanor turned around to look at Claire, who appeared terrified, and then Dax, who looked excited. They continued walking, ducking under sharp branches that stuck out of the trees. They took steps over rocks, moss-covered logs, and even a tree trunk.

"I don't see any bananas yet," Gregory called from the front of the line.

"Really? Are you sure?" Claire asked.

"We need to keep looking," Dax added. "I know we can find them if he leads us!"

"It has been a strange day," Gregory continued. "I was having a great time with my friends, the other gorillas in the jungle. We call ourselves the Silverback Squad. We were swinging from some vines, eating delicious bananas, you know, those jungle things. It was going really great. But then…"

"What happened next, Gregory?" Eleanor asked.

He reached forward to grab a jagged tree branch growing from a tree. With one powerful motion, he ripped it off and tossed it into a nearby bush. "Oh, you were asking me a question. That's right. Well, I was having such a perfect day, and so I decided to have a little nap. I wanted some peace and quiet. Do you understand what I'm saying?"

"We do! We do!" Dax called.

"After I woke up from the nap, I went for a walk, kind of like how we are right now."

"You really are a master storyteller," Claire said.

"Thanks for saying that. I just hope it makes sense."

Eleanor considered it more important to be kind to Gregory than argue with him. "You said you went walking for a while, and that you ended up going to sleep again later," she said. "Is that right?"

"Yeah. Then I woke up and met you three. You and I talked for a while, and then we decided to go get some bananas. That's what we are doing now." He turned his head around. "Do you remember?"

"Yes, we remember," Eleanor said in a sweet voice.

"You said that this is the Togetherwood place and that I'm not in any jungle. I don't know, though. I feel like it's the jungle."

"What do you mean?"

Gregory scratched his head slowly. "This place has trees, and they are all green. There are different animals, too. It makes me think of where I come from."

"It is true that there are trees," Dax said.

"Do you see that?" Eleanor asked suddenly.

The others stopped walking.

"Look up," she continued.

Dangling from a tree a few meters off, long and worn, was a white rope, It gently swayed with the light breeze. Several glowing rays of sunshine finally broke through the tree canopy above, lighting up the area. Birds could be heard chirping in the distance.

"Look below!" Dax cried.

The path in front of their feet disappeared altogether, revealing bushes of thorns below. Sharp and dense, they reminded Eleanor of crossing the thorny thicket with Ryder.

"Ugh, not these again," Claire groaned.

"I do not think we can continue going this way," Eleanor said, pointing at the sharp thorns.

Gregory stood up straight. "What do you mean?"

"There is no path to take. If we keep going, we will fall into those prickly bushes."

"We can use that," Gregory said, pointing to the rope hanging from the tree.

"What are you talking about?" Claire asked.

"We can swing from it."

"Swing? Do you even know what that is?"

"Yes, I do. That is a vine. Me and my friends, all of us in the Silverback Squad, like to swing from these when we have nothing to do. We like to take one and then jump to another." He looked at the others. "Now I know for certain that I am still in the jungle."

"That all sounds fine," Claire began, "but please tell me how many white vines you have seen before. Because, to me, that is a rope."

"You are right. It is white. It must be very rare."

"That makes sense," Dax said.

"Whatever it is," Eleanor said with a smile, "I must say I am a little nervous about using it. Do you really think it is a good idea? How do you know it will hold your weight?"

Gregory shrugged. "I know my vines when I see them."

Without saying another word, he leapt from the edge of the path, soaring through the air. He grabbed the rope with one hand, swinging away while roaring.

"That's unbelievable!" Dax exclaimed. "Do you see what he's doing?"

"Unfortunately," Claire replied.

Eleanor scratched the back of her head. "That is remarkable. He does seem to know what he is doing." Her eyes brightened as she looked at the others. "Maybe we can learn from him."

"What," Claire began, "do you think it's a vine, too?"

"No, but I do think it might be able to help us keep going."

"I want to keep going," Dax said.

"Can you hear me?" a voice called.

The travelers turned their heads up to look across the gulf of thorns and see Gregory standing on the other edge on a new trail. He held the rope with his right hand.

"I saved the vine for you. That way, you can use it to cross over, too."

"I don't see a vine anywhere," Claire answered. "All I notice is you holding a rope."

"Oh," Gregory turned to look at it. "This is a vine. Like I said, it's white and feels kind of rough, but I know what it is." He tilted his head. "Do you believe me?"

"You certainly are an expert," Eleanor replied. "Will you toss it back to us?"

"Yeah." He let go of the rope. Like the pendulum of a clock, it swung towards the travelers, and Eleanor had to grab it fast to make sure it did not get away from her.

She looked at Dax and then Claire. "Do I jump now?" she asked.

"When you leap with it, you can start to swing," Gregory explained. "It is important to not let go of it."

"That makes sense!" Dax said.

"One more thing," Gregory continued.

"What's that?" Eleanor asked.

Standing up straight, stretching out an arm and placing his hand on a tree branch, Gregory said, "It is very important that you roar when you swing."

"I will certainly do that," she said with a smile.

Claire crouched down and stared at the thorns. "Good luck ever getting me to do that."

"Now it is time for you to swing," Gregory said to Eleanor.

She stared at the thorns and noticed her arms tremble. Terrified, she thought about falling into them. She then looked across the gulf, back at Gregory, who was leaning against a tree.

"If you hold on to the vine and roar, then you will swing and be successful," he said.

"I can do this," Eleanor whispered to herself.

"You can! You can do it!" Dax jumped several times.

Though she was afraid, Eleanor did not allow it to stop her from jumping off the edge of the trail and soaring towards the center of the thorn gulf. The sound of her screaming filled the entire forest. Then, remembering the instructions, she did her best to roar. She couldn't help but laugh when she heard herself.

In the blink of an eye, Eleanor was holding the rope on the other edge near Gregory. She wanted to jump off, but was not quick enough. She began to sway back towards Claire and Dax. Then she moved towards Gregory again, the rope and her body spinning slightly.

"You need to let go of the vine to stop swinging," Gregory called.

Roaring, and then laughing, Eleanor answered, "I know that! It's just…it's just so much!"

The next time the rope moved past Gregory's edge, Eleanor let go and landed on the ground with a light thud. She noticed she was breathing heavily. Gregory reached for the rope and held it in his hand.

"That was a great swing," he said.

"It was," Eleanor beamed. "Thank you for teaching me."

"Who will go next?"

Claire, irritated, looked at Dax.

"I would like to be the next swinger," he said.

"I will send the vine to you now." He let go of the rope, and it traveled across the gulf.

As though catching a Frisbee in the air, Dax jumped up and bit it, securing it with his teeth.

"I hurr thurr vyyy…" he said with the rope in his mouth.

Claire licked her left paw and groomed herself, while Dax moved towards the edge.

Gregory said, "It is important to m-"

Before he was able to finish, the air was filled with the sound of Dax growling and grunting as he swung over the thorns. His entire body spun as it dangled in the air. Like Eleanor, he reached the other side but did not let go, instead continuing to swing.

"There is no positive outcome to this," Claire said as she watched Dax come back towards her.

Dax swung from one end back to the other, again and again. It was only seconds later that the rope came to a halt, becoming still and leaving Dax to hang from it in the middle of the thorn gulf.

"Whaa durr I durr?" Dax asked.

Gregory turned towards Eleanor. "This happens with vines sometimes. I know what to do."

In a burst of powerful energy, he jumped off the edge, grabbing the middle of the rope just above where Dax dangled. They both immediately began to swing. Gregory held on with one hand while he used his body to increase the momentum, the sound of him grunting audible.

"We err sweeengeng!" Dax cried.

A moment later, the rope was moving at full speed once more. Gregory, without hesitating, jumped off and landed on the dirt next to Eleanor. He reached out an arm and grabbed the rope the next time it was near, holding it steadily in place.

"If you let go, then you will fall and land on the ground safely," he said.

Dax opened his jaw and collided with the earth, rolling over onto his back while wearing a massive grin.

"That was so great! That was the best!" he shouted.

"Are you sure about that?" Claire asked from the other side of the chasm.

"Yeah," Dax replied. "I had a lot of fun!"

"We are glad you made it over here," Eleanor said. "Next time, please remember to let go sooner." She turned to look at Gregory. "Your swinging abilities really are spectacular."

Gregory looked at the rope in his hand. "It's a jungle thing."

"What about me?" Claire called.

Gregory held the rope out and gestured with it. "I will let go of this vine. Then it will swing over to you, and you will be able to use it."

Claire's tail sliced through the air slowly. "What kind of a jaw do you think I have?"

"I, uh," Gregory looked at the rope, then at her, and then back at it. "Huh. When I swing with the Silverback Squad, none of them are cats."

"I'm sure that's true. But the thing about me is that I am a cat."

"She is an orange cat," Dax added.

"Do you have any other ideas about how she might get across?" Eleanor asked. "Given how skilled you are at swinging, I know you must have another way to help her."

Gregory scratched his head. "Hmm. I'm not used to thinking about this. Normally, I just swing."

"Maybe you can jump across," Dax suggested.

Claire sighed.

Gregory stopped scratching his head and lowered his hand. "I have an idea about how to help you. I think it might work."

"I usually prefer ideas that always work," Claire answered.

"If I swing back over to you on the vine, then I can carry you in my arm and cross over again. Does my plan make sense?"

"You want to carry me across while you hold on to a rope with one hand?"

Eleanor looked across the thorny chasm and then at Gregory. "I think if you are cautious, you will be able to do it. We have all seen how excellent you are at swinging."

"It's true!" Dax exclaimed.

"I really don't have a choice, do I?" Claire asked.

"Just make sure to roar," Eleanor replied, nodding her head.

"I will go now," Gregory said. He jumped off the edge, swung over to Claire, and jumped off while still holding the rope. As he crouched down, he said, "I will pick you up."

"You don't need to do that," she said, arching her back. "I am perfectly capable of walking onto your arm."

"Now we are ready to finish swinging across."

"What an amazing gorilla!" Dax called. He turned towards Eleanor. "Do you see him?"

"Yes, I do."

Gregory held his left arm out, cradling Claire like a beach ball. He grimaced as her claws dug into him more and more. With one final step, he jumped off the edge and began to swing. The sounds of his roaring and Claire's yowling rang out. Gregory jumped off and Claire flew out of his arm instantly.

Shaking herself, she said, "We will never do that again."

"I was able to bring you over," Gregory said. "I think that is a good thing."

"Where do we go now?" Dax asked.

Pointing her finger towards the trail ahead, Eleanor said, "I think we should continue this way."

"It's true," Gregory agreed.

"What are we waiting for?" Dax shouted. He sprinted off ahead.

"He really only comes in one speed…" Claire said to herself.

The path spread before them, the coverage of tree branches above now less thick than earlier. While walking, Eleanor turned her head to look about, observing a blue horizon that must have been the sea, a light green patch that was the meadow, as well as the countless trees spread out in every direction. She also saw something far off in the distance that appeared dark gray, though she was unsure of what it was. It was clear that the four of them were moving up a slope, approaching a new area. Where was the Loneliest Hollow? What was the story of that place, and who lived there? How would getting there lead to them making it back home? It felt to her as though they were moving closer and closer to the answers.

With a turn to their right, the travelers found themselves standing in a clearing. Light green grass mixed with patches of brown dirt to create a display as dazzling as a painting full of colorful splashes. In the center of it all stood a single tree. On its many branches hung bright red apples which gleamed in the sunlight.

Dax jumped forward, his tail wagging fiercely. "It's a tree! Look at the food hanging on it. They're-"

"I know what those are," Gregory said. "Those are bananas."

"You've got to be kidding me," Claire said.

"What?" He turned to face her.

"Those are not bananas, They're apples. They're apples because they are growing on an apple tree, which is growing in the woods and not the jungle, which makes sense because we are in the woods, not the jungle."

"Hmm..." Gregory pointed at Claire and asked, "Eleanor and Dax, do you think everything is OK with her?"

"She seems upset," Dax observed.

"I think she is maybe feeling frustrated and also hungry," Eleanor reasoned, turning towards Claire. "It is all right. I understand what you mean, but I really think the important thing for us all right now is to get something to eat, no matter what fruit it is!"

"The voice of sanity has spoken, and will continue to hold its peace," Claire muttered.

"I sure am hungry," Gregory said.

"Me too," Dax added. "Do you want to race? Let's race!" He ran towards the tree, reaching it in the blink of an eye.

"You sure are fast," Gregory said. Using his long, lanky arms, he ambled towards the tree, coming to a halt at its base. "I was the captain climber in the Silverback Squad."

He reached his arms out and launched himself up like a catapult.

Dax, still on the ground, looked up and his jaw fell. "Look at him climb! That's amazing! He must not be from around here."

"At least someone else is starting to wake up," Claire said.

"Let's go join them," Eleanor called, following them.

By the time Eleanor reached the tree, grabbed a bough, and began to climb, she heard Dax yelling:

"So fast! He got up there so fast."

Eleanor tilted her head up and saw, just barely, Gregory hanging at the top. The thin branch he was holding onto was rocking gently. He plucked an apple and inspected it closely.

"Hmm…it's not fully ripe. That explains why it's so red. It's not formed all the way, either, so that must be why it's very round. Still, I think this will be a delicious banana." He took a bite and made a loud crunch sound. "It IS a delicious banana."

"I want one, too," Dax cried.

Midway up the tree, Eleanor said, "Perhaps you can bring more of them down, Gregory?"

After tossing the apple core, Gregory replied, "Yes, I can do that."

He held the tree trunk with both hands, let loose another roar, and shook the entire tree forcefully with all of his strength. Eleanor felt herself move back and forth and feared that she might fall. As she looked up again, she saw several red flashes followed by multiple thud sounds.

"It's raining apples!" Dax exclaimed, still on the ground. He turned towards Claire. "Do you see this?"

"I do."

Dax hopped to one side and then another in order to dodge the cascading fruits. "There are so many of them."

Seconds later, the tree was still. Eleanor looked around and realized there were no apples hanging anymore. All of them were on the ground, surrounding Dax and Claire.

"They're everywhere," Dax said.

"You really are a remarkable climber," Eleanor said to Gregory as she tried to catch her breath.

"Thanks for saying that."

"Should we climb down now?"

"Yes," he nodded. He let go of the tree, jumped high into the air, and met the ground below with another thud. He stood up tall and straight, and then beat his chest powerfully.

"How did you get all those apples?" Dax asked with wide eyes after he stopped.

Shrugging slightly, Gregory replied, "It's just a jungle thing."

After a few minutes, Eleanor made her way down and joined them once more. She gestured with both her arms at the apples, "Should we eat these?"

"Yes!" Dax took hold of one in his sharp teeth and bit into it.

"I think I'll sleep instead," Claire said with her eyes still closed.

Eleanor pulled off a part of her apple and handed it to her. "I think it would be good for you to at least have some."

Claire opened her eyes and sniffed it. "Fine," she said. "But I'm only eating this if you can promise me it's an apple."

"You will certainly enjoy this apple, and I think Gregory is enjoying his bananas."

Claire licked the slice slowly. Her breathing became deep and she started to purr.

Between Dax and Gregory rested two piles of apple cores.

"Those were delicious," Dax said. "I think my stomach is at its limit."

Gregory patted his belly. "They were delicious. They were yummy. They were...they were..."

A pause followed. Gregory looked down at the earth and shook his head slightly. As Eleanor looked, she noticed that a few tears were streaming from his eyes.

"What's the matter?" she asked. "Are you all right, Gregory?"

Both Dax and Claire were silent.

Sniffing, he answered, "It's no use."

"What's no use?"

He waved his long arms and said, "This. I know the truth. This is not the jungle. I was pretending that it was, but I just don't think I can do that anymore. I know I'm very far away from home."

"Finally," Claire said. "Thank you."

Eleanor looked at her briefly with a stern expression. "You don't need to pretend anything at all when you are with us," she said to Gregory.

"But you don't understand. I do need to. I need to lie to myself."

"How come?" Dax asked.

Gregory placed his hand on his forehead. "Because I'm scared and I'm sad. I'm not where I belong."

"Of course you don't belong here," Claire said. "So are you going to tell us how you got here or what?"

Gregory was silent.

"You don't have to tell us," Eleanor added, folding her hands and letting them rest. "If you would like to tell us your story, we would be happy to listen. But if you would rather not, that is fine, too. We are here for you either way."

"It's true!" Dax cried.

"You seem like great friends. I think I will tell you how I got here," Gregory said as he sat down. No longer were there any tears in his eyes. "I used to live in the jungle. It was a nice place and I liked it. I spent time swinging around with my friends, the Silverback Squad, and I looked for bananas most days."

"We have certainly heard of the Silverback Squad," Claire said.

"They are my friends. I really like them a lot. You three kind of remind me of them. Anyway, one day in the jungle, these men showed up. They captured me and put me in a cage. Then

I went on a plane to this place…hmmm….I can't remember what it was called. There were a bunch of cages, and all day there were humans walking by to stare at me and take pictures."

"I know what that is," Dax said. "That's a zoo!"

"Yes, they put me in a zoo. I was upset because I missed my friends. I thought I would never go back home again."

"That sounds pretty familiar," Claire replied.

"Huh?"

"I can explain what my friend is saying," Eleanor added. "We are also lost here. We miss our homes and are looking for them."

"Really? That makes me feel a little better."

"I just can't wait to get home," Dax said, his tail wagging quickly.

"You are not alone," Eleanor continued. "What happened after you went to the zoo? Why are you here now?"

"I wanted to get out of that zoo so bad. So one day, when the guard guy wasn't looking, I figured out a way to escape by climbing up a tree and making a big jump."

"Wow!" Dax exclaimed.

"Sounds like the design for zoo security could be improved," Claire said.

"It was a great jump," Gregory continued. "Then I started to walk around, but I didn't know where I was, so I was scared again. There were humans everywhere, and these big metal square things that move really fast." He tilted his head slightly. "Do you know what those are called?"

"I think you are describing a car," Eleanor replied with a smile.

"Thanks for that. I had to avoid a lot of those car things. I had to jump a lot. I kept wandering around. After a while, I was going to turn around and head back to the zoo, but then I saw all these trees. They looked different from the ones in the jungle. It was a lot colder and the birds sounded different, too."

"You were in the forest."

"I think so. I kept going through the forest and later on, I found this brown box. I wanted to take a closer look at it, so I climbed inside. But once I got in, all the flaps closed, and when I climbed out, I was somewhere else."

"We had the same exact experience. We also found cardboard boxes."

"I thought if I told myself it was the jungle enough times, then it would work." He lowered his head. "It didn't work, though."

"It makes sense that you did that," Eleanor replied. "You were really struggling and alone, so thinking that way probably made you feel better."

"I guess it did for a while. But then I ran into you three, and things got more complicated. Now I just don't know what to do. Do you understand what I'm saying? I don't belong in this Togetherwood place. I don't belong anywhere."

The trees surrounding them stood still. Eleanor noticed the warmth of the sun on the back of her neck. She looked at Gregory and saw that he really did appear lost, as though he had no idea where to go.

"I hate to interrupt your moment of sorrow and everything," Claire finally said while pointing at a nearby tree, "but do you see that?"

"See what?" Dax asked.

Claire continued to point. "Up there…I see something blue. I think it's a bird." Her pupils narrowed until they were slits. "That's a bluejay."

Eleanor placed a hand at her forehead and focused her gaze. "You're right, Claire. That is a bluejay in that tree. Why is he not moving, though?"

"Maybe he's asleep?" Dax reasoned.

"Who cares?" Claire said. "It doesn't affect us."

But as she was saying this, Eleanor meanwhile noticed that Gregory seemed to be listening to something very closely.

"What is it, Gregory?" she asked.

"I think I hear chirping sounds," he replied. "But they don't sound normal. I think he might be in trouble. What should we do?"

Dax hopped several times. "You could go rescue him! You're the fastest tree climber anywhere!"

"I don't know," Gregory replied, lowering his head. "All I did was get lost here and then lie to myself."

"That doesn't matter. I know you can go save the bluejay and be a hero!"

Gregory stood up straight. "You might be right. I know what to do. I need to go check on him."

Using his long arms, he propelled himself again towards the tree. Without hesitation, he grabbed the first branch he saw, flung himself upward, and climbed with all his strength. Eleanor listened to the chirping and agreed to herself that he did seem distressed. She looked to where the bluejay lay, and suddenly Gregory was next to him. A moment later, he leapt from the tree and landed just meters away from them. Gently, Gregory lowered the bluejay to the ground.

"Did you see that jump?" Dax asked. "It never gets old!"

"You may have rescued him," Claire replied, "but what are you going to do now?"

"Hmm...I know exactly what to do," Gregory answered. He beat his chest with his fists harder than the others had ever before heard. Eleanor felt as though the ground beneath her shook, though she knew this was not possible.

"I've got him!" Gregory yelled while beating his chest at full speed. "I found the bluejay!"

At last, he stopped. Next came silence except for his deep breathing.

"Great job," Claire said. "You transferred an injured creature from one place to another. You accomplished absolutely n-"

She was interrupted by the sound of fluttering above. They all looked up and saw four bluejays flying above. Tracing the sky in circles, one of them dove towards them, and the others in turn followed after. All four of them stood in a circle around the injured one.

One of the bluejays said, "Oh, gee! Can you guys believe it? We found our little buddy!"

"Oh my goodness!" a different bird cried.

"Wowsers!" another added.

"Jeepers!" still another added.

The bird who appeared to be the leader looked up at Gregory. "Hey, mister. Did you find our little buddy?"

"Yes, I did. He was up in that tree," he answered while pointing.

"Did you hear that?" one of the other bluejays called. "He was injured." The other birds exclaimed again:

"Whoa!"

"Wow!"

"Wow!"

"You saved our buddy, mister," the leader continued. "Hey, what's your name?"

"My name is Gregory. What are your names?"

"I'm Larry," the leader replied. The other birds continued:

"I'm Gary."

"I'm Terry."

"I'm Barry."

"Wait, don't tell me," Claire said, pointing to the injured bird. "Is that Cherry?"

"Him?" Larry replied. "That's our buddy. His name is Simon."

Claire blinked several times.

"You really helped us out, mister," Larry continued. "We were looking all over for him, and you saved him!"

"You did save him!" Barry called. "Thanks, Gregory."

"It was no big deal for me," Gregory answered with a slight grin.

"Sometimes Simon's wings get sore if he flies for too long," Larry said. "But now that we found him, we will make sure he is fine in no time."

The injured bird opened his eyes and chirped several times lightly. "I am OK, guys. I am A-OK."

"Did you hear that?" Gary called. "Yahoo!"

"Yipee!" Barry cried.

"Oh, boy!" Terry exclaimed.

"That is great to hear, Simon," Larry said.

"It's thanks to you, Gregory," Barry said. "You're a hero!"

"He is a hero!" Terry echoed.

"It's true!" Dax added.

"What's your name, mister?" Larry asked him.

Eleanor cut in and introduced the three of them.

"You all seem really swell," Larry replied.

"Not as swell as Gregory here," Eleanor replied.

Everyone looked at Gregory, who asked, "Do you birds like to go on adventures?"

"We do," Larry answered. "We like to fly all over and see new things."

"I also like to explore," Gregory replied with a bigger grin. "Do you like to have a good time?"

"I want to have a good time," Barry said. "That sounds like everything I want to be a part of."

Larry turned to look at the others and then said, "Yes, we do like to have fun. Do you, as well?"

"Yes, I do," Gregory answered.

Then Larry flapped his wings several times as he stood up. "Well, if you also like to explore and have a good time, then here is what I want to do for you. Mr. Gregory the Hero, I would like to invite you to join the Bluejay Brothers."

"Bluejay Brothers...hmm. I don't know."

"Why not?" Gary asked.

"Well...umm..." he turned towards Eleanor. "I don't know how to say this...it makes me kind of uncomfortable..."

"You can tell us," Terry said. "What is it?"

Gregory scratched his head. "The thing is, I'm not a bluejay. In fact, I'm a gorilla."

Larry turned to talk to the others. Then he looked at Gregory once more. "You may be a little bit bigger than most, and you may not have blue wings, but Mr. Gregory the Hero, you are just as much a bluejay as anyone I've ever seen. So what do you say to my offer?"

"Please say yes!" Gary exclaimed.

Gregory stood up, beat his chest ferociously, and then crouched back down, becoming still. "I will join," he said.

"Oh, boy!" Larry cried. "That's great news!"

"Hooray!" Gary called.

"Wowsers!" Larry exclaimed.

"Hooray!" Barry called. "We've got a new bluejay in our brotherhood!"

"This is very unexpected," Claire said to herself.

"Now that we successively recruited you," Larry began while pointing with his beak at a cliffside in the distance, "we were thinking we would explore that area over there. Who knows, we might even find some berries along the way. What do you say, new member?"

"That sounds great," Gregory replied.

"But they are birds," Claire said. "How on earth is he supposed to keep up with them?"

"I'm sure he can move as quickly as them," Eleanor reassured.

"Yeah, he can swing faster than any bird," Dax reasoned.

Gregory scratched his back. "It's true. If I swing around on vines, I can keep up with anyone."

"That's great to hear," Terry replied. "Are you ready to go?"

"I'm ready. I just need one moment." He turned to face the others. "I want to thank you three."

"What for?" Dax asked.

"You were great friends to me. You were there for me when I was feeling down. You were nice to me and made me feel like I belonged, like I wasn't the only one lost here. Even though this isn't the jungle I used to know, that doesn't mean I'm lost. This can be my new jungle!" He grinned. "You really supported me. Look at me now. I'm a member of the Bluejay Brothers!"

"I guess sometimes in life you get what you don't deserve," Claire replied.

"We were happy to travel with you," Eleanor said while beaming. "You were brave and open with us, and now it looks like you have a new life."

"I will always remember you," Dax said. "You climbed so fast, beat your chest so fast, swung on vines so fast. I will always remember that you were really fast!"

"And I want to say a special thanks to you, Dax," Gregory said. "When I felt like I was useless, you told me I was a hero. Thanks for saying that."

"It's true!" Dax exclaimed.

Gregory's grin grew even bigger. "I should get going now. Goodbye!"

Eleanor, Dax, and Claire said farewell to the Bluejay Brothers and then continued on, exiting the clearing and passing through a gate of thick trees. They were now in an even deeper section of the Togetherwood.

"This is useless," Claire sighed. "We're never going to arrive at this stupid hollow."

"I think we will get there any minute," Dax said. "I just know it!"

"I think you are right, Dax." Eleanor said. "Let's keep going."

The air became foggy, a mist filling the dark space between the trees. Eleanor now was barely able to see more than a few meters in front of her white sneakers. When she turned left, she noticed a massive, ominous cave cloaked in the shadows of the trees. On top of the cave entrance was perched a familiar owl.

"Great…" Claire said. "What's this weirdo want now?"

"Hi, Octavious!" Dax called. "We missed you. We hope you and your family are safe and very happy!"

The three travelers came to a halt at the beginning of the cave. Octavious scrutinized them closely and then said, "Close."

"To what?" Claire asked.

"I think he means the Loneliest Hollow," Eleanor said. "Is that right?"

The owl nodded. "Shadows…the forsaken one…friendship…home."

"What do all those words mean?" Dax asked, looking puzzled.

Eleanor scratched her chin. "It must mean that we need to keep going, no matter how dark or scary it might seem. If we continue on, we will find out what's there, and then we can get back home. Is that right, Octavious?"

But when she looked to the top of the cave again, there was no sign of the owl; he had vanished.

"How helpful," Claire said.

"We found out what we needed to know. We are close. Let's keep going and get out of here."

Claire looked uneasy. "We need to go inside of this cave? Why?"

"It must empty out on the other side somewhere, like a tunnel."

"Let's go!" Dax shouted, his voice echoing in the mist.

Eleanor, Dax, and Claire went inside the cave, moving hopefully closer still to the Loneliest Hollow.

12.
ANOTHER INTERLUDE, AN ARGUMENT, AND A HORRIBLY MISPLACED STEP

Eleanor, Dax, and Claire moved through the cave in complete darkness. Only the sounds of Eleanor's steps and Dax's steady panting could be heard.

"I really am not able to see anything at all," Eleanor began. "Claire, do you think you could help guide my way?"

"I suppose so," she answered, her eyes wide open and alert. "I suppose having a cat's night vision is a gift of sorts."

"Being a dog is also a gift," Dax said. "I can kind of see in the dark a little."

"One animal's gift is another's curse, I suppose."

"This place is very different from all the others we have been to."

"It is, and I don't like it at all."

"It's OK," Dax continued, "we'll be out of here soon enough. I just know it!"

"Eleanor, turn right," Claire instructed.

"Thank you for saying that!"

"Wait," Claire's voice sounded hesitant. "Eleanor, please stop walking."

"All right."

"I will stop, too," Dax said.

Eleanor placed her hands on her hips. She noticed that, whether she opened her eyes or closed them, everything continued to appear equally black.

"Be quiet, you two..." Claire said at last. Eleanor thought for a moment that she saw Claire's ears perk up, though she knew she couldn't.

"What is it?" Dax asked.

"Is everything all right?" Eleanor added.

"I thought I heard something," she said, "but I don't know what it was."

"Let's keep going!" Dax whispered loudly.

"I don't like this."

"I'm sure we will be through this soon enough," Eleanor said. "If you hear anything else, we can always reconsider and turn around."

They continued to pass through the cave with Claire in front, following any instructions she gave. Though she was nervous about colliding with a smooth, rocky wall, Eleanor trusted her friend, taking small steps all along the way.

"I don't like the dark," Claire said suddenly.

"That's silly, Claire," Dax said. "You can see!"

"Still, I don't like the feeling of being somewhere where things try to hide. This cave has so many turns. It's disorienting."

"I think I know what you mean," Eleanor agreed. "It can be frightening to be somewhere like this."

"That owl Octavionon keeps talking about that hollow place. I wonder if it's really dark inside of it, too," Dax said.

"I think you meant Octavious," Eleanor corrected.

"Yes, I meant him!"

"None of that matters," Claire replied. "I just want to get out of here. We all need to turn to the right here."

"Do you remember what I said about interludes back when we were in the tall grass?" Eleanor asked. "They are the piece of music that links two other sections together."

"So?"

"Well, maybe this cave we are walking through is just like that, a little tunnel between two different places."

"It doesn't seem little to me."

"Perhaps it does have a few turns to it-"

"We need to stop," Claire said, her voice cutting off.

"What is it?" Dax asked.

Silence again followed. To Eleanor, the quiet felt full and absolute.

"We need to turn around," Claire said finally.

"Are you sure?" Eleanor asked.

Her voice a bit fainter now, Claire answered, "Yes, I am perfectly sure. I don't like this place at all. I keep hearing rocks sliding, and I feel like there is something waiting to devour us on the other side of this cave."

"Is it a monster?" Dax asked.

"I don't care what it is. I am not going to find out. I want to get out of here."

"But why?"

"Why?" Claire's voice was louder now. "Are you so clueless that you're unable to comprehend even one sentence of what I'm saying to you? Are you really that dumb?"

"No way! I'm not dumb!"

Claire exhaled loudly in exasperation, continuing to walk back the way they came. "Just forget I said anything. You go ahead and continue. You clearly don't care at all about living, or even about me and how I feel. Go ahead! Besides, this is all your fault, anyway."

"Huh?"

Claire groaned. Eleanor turned towards where she heard it, but what followed next was only silence. For several seconds, no one spoke, making Eleanor almost feel as though she were alone in the cave.

"Are you all right, Claire?" she asked.

"It's your fault, Dax!" Claire screamed with a voice that was high and shook. "The only reason we are here is because you were stupid enough to go look for a lost ball in the woods. There was no reason, absolutely no reason at all to go after it, but you went ahead anyway. You convinced me to climb inside of a box because you thought a ball was in it, and that's why we're here, with no hope at all."

"I didn't know we would get lost," Dax answered in a soft voice.

"Oh? Did you say you didn't know we would get lost?" Claire shouted. "Well, I'm just so glad to hear you say that. What a relief. Now all my problems are solved!"

"I don't get it. We're still lost here. Our problems a-"

Claire sighed so loudly, it reminded Eleanor of a gust of wind. "You just don't get it, do you? You have no idea what others are thinking or what they are feeling. All you care about is yourself. So, what happens when our owner tosses a little red ball too far into the woods? You go after it. And what else do you do? You beg me to join you. 'C'mon, Claire. It will be fun! We can go find it and see a new part of the woods.'"

"But it has been fun."

"No, it has not been fun, Dax. After you somehow tricked me into following you down here, after we slid down that muddy gully, traveling way deeper than any sane animal should ever go, then you still insisted that we keep going, that we were so close. You looked at me like you were going to be miserable for the rest of your life if we didn't press on."

"Thanks for not giving up."

"You're not at all welcome," she answered, her voice now calm and steady. "Even though I knew better I still went along with you, past one thorn bush, then across a creek, then up a hill. 'Let's just go past that tree, Claire,' you said. 'It's right around that bush, I just know it!'"

"We were close to finding it, weren't we?"

"No, we were not close to finding anything at all. All we did was lose ourselves, and now we're here, in a pitch-black hole in the center of an uncaring universe. We will be lost here forever, and our owners will never know what happened to us. Is this what you wanted?"

"At least we got to meet Eleanor."

In the pause that followed, Eleanor said, "Though I know you are feeling a lot of intense and difficult emotions, I do need to say that I have enjoyed traveling with you two. I do not know what I would have done here in the Togetherwood if I was lost by myself. I am very glad to be your friend, no matter how difficult our journey has been."

"I'm starting to think you don't understand, either," Claire answered. "Do you think this is a fun playdate we're on? Is this a game for you? It's only a matter of time before something goes wrong, and it's all over for us. It's all your fault, Dax!"

"I didn't want us to get lost. I'm sorry, Claire."

"But you know what?" she answered slowly, speaking in a voice so soft the others had to focus to hear her. "It isn't actually completely your fault."

"It isn't?"

"No," she sighed. "Even though you were foolish and reckless enough to play fetch deep in the woods no matter the risk,

I wouldn't be here lost with you if I hadn't been foolish enough to join you." For a moment, she didn't speak. Eventually, as though talking to herself alone, she said, "I was the bigger fool. I was the one who knew better and still went along with the idiotic decision to get lost. I could have avoided being here. I... I could be sleeping on my blue cushion." She started to sob, her voice sounding desperate.

Eleanor heard Dax take several steps towards Claire.

"What are you doing?" she asked.

"I want to sit next to you. That way, you can know that everything will be OK."

Claire was already several meters away from them, walking back the way they came. "I don't want you to sit next to me," she said. "I'm done traveling with both of you. I can't take this anymore."

"What? But what are we supposed to do?"

"Claire, you are our friend," Eleanor pleaded. "We have been through so many experiences together. Perhaps we can talk about this more?"

"I don't have anything to discuss," Claire replied. "What I know is that it's not my problem anymore what happens to you. I'm tired of having friends drag me around like this. I'm going to find my own way back. You two are on your own now."

"Claire?" Dax called. Then he turned towards Eleanor. "What do we do now?"

"I don't think I know," she answered. "We will need to let her go."

But Dax was already running after her. "Wait up! Don't leave!"

There was no sound from Claire. Within seconds, Dax also disappeared, leaving Eleanor all alone in the darkness. Frightened, she felt that she needed to try to follow after even though she was unable to see anything at all.

"Are you two there?" she called, walking with her hands stretched out in front of her. "Where are you?"

Just barely, she was able to hear Dax shouting:

"Wait up, Claire! Everything will be OK! I won't lead you after any more red balls, I promise!"

But despite her efforts to follow them, Eleanor knew that they were moving farther and farther off, and soon she struggled to hear the sound of any voices. She finally came to a halt and stood still. She suddenly began to breathe rapidly, full of panic, and feared that she was going to faint. Crouching down low, she wrapped her arms around her knees and hugged herself tightly. For several minutes, she remained this way, not moving, staring into darkness.

Terror seized her. She stood up, flailed her arms, and ran as fast as she could without thinking. She was so scared that she would be alone in the cave that to run, to sprint anywhere was better than anything else. On and on she ran, and surprisingly, she did not collide with anything. If only she could see a light, something to indicate the end of the tunnel, then surely she could find her way back home.

Seconds later, Eleanor heard a scraping sound. She felt the sensation of her feet slide off of an edge, and realized at once that she was falling off a cliff. Her scream filled every corner of the cave.

13.
THE MANY STORIES OF FABLE THE FOX

For what felt like an eternity, Eleanor plummeted down, deeper towards the heart of the cave. Yet, just as suddenly as it began, she felt the cold splash of water. Her nose began to sting at once. She reached out with both her arms, her whole body feeling like it was made of ice, and paddled up towards the surface. She could hear the soft currents flowing around her, and she almost believed she was now in some sort of dream world.

At last her hands broke through, and she felt the stiff cave air above. Once her head was above the surface, she took in perhaps the biggest breath of air she had ever taken in her whole life. She wiped her hand against her forehead to move her wet hair. As she looked around, she realized she was in a pool of water, an underground lake.

Thankful to have something to break her fall, Eleanor wondered how it was that she was able to see anything at all, given she was in such a dark place. But she did not have long to think about this before she noticed the incredible answer. On the other side of the lake, burning brightly, was a fire. She saw orange sparks fly from it, the smoke rising steadily upwards, a deep crimson blaze. Amazed and in disbelief at what she was looking at, yet also overjoyed to be seeing something, anything, she called out:

"Is there someone here?"

Other than the rippling of water and the crackling of the fire, there was nothing to be heard. Filled with curiosity, she swam towards it, reaching out with her right arm and then her left, kicking steadily. Swimming, after all, was one of her very favorite activities, especially back when her father took her to her lessons years ago. Yet here, in the middle of a lake deep down below the whole world she knew, those happy memories were from a different world. Behind the bright fire, she noticed where the orange wall faded into shadow.

At last, her left hand scraped against pebbles. Eleanor turned around, seeing only darkness. There was no telling how big this area was. A particularly loud crackle sounded and caused her to turn her head around with a jolt. Who had made this fire? By pressing her hands against the ground, she was able to lift herself up onto the rocky shore. The fire, which moments ago felt so distant to her as she waded in the water, was now very near to her, burning only several meters up the slope.

She walked towards it, careful to take each step slowly and cautiously. If there was a fire down here, she reasoned, then surely someone had made it in the first place. And if this was the case, then that must mean that the way out of the cave was closer than it seemed.

Now she stood next to the fire. Captivated by the embers that swirled up and disappeared into smoke just above her head, she simply stared at it for a moment. At the base beneath it were branches placed in a criss-cross pattern, and Eleanor considered the stacking to be very organized. After carefully placing her hands near it for warmth, she started to walk around, looking for any sign that someone else was near.

Moving in a circle around the fire, she was struck by just how much more she was able to see now. Across the flame, she observed the lake in the distance, resting perfectly still. It was dim, pressed down by layers of darkness. She looked towards the water, at the fire near her feet, and then back at the water once more. She really was all alone here in the cave, she thought to herself.

At once, Eleanor slumped down and cried. Her tears streamed down her cheeks. Why had she allowed Dax and Claire to become separated from her? Why had the three of them entered this cave to begin with? Why had she been so foolish and followed the wrong path to begin with when she knew it was wrong? If she chose to disobey her parents, then that must mean that she was bad, she reasoned, a daughter who only wanted to hurt them. Why would she be such a daughter?

"What did you do to fall down here?" a voice asked.

Eleanor started and softly shrieked. Sitting on the other side of the fire, looking at her with an attentive gaze, was a fox.

"Who...um, who are you?" she asked in response, able to feel her beating heart slow down.

Without speaking, the fox walked around the fire, her tail perfectly still. Eleanor now saw that her eyes were orange, and her pupils were big.

"Why are you here?" she asked.

"I fell," Eleanor said quickly.

"You were in the cave up above?"

She nodded.

The fox looked up above into the darkness and then back at Eleanor. "This, my dear, is not a place you want to be."

Eleanor wiped away her tears as the fox continued:

"Are you all right?"

"Yes, I am. I just became separated from my friends, that's all."

221

"Do you know where they are?"

"We were up above. But I was walking in the dark, and I stepped off the edge. The next thing I knew, I was-"

"Down here," the fox finished with a slight smile.

"Yes, and now I don't know what to do." Eleanor made a sniffing sound. "What do we do?"

"What do we do?" the fox echoed while walking around the fire towards her. She stood next to her and said, "We need to find your friends."

"But how?" Eleanor asked with a strained voice. "We are trapped down here in the middle of the cave. There is no way out of here."

"There is a way out."

"There is?"

Smiling again, the fox asked, "How do you think I got down here?"

Eleanor moved to stand up. With the light from the crackling fire, she was able to watch droplets of water fall from her legs when she shook them. "My name is Eleanor. What is yours?"

"Me? I'm Fable."

"It is nice to meet you, Fable. You must understand, I was very distraught a moment ago, so I am glad to not be alone anymore."

"I understand that feeling."

Eleanor gazed at the embers pouring out of the fire, how they twirled in the air before meeting the wet cavern floor. She could see that the ground was uneven; there were many dips and bumps in every direction.

"How do we leave here?" Eleanor asked.

"Do you like to hear stories?" Fable asked, her eyes twinkling.

"I do."

Fable raised her head up. Her eyes stopped blinking as she gazed across the fire at Eleanor. She began:

"Once, there was an old man who traveled the sea in a small wooden boat. His name was Ernie. He had a long beard, and he liked to wear an orange bandana around his head. He spent his days sailing to the farthest corners of the known ocean. Over the years he visited countless islands, meeting many people along the way, and finding plenty of treasure. Ernie had no fear. No wave was too big for him, no storm too menacing to scare him off. Whenever he docked at an island, he enjoyed visiting the local pubs.

One day, while drinking a glass of apple cider, he met a man who had a challenge for him. This man, named Raphael, told Ernie that there surely was no way he could ever sail to the nearby circle of jagged rocks, claim a treasure chest hidden on one of them, and survive to tell anyone the tale.

'It simply cannot be done,' he told Ernie. 'It is best that we all accept our own limits, knowing that some places are beyond the reach of any boat.'

Well, Ernie only had to hear there was a challenge to know that he accepted it. 'I will have the chest back before the end of tomorrow,' he replied. 'Then you will know that the brave have no limits.'

So he prepared his seasoned boat and made his way towards the area where the treasure was rumored to be. As he was sailing, a massive storm met him. The waves crashed into his boat and the gusts of wind turned his sail every which direction. Unconcerned, brave as always, Ernie worked to steady the sail while using his telescope to inspect the distant rocks. He was hoping, still, to find his prize. It only took one moment for everything to change for him. During one careless moment, he tripped on the slippery boat floor and his head struck it."

Eleanor softly gasped.

Fable's eyes twinkled once more. "When Ernie finally regained his consciousness, he was standing on a lone jagged rock, the waves splashing near him from every direction. He had no telescope. He had no map. He had no boat. With a sigh, he stared out into the distance, unable to see anything at all, wondering how he could have been so foolish as to end up marooned in this way. Just as soon as he lowered his head and let his shoulders slump, convinced that he would die alone and unknown, a failure, something happened. He felt a breeze against his chest and looked up to see a seagull flying overhead.

'Just swim,' it said to him.

'Just swim?' he repeated.

'That's all you need to do,' the seagull continued.

For a moment, he felt unsure, but knowing that he had nothing to lose, he decided to give it a try. Ernie dove into the frigid, dark blue water. He felt the freezing currents against his whole body. He had no idea where to go, no sense at all if it was even possible to survive, but still, he made stroke after stroke. He continued in this way until, finally, his hand met the sandy shore of an island he knew well. He kissed the land in joyful ecstasy and looked up at the clearing sky.

At that moment, Raphael from the pub walked by, asking Ernie where the treasure was.

'Did you fail the challenge?' he asked. 'Did you find nothing at all?'

'No, I found plenty,' Ernie replied. 'In fact, I gained the one thing I truly needed to.'

As Raphael walked off puzzled, a seagull flew by, and Ernie couldn't help but say to himself, 'Just swim. That's all I had to do.'"

Fable became still. The cave now felt less dark to Eleanor as she looked, mesmerized, into the bright flame. At last, she said, "That story was remarkable. Is it true?"

"I will not answer that."

"You have a special way with how you tell stories," she continued. "When you were speaking, I felt as though I could see it happening. I felt like I was with Ernie. It was so vivid and very wonderful."

"I appreciate your kind words. I like to tell stories. I think they tell us a lot about the world we live in."

"I agree!" Eleanor exclaimed. "My mother and father taught me to read when I was little, and I love to read books."

"It sounds like your parents raised you well. Do you know why I told you about Ernie?"

Eleanor placed her hand under her chin.

"You asked how we leave here," Fable continued. "I'm sure that Ernie asked himself a similar question when he was alone, abandoned on the rocks. But I think sometimes all we need to do to get out of the place we are stuck in is to just start moving. I knew you were upset when I first saw you, and so I wanted to tell you this story. I'm glad you liked it. I've been practicing it down here for a while."

"Down here in a cave?"

"Yes, I like to recite stories somewhere dark, and of course, I need to have a fire, too. Moving is what Ernie did, and that's what we will do now. Lucky for you, though, I know where we need to go next."

"Which is where?"

Fable nodded her head towards a cavern wall on the other side of Eleanor. "Over there."

"Are you sure? I do not see anything over there."

"Yes, I am sure." She silently moved past Eleanor. Now sitting next to the wall, Fable said, "I know you can't see in the dark, but I can. If you crouch down low, there's a little tunnel here."

"I can't see it, but I do trust you."

"I'm glad." Fable lowered herself down and moved through a hole. "Follow me, then."

It was uncomfortable for Eleanor, still dripping wet, to crouch down and search for the entrance to the tunnel in the darkness. Her hands traced the rough, rocky wall until they passed through open space. Lowering herself still further down, she moved her head until it cleared the entrance of the tunnel. She heard the faint scraping sounds of Fable moving a few meters ahead.

"Please follow me," she called to Eleanor. "I know it may seem frightening, but you will be fine."

"I am coming," Eleanor said softly.

Feeling exhausted caused her to crawl slowly, frequently reaching out with her hands to ensure she wasn't going to brush against the tunnel wall. Why, she wondered, was she unable to see any light on the other side? After all, this was supposedly the way out of the cave, wasn't it? Vowing to not ruminate too much on questions she couldn't answer, Eleanor continued along, and it was only seconds later that the final traces of light from the fire behind her disappeared completely.

"Please stop, Eleanor."

"How come?" she asked, breathing heavily.

Though unable to see, Eleanor could sense that Fable's orange, furry face was not far from her. "This is the part where you need to turn."

"The tunnel has a turn in it?"

"Yes, it does."

Eleanor placed her hands on both sides, hoping to discern which way to go. Sure enough, her right hand swished through the air and landed on the rough cavern floor.

"It must be this way. Is that correct, Fable?"

"That's right. You are doing very well for being unable to see."

Eleanor smiled for the first time since she entered the cave. "Thank you."

After she shifted her entire body to the right, she wasted no time in continuing to crawl. Her heavy breathing and the sounds of her legs shuffling filled the tunnel.

"Are you still there, Fable?" she called.

"I am right here, yes," a voice replied from a few meters ahead.

"All right."

"Just keep going. We will be back in the daylight soon enough."

"I will," Eleanor answered. "D—"

"—Go ahead and stop again," Fable interjected.

Weary, Eleanor lowered her head. She took several deep breaths and then placed her hands against the tunnel walls. "What is it now?"

"Can you hear me, Eleanor?" Fable's voice sounded as though it could be coming from anywhere.

"Yes, I can hear you."

"Good. Then look up."

"Why?"

"Because that's where I am."

Eleanor then realized Fable's voice was coming from up above on a different level of the tunnel.

"How did you get up there?" she asked, astonished.

"The same way you will. By climbing!"

"Climbing?" Eleanor asked.

"Well, I suppose that you, being a human, will have an easier time than I did. Why don't you try standing up?"

"Are you sure?"

"I am, yes. Stand up."

Silence followed. Eleanor lowered her head. She froze in place and sighed.

"Are you all right?" Fable called.

Eleanor shook her head slightly to the side. "I am. I wish I could see, though."

In the darkness, she heard Fable ask, "Do you mind if I tell you another story?"

"That would be great."

Fable took a deep breath and began:

"Once, there was a boy named Francis who enjoyed riding his sled high up in the white mountains. Francis lived in a small, quaint village that was often hidden beneath sheets of snow.

As Francis came home from school one afternoon, his father spoke to him sternly, saying, 'There have been sightings of a snow wolf at the village. You absolutely must be careful, son.'

Francis asked, 'But why do I need to fear it?'

His father sighed and looked at him, saying, 'One day you will understand certain things about this world.'

So the next day, Francis left school and walked through the village towards his home. The shingles on the house roofs were worn, and the lights in the town center felt a little dim to Francis. He walked alone with his books under his left arm.

When he turned a corner, he saw Roland, another boy in his school. Roland stood up straight, a full head taller than Francis. On his face, he wore a sly grin as he said, 'I think I found my new favorite target.'

He reached down and picked up two snowballs from the powdery ground. Instantly he threw them at Francis, and they pelted him hard in the middle of his face. Francis felt a cold rush in his head. He turned around and began to run away from Roland. Turning left and then right, moving up a slope away from his home, Francis ran with all of his strength. But he heard behind him the sound of heavy breathing and laughter.

'Why are you trying to get away?' Roland called. 'Don't you know I'm your best friend?' Francis ducked down and saw another snowball soar overhead."

"How will he escape?" Eleanor whispered to herself.

"Francis was hit in the back by another snowball. He took a turn to the right and ran past a shopkeeper. Moments later, Francis tripped and fell to the ground. A sharp pain moved through his right ankle, and he realized that he could no longer run. He grabbed his foot in agony and winced. Looking up, he saw that Roland was now standing up above him, holding a single massive clump of snow in his two hands.

'You know I'll always be there for you when you fall,' he said.

Terrified, Francis raised up both of his hands to shield himself from the snow. At that moment, both Francis and Roland heard a howling sound. Now even more frightened, Francis closed his eyes.

He next heard another howl, followed by Roland shouting, 'Help! I'm going home!'

Francis heard a second voice call from behind, 'You shouldn't mess with others if you don't want to get messed with!'

Something white flashed across the sky. Francis raised himself up and saw a snow wolf, crouched over and ready to pounce, staring at Roland. The bully was standing frozen in place, his eyes big and his whole body shaking.

The wolf turned to look at Francis and winked. Then it stared at Roland once more, saying, 'I think if I say it once, you will get the idea: stay away from this kid or else I'm going to chase you out into the middle of the tundra.' He tilted his head slightly. 'Do you hear me?'

Roland's teeth clattered as he tried to speak, but no sound came. The wolf tilted his head up at the starry sky and howled once more. Roland sprinted off at once.

Francis remained seated on the snowy ground until the wolf walked over to him. 'You can call me William. Go ahead and grab me,' he said to Francis.

Frightened of what would happen next, Francis grabbed the wolf's torso and felt a burst of energy pull him up and back on to his feet. He took a deep breath and said, 'That was marvelous!'

He lowered himself down to pick up his books and when he looked at the wolf again he noticed his dark eyes, his regal white fur, the way he stood with confidence.

'But why would you want to help me?' Francis asked curiously. The wolf's breath was visible as it exhaled.

'Because,' he answered, 'I get tired of people thinking of me as some villain. Like you, I know how it feels to be stepped on, and I want to see a little less of that in the world. I would rather be a hero.'"

"Wow!" Eleanor exclaimed.

"Do you know why I told you the story about Francis and William?"

"I do not. It certainly was a wonderful story, though!"

"Because sometimes we don't expect to find ourselves in trouble, and so we need others to help us up. Why don't you go ahead and try to stand?"

The sound of rocks scraping against the ground reverberated through the tunnel. Now crouched on her feet, Eleanor took a moment to position herself properly. She placed both her hands against the sides of the tunnel, focused on her legs, and stood up, amazed that her head didn't strike any sort of ceiling.

"I didn't hit anything!" she exclaimed.

"Of course you didn't. I can see, remember?"

Faintly, Eleanor was able to notice cracks on a dark rock wall a dozen meters in the distance. It then dawned on her that she was finally able to see.

"We need to go that way," she said while pointing. "Is that correct?"

"Very good. You can keep following me."

Eleanor occasionally felt the brushing of fur against her hands. Being able to see something, anything, emboldened her. She now believed that she would be able to leave the cave once and for all. Carefully, she reached out her hand and lifted herself up onto the ledge, pulling herself forward until her knees rested on the second level. As she crawled forward through the narrow tunnel, she realized that the cracks on the walls were slowly becoming more and more vivid. Small rays of light ran against them, illuminating the faded cavern wall. Eleanor saw that Fable was now at the end of the tunnel. The next moment, she turned to the right and disappeared.

No longer afraid of anything, Eleanor called, "I will be right there!"

She reached towards the wall with her hand, placing her palm against it. Taking one final look back over her shoulder, she saw only pure darkness. When she faced forward once more and leaned to the right to look around the corner, she couldn't believe what she saw. Bright, lovely yellow light flooded her view so suddenly that she had to place her left hand to her eyes and look down. She smiled and giggled to herself. How could she have been so faithless, so despairing? Of course she would find her way out of the cave!

"We still have a little longer to go. As you can see, though, we're certainly close," Fable's voice rang.

Eleanor continued to crawl, feeling that each time she shuffled forward with her knees, she was moving closer to home. At last, she saw the stone ceiling above pass by as she emerged outside, standing on a dirty path that was dotted with boulders. It became obvious at once that she was in the Togetherwood; down by the edge of the path was a dense grove of tall trees. As she looked around, she realized that she did not have any sense at all of where, exactly, she was. Nevertheless, she was overjoyed to be back outside, above the darkness and the loneliness.

"You really did save me, Fable."

"You were the one who did the crawling."

But then Eleanor's situation hit her once more. She crouched down and stared at a nearby rock, silent.

"What is it?" Fable asked

With her arms wrapped around her knees, Eleanor looked up slowly at her and replied, "It's just...you need to understand that I was with my friends, and now I do not know where they are."

"Who are they?"

"Well, there's Dax. He is a dog, a black Labrador. My other friend is Claire. She is an orange tabby cat."

"You said you were separated from them in the cave?"

"Yes, I was walking, and I fell deep down into that lake. That is when I met you, Fable."

"That's right. Will you wait there for a moment?"

"Here?" Eleanor pointed at the ground.

"Yes, I will be right back." Fable lowered her head down towards the dirt and took several steps along the path, sniffing continually. Though Eleanor felt a small amount of dread when she considered being alone again, she trusted that Fable would not leave her behind. The fox took a turn around a big boulder and was gone for a moment. Seconds later, her head reappeared as she exclaimed, "Please come over here, Eleanor!"

When she met her at the boulder, Fable continued, "I think I know where your friends went."

"Do you?"

The fox pointed at two sets of paw prints in the dirt, one much larger than the other. "Do you think these belong to them?"

Eleanor lowered her head to examine them more closely. Though she was not an expert in paw prints, she had no doubt at all that they belonged to a cat and a dog. Both sets moved as two parallel lines deeper into the dark depths of the Together-wood.

"Those certainly are theirs," she said.

Fable looked down at the trails and then at Eleanor. "Do you know where this leads?"

"I do not, but I know that I want to go there."

"Why is that?"

Eleanor crouched down so that she was next to the prints. "I want to go wherever my friends went. I want to find them, no matter the cost."

Fable looked at her. "I know that you care for your friends. I really do think that is beautiful. However, I do not think this is somewhere you want to go to."

"Why is that?" Eleanor pushed her hair out of her face. "I know we had been traveling to the Loneliest Hollow."

"Maybe it would help if I told you another story," Fable said as she crouched down, her fluffy orange tail hovering in the air. She began:

"Once, there was a young woman named Lyla who lived in an old cottage near a meadow. On a bright morning, she stepped outside and noticed a letter pinned to her door. It was from a man who she had not spoken to in many years, a man who at one point had meant very much to her.

'I now live in the heart of the desert,' the letter began. 'It is not the sort of place you may imagine. I live in an oasis, near a small river that carves into the sand, where a few trees have sprung up. I want to see you, Lyla. Things will not be as they once were. Please come visit me as soon as you are able.'

Lyla felt a few tears in her eyes as she read this. At first, she told herself there was no way she would go. To return to him, to go to the desert, was utter madness, she told herself. Still, as one day bled into the next, Lyla found herself thinking about this man, Charles, more and more. Despite her best efforts to feel otherwise, she did long to be with him, to believe in a new life.

So Lyla one day packed her things, left the green meadow, and crossed the eastern bridge that led to the desert. When she stepped off the bridge on the other side, she saw a small man crouched near a boulder.

Lyla sought to walk past him without speaking, but the man called to her, saying, 'What am I to do? Days have passed by, and he is nowhere to be seen.' Lyla asked who it was that the man was referring to. 'I am speaking of my brother,' he replied. 'It was a week ago that he went to the desert to visit the market, and now I do not know where he is. Will I ever see him again? Anyone who crosses this bridge must know that the wise thing to do is forget the desert, turn around, and cross the bridge once more.'

Lyla considered what the man told her and decided to continue on her way. Over time, the ground under her feet became dry and dusty. The sun shone on her back all day long. Lyla continued to walk, viewing the horizon ahead of her, blurry in the relentless sun rays. Eventually, she came across a woman who lay on her back on the soft sand. Lyla crouched down and noticed she was quite still, though breathing slowly. Small beads of sweat were on the woman's forehead, and so Lyla reached into her pouch, grabbed her container of water, and poured it on the woman.

'Ah!' the woman exclaimed. 'Water is all that I needed, and now I have had some. It is so hot here. Only the most foolish would continue onward.' Lyla looked intently into the woman's eyes, seeing the fear in them. For a moment, she considered turning around, but then she remembered Charles' letter."

"What happened next?" Eleanor asked, full of curiosity.

There was a gleam in Fable's eyes. "Resolved once more to continue on, Lyla kept walking towards the desert. The sun now was unbearable, a small circle in the sky that blazed down on everything in its path, torching it all endlessly. To remain cool, she traveled by night in the dark sand, finding places to sleep during the day until the sun hid away from the world once more. For days, she moved in complete isolation, not seeing anyone at all.

Then one day she encountered an old man crawling in the sand. He had a long beard, and he stared at the grains of sand as though they had secrets to tell. 'It nearly killed me,' he said. 'The desert nearly swallowed me whole, never to return to my family. How happy I am to be here, crawling back towards the world I know. Anyone would be wise to turn around here.'

Lyla still continued to walk east. Then one day during twilight, when she first set out, Lyla saw what she was seeking in the distance. She was able to make out, just barely, the silhouette of a tree on the edge of the horizon. She believed it was a sign of the oasis, and so she set out with more speed and resolve than ever before. But as she went on, it did not appear that the tree was moving any closer to her. It was as though it were frozen in place, hovering far off. She was desperate, and so she ran with all her strength. In the blink of an eye, she collapsed and fell down, crashing into the sand. She lost consciousness immediately.

When she next opened her eyes, she was lying on her back at the bottom of a steep sandy slope in the heat of the day, looking at a camel who did not blink.

'So,' he said to her. 'Are you another one who did not see what was so plain, what the desert was telling you since the bridge?'

Lyla nodded in horror.

'I see,' he continued. 'I think now is the time to open up your eyes, turn around, and head back. If you wait much longer, you may not have the chance to warn others.'"

Eleanor wiped her eyes with the palms of her hands, as though awaking from a dream. "What an amazing story! You really are skilled."

"Thank you," Fable replied. "I do think the best stories have a life of their own." She leaned her head in towards Eleanor. "Do you know why I told you about Lyla?"

"No, I do not."

Fable gestured at the trees surrounding them. "You mentioned the Loneliest Hollow. If you look a little more closely, you can see that we are, in fact, very close to there. This place is not for us. We are not safe here."

"Are you sure we are close?"

"I am. I can see the signs all around us."

"Then that means I should be close to them!"

"I am sure Lyla felt the way when she thought she was near the oasis where Charles lived. However, wanting to be somewhere, when it is known to be treacherous, is not wise. Danger will often warn us to turn back long before we meet it, and we would benefit from remembering this today."

Eleanor did not reply, but frowned as she stared at a boulder.

"The sun is beginning to move towards setting in the next hour," Fable continued. "However, if you look at any of these trees, what do you notice?"

"I see that they are casting shadows."

"Yes. But do you see how long the shadows are?"

Sure enough, when Eleanor looked at the gloomy shadows of each tree, she realized that they were much longer than what would have been expected. The dark silhouettes spread out from the trees dozens and dozens of meters ahead, trapping much of the grass in a deep blackness.

"Why are they like that?" she asked, her voice shaking slightly. "Is it because of the one who lives there?"

"It is, yes."

Eleanor stood still. "But you said these tracks belong to Dax and Claire. I need to find them. I need to!"

"Why do you want to go there?" Fable asked, wrinkles visible on her face.

"I already told you. I need to find my friends. We have traveled together and seen so many amazing things. We all wanted to leave the Togetherwood. How could I go home and know they were still here? They could be in danger."

"If they did indeed go to the Loneliest Hollow, then I am certain they are in danger. Do you want to be like them?"

"If that is what I need to do to be with them, then yes, I do!" Eleanor exclaimed. "I am not going to stop. I will find them."

Without turning back, Eleanor marched past the long tree shadows in the direction of the paw prints. The air suddenly felt colder. She had to squint slightly in order to keep track of the paw prints, which occasionally shifted direction.

When she looked up, she saw the sun moving deeper past the lines of trees, turning scarlet. Thoughts raced around in her mind restlessly. Was she also headed towards danger? Would she be able to find Dax and Claire? What she said to Fable was indeed very true: the three of them had seen much. They had experienced many challenges and made countless friends along the way. Eleanor thought of Dax, of him jumping in the air and shouting, him sprinting fearlessly into whatever came his way, his simple way of seeing the world. Then she thought of Claire, who could be so prickly but really did care about others, who made such astute observations, how her tail would slowly sway through the air. Eleanor did not want to imagine going home if she wasn't able to do it with them alongside her.

But she did not have long to think about them. When her right foot stepped on the shadowy ground, she suddenly felt an intense coldness moving up her leg. It was as though she had stepped in a river of glacial water. Out of instinct, she tried to raise her leg up, but she found that it was completely immobile. Now the cold feeling was moving up her legs, to her waist, and then to her chest. Though she wanted to scream, no sound left her mouth. She became still. The cold feeling, colder than anything she had ever known, colder than falling asleep in the snow, now overtook her. She felt her body lean forward, and then in one motion she hit the ground and everything became dark.

"You will be all right, Eleanor," a voice called. "Everything will be fine."

Her eyes opened slowly, and at first, everything seemed blurry. After a few seconds, had passed, she raised herself up off the forest floor so that she was sitting. Right across from her was Fable, whose eyes had a tenderness in them.

"What happened to me?" Eleanor asked, feeling foggy. "I was walking, and then everything changed."

"You stepped in one of the shadows, into darkness," Fable answered. "It's an easy enough thing to do. I was able to pull you out of it."

"But why did everything become so cold? What happened?"

Fable took several steps forward, her orange fur brushing against her. "What you need to understand is that this place, the Togetherwood, is not like any other place."

"I certainly knew that."

"I assume you came here through a box. Is that right?"

Eleanor nodded.

"Yes, there is no way to understand where the boxes appear or when, and, as you know, they can only be traveled through once before they break down. The Togetherwood is a world where what may feel normal or ordinary becomes just a bit more enchanting. It is here that humans finally can understand animals, and the very flow of time is altered. You may spend months wandering here only to return home and find you were gone mere minutes. There are many other magical forces at play as well." She lowered her head to the ground. "I cannot fully explain it."

"That does make sense. As I traveled with Dax and Claire, this world did seem to be somehow different."

"There is an important story I wish to tell you. It was a couple of years ago. A boy became lost here, just like you did. As you know, once one is here, it can be horribly difficult to ever leave. He entered the Togetherwood all alone, and he wandered for a long time. I have heard stories that he crawled through mud, screaming in the rain for someone, anyone to rescue him."

"What happened to him next?" Eleanor asked.

Fable took a deep breath. "This boy, named Liam, continued to wander in desperation. Eventually hopeless, he arrived at the very place we are now walking towards. It is called the Loneliest Hollow. It is a massive, abandoned tree resting on the very edge of the Togetherwood. The boy came to this rotten tree, which is completely empty in its center, and I understand that he lay down on his side, prepared for the end. But that is not what happened."

"Is he still alive?"

"It is much worse than that. As he lay on the wood of the hole in the tree, the shadows, the powers of loneliness swept over him until they filled him with darkness. Liam became possessed by these forces, and this is precisely what you came into contact minutes ago when you stepped in that shadow. The Loneliest Hollow has its name for a good reason. It is said to be the most forsaken, abandoned place one can find anywhere. I have heard stories of animals visiting it and, while moving near the tree, suddenly feeling an indescribably painful loneliness, as though they were permanently hopeless, as though their life had no value or meaning at all."

"That sounds horrible," Eleanor said.

"As I said, you do not want to go there. The Loneliest Hollow is a dark place, but most of the Togetherwood is not affected. There are many fascinating animals roaming the different areas here, but we all try to go about living our lives the best that we can. Still, it does seem as though these shadows are growing bigger with each passing day."

"I need to go there," Eleanor said.

Fable smiled slightly. "I think I know what you are going to say. You want to help your friends."

"I need to find them and make sure they are all right."

"I know. But we can't continue going this way. Don't you see the black silhouettes filling up the ground? I have liked traveling with you, Eleanor, but if you step into one more of those shadows, it may not be as easy for me to pull you out of it."

Eleanor looked at Fable with a determined expression. "I know that you enjoy stories, Fable," she said, "and you are a wonderfully talented storyteller. Now I think I should tell you one of my own:

"When I was completely alone here in this forest, I met a dog and a cat who were my only friends. All three of us wanted to leave here, and so we traveled together. We met a frog who was a professor, and he helped us create a boat out of lily pads to cross a pond. We came across a fish who at first glance seemed awfully sad and gloomy, but when we traveled with her, we realized she was frightened and looking to conquer her fears. We encountered a duck who served in the armed forces with his troops, and worked with him to bring peace to the estuary, where he was at war with some very hospitable beavers. We met an explorer badger who was unquestionably brave, and he showed us how to fill out every last corner of his map. Then we came across a raccoon who seemed to enjoy stealing things and tricking others, but he actually was looking for redemption and a better way to enjoy life. Later on, we found a deer who was trying to find transcendence in a beautiful meadow, and she helped us reunite with our lost friend while we collected flowers. Next we encountered a mother bear who was looking for her cub, and we all came to realize that the two of them had much to learn about each other. What came next was astonishing. We met a gorilla who was missing his jungle, and as we got to know him, some bluejays helped him find a new one. After that, the three of us ended up lost in a cave, and with one misplaced step, I fell way down into that lake. That was where you and I met, Fable, and I really have appreciated your help, your kindness, and your stories. But I think now is the time to put away stories and get back to reality because my friends need my help!"

Fable blinked several times. "I think you may be a natural storyteller as well, Eleanor."

"This is a story that is completely true, too."

Fable looked at the cave in the distance and then at Eleanor. "I think you are teaching me something. I have spent too much of my life hiding in stories, afraid of living my life. Maybe now is the time to change that. For all we know, there may be a box for you there as well."

Eleanor nodded. "Either way, I need to find Dax and Claire. I know I can do it! Will you join me and head towards the Loneliest Hollow?"

"Yes," Fable replied as she moved around a shadow on the ground. "With a story as captivating as that one, how could I resist helping you finish it?"

14.
THE BOY IN THE ROTTEN TREE

As Eleanor walked with Fable, she realized that night now filled the skies above; the horizon was dark blue, like water near the bottom of an ocean. Stars sprinkled across and there were thick patches of clouds.

Suddenly, a sliver of light broke through the clouds and the moon began to glow down on the Togetherwood. Its brightness was striking, shining with a brilliance much stronger than Eleanor had ever before seen. She felt relief to see such a great source of light. Somehow, it made her feel more confident that they would be successful.

She saw Fable come to a halt and gesture up at the round moon. "With that shining down on us, we will need to continue to be sure to step around any shadows."

"I understand," Eleanor replied. There was a pause, and then she continued, "I do think we are close to them."

"You think so?"

"Yes, I do," she pointed her finger in the distance past the dark patches on the forest floor. "There is something about this place…it is as though they are with me now."

"Well, we must keep going, then," Fable said.

The air was cold. Beneath their feet, the shadows now were stretched out so much that Eleanor had to look carefully where she placed each step, practically jumping from one patch of grass to the next. They walked quickly, sensing that no time could be wasted. With each passing minute, Eleanor knew that the ground was becoming darker.

A few meters ahead of them was a thick tree with a rope dangling from it. When Eleanor came closer to it, she realized that a thick tree branch was connected to the bottom of the swaying rope.

"I know what this is," she told Fable.

"It is used for play, isn't it?"

"Yes, it is." Eleanor reached out a hand to hold the branch in her hand. "When I was younger, my father would play with me on the swing set we had in our backyard. I remember he would push me high up, and I would try to kick the leaves off of the trees in front of it. My brother Edward played this game, too." She pushed the swing and watched as the branch collided with the tree, faltered, and then moved in another direction. "I had so much fun with both of them," she sighed.

"I think I can imagine the appeal of a swing like this."

Eleanor looked towards the top of the tree. "But who does it belong to?"

Without answering, Fable stepped towards the base of the tree. She moved her head to look around the other side, her ears perking. "I think I know," she answered. She gestured at Eleanor with a paw. "Come over here."

Eleanor carefully walked towards Fable. Now standing before the tree, she slowly reached her head around it to see what was on the other side. The ground steadily sloped down to form a deep valley. There was no grass to be seen, but rather dirt and boulders. In the very middle of the valley, hardly standing at all, was a single, worn tree. So dark that it nearly disappeared in the blanket of the night, Eleanor was amazed by how bleak it was. Each branch protruding from the tree seemed ready to break and fall off at any moment. Eleanor turned to look at Fable with wide eyes.

"It really is frightening," she began.

"No one knows how it got to be there," Fable said, "or for that matter, even why such dark power comes from it. What we do know, though, is that it exists, and maybe that's all that is needed."

Eleanor stood still, looking at the Loneliest Hollow, unable to take a step.

"Are you still wanting to go down there?" Fable asked.

Despite the fear and trepidation she felt, Eleanor nodded.

"If that's the case, then we shouldn't delay too much, should we?"

With the moon's gentle light pouring down on the valley and no trees anywhere near, there was no longer a need to hesitate while walking. Eleanor adjusted her steps to the slight changes in the slope, making sure she avoided any rocks. She was soon able to see how the other side of the valley rose above her like a wall slowly climbing up into the sky.

At last the ground became flat. Eleanor looked up and saw it, the Loneliest Hollow, stretching towards the night sky like a monster desperate to escape the sinking valley.

"It really is gigantic," she whispered.

Fable nodded and then pointed towards the ground with a paw. "I can still see signs of your friends' tracks, which means we are in the right place."

"I think I hear something," Eleanor said. She placed a hand at her ear and turned her head to the side. "Is it…I think…" she smiled.

"What is it?" Fable asked.

"That sounds like my friend, Dax. He's the dog!"

Fable nodded twice. "Perhaps that means he isn't far inside."

"But how do we enter the Hollow, anyway?"

"I almost forgot," Fable said while taking several steps to the left. "Humans aren't able to see much in the dark. Please follow me."

Feeling less afraid now, Eleanor went after Fable as they made their way around the tree trunk. It was amazing to her just how enormous it was, bigger than any tree she had ever seen. She placed a hand against the trunk and felt the edges of bark. Nothing about it seemed unordinary, but still, she felt strange. Fable came to a sudden stop, startling her.

"This is the way in," she said while pointing her paw at a gaping hole.

When Eleanor looked inside, she was immensely grateful for the moonlight from above. Covering the wooden floor in a ghostly sheen, it enabled her to see the vast curving walls of the Hollow inside. When she looked up, she realized the tree had no ceiling; she saw the open night sky above. Then she heard a voice call:

"Is someone there? Anyone? I'm starving! I can't just eat apples for dinner! I need a dessert, too! Maybe a cookie?"

Eleanor smiled as she recognized a shifting black figure on the other side of the tree.

"Is that you, Dax?"

"I don't think one cookie will be enough. I think I need a dozen!"

The sound of her steps echoed through the empty space of the Hollow. She ran over to where he was and stopped when she noticed rows of thorns separating them.

"It is you, Dax," Eleanor said. "I'm so happy to see you!"

"Me too," he answered. "I was shouting and talking, but it was just me. I like talking to you better."

"That's sweet, Dax."

"Who is that fox?"

Fable approached them and introduced herself.

"It's nice to meet you," Dax continued, "Are you a story?"

"What do you mean?" she asked.

"Your name is Fable. A fable is like a story." He turned to look at Eleanor. "Am I right? I'm sure I am!"

"She is not a story," Eleanor explained with a smile. "She is a fox. She does like to tell stories, though."

Dax stared at them with a thoughtful expression. "That makes sense!" he said at last.

"I did tell her a few of my very favorites while we were looking for you," Fable said. "She even told me one of her own."

"That's great!" he exclaimed before lowering his head. "I'm glad you're here. I hate being alone. It reminded me of being at the shelter. I wanted to be happy, but I was scared!"

Eleanor smiled. "Don't worry. You don't have to ever sit in an animal shelter again. Do you know where Claire is?"

"Hmm. I'm not sure. Can you help me?"

"Unfortunately, we can't," Fable said. "Perhaps the memory will r-"

"That's right!" Dax cried. "I remember what happened. Claire was upset about something. I was looking for her outside that cave place. But after I found her, I realized that you were lost! We went back inside the cave and looked for you, but you were gone. It was dark in there!"

"It was dark," Eleanor agreed. "I suppose you both went to the Loneliest Hollow because you thought that was where I went. Is that correct?"

"Yes, it is very correct!"

Fable adjusted her paws and sat upright. "I think it is important for you to know, Dax, that Eleanor was very concerned about you. She was prepared to go anywhere to find you, no matter the cost. You must be a really good friend."

"I am a good friend," Dax said. "She was a good friend first, though." He stood up straight. "Can you help me get out of here?"

So excited to have found him, Eleanor had momentarily forgotten that Dax was standing in a small hole, with rows of thorns keeping him stuck.

"How did you end up here, Dax?" she asked.

Dax stared at the ground. "That's a great question. That boy was really mean to us! Maybe he was hungry, too, or maybe he wasn't. Anyway, when we got here to look for you, the boy showed up and said some things."

"What did he say?"

Dax paused in concentration. "I don't remember. But then he attacked us by making the ground be really dark. I don't know what happened to Claire, but I woke up here. I hope she's OK!"

"Me too," Eleanor continued, looking around at the dim wooden walls as she spoke.

"I'm sure she is also somewhere in the Hollow," Fable said.

Dax turned towards Eleanor. "If you set me free, I would be really happy!"

Eleanor scratched her head. "We will certainly do that, Dax. But how? These thorns are awfully sharp."

"I know!" Dax exclaimed while pointing behind Eleanor, out to the entrance of the Hollow.

"What is it?"

"You could go out there and get a tree branch or something. You could use it to push the thorns. You remember that criminal raccoon guy? You used a tree branch to break him out!"

"Am I missing something?" Fable asked with a smile.

"That's right," Eleanor replied. "If I take a look back outside, I should be able to find something to get you out." She turned towards Fable. "We will be right back."

"OK! I'm right here! I'm imprisoned."

Eleanor and Fable walked across the circular room until they were outside the Hollow. The quietness of the night struck Eleanor in a new way, the sounds of her footsteps the only thing she could hear.

"This doesn't feel right," Fable began.

"What do you mean?"

Fable pointed at the Hollow again, resting under silvery moonlight. "I don't think I can fully explain it, but I feel very unsettled being here."

"Why is that?" Eleanor noticed a big tree branch nearby. It must have fallen off the tree at some point.

"Why were we able to go in there so easily? Where is he?"

"Are you referring to the boy? I don't know the answer to that," Eleanor replied, placing her hand under her chin. "It must simply mean we are lucky. Once we help Dax out of the Hollow we can go find Claire."

"What will you do after that?"

"After that, we will need to find the boy. The owl Octavious told us to go and talk to him."

"Do you really think going and talking to him will help you find your way out of here?"

"I do," Eleanor said with determination in her voice. "I trust Octavious."

Fable was staring at the ground as they approached the Hollow again. Once inside, Eleanor looked across towards the thorns. Dax was nowhere to be seen.

"Dax? Where are you, Dax?" Eleanor ran over to where the thorny strands had kept him. She turned towards Fable, who sat near the entrance.

"I see that he escaped," she spoke.

"But where did he go?"

Fable moved closer towards the thorns. "I think I see an explanation."

Eleanor joined her. "What is it?"

"There," Fable answered while pointing her paw. "On the other side of the thorns, there in the back. It looks like he was able to make a hole in the tree and crawl out through it."

"I find it hard to believe that Dax could bite his way through a tree. Then again, though, I do know he has an incredible amount of speed and energy."

"I was able to see that as well. He does like to shout, doesn't he?"

"He does," Eleanor agreed. "He is a wonderful friend."

"I have no doubt about that. Perhaps we should step outside again and look for him."

Eleanor nodded. "Let's go."

Outside, the air felt colder as the thickness of night covered the Togetherwood more and more deeply. Desperate to find Dax, Eleanor ran in multiple directions, placing her hands around her mouth as she called his name through the valley. She eventually came to a halt and crouched over, catching her breath.

"Where could he be?" she asked. "I just don't know."

Several tears formed in her eyes as she sat down on the hard dirt. Exhausted, afraid, and full of sadness, she did her best to not cry. She turned to look at Fable.

"He is gone, isn't he?" she continued.

"Not necessarily," Fable replied. "This is a big area, and we have only begun to look."

"I shouldn't be like this."

"Whatever do you mean?"

Eleanor looked at Fable, her eyes red and several tears still on her cheeks. "I get so upset. I let my emotions overtake me and I become pathetic. I feel so weak."

Fable's tail made a swooshing sound as she sat down next to Eleanor. "I don't know if you're right in saying that, Eleanor."

"Why?"

"Because," she continued, "I don't see how missing someone you care for is weak. I don't think there is any truth to that."

A slight smile formed on Eleanor's face. "Maybe you are right. Still, though, it is how I feel."

Fable's ears perked up.

"Did you hear something?" Eleanor asked.

"Yes, I did." She turned around and looked towards the Hollow. "I think there are voices on the other side of it."

Eleanor was also able to hear two faint voices. She closed her eyes and concentrated as she listened to them:

"I did see her! It's true!"

"I'm sure you did. You would also chase your own tail for three hours and tell me it was a squirrel."

"I would never do that. The last time I saw a squirrel, I got locked up!"

Full of relief, Eleanor wiped the last tears from her eyes, ran around the Hollow, and called out, "We are over here, you two!"

Dax hopped in the air several times when he recognized her. "See? She is here! Everything I said was true."

"I guess I don't mind him being right," Claire replied.

When Dax and Claire reached Eleanor, she crouched down and held out her arms to hug them. "I missed both of you so much!" she exclaimed.

"Me too!" Dax's tail wagged rapidly as it hit against Claire.

"I didn't mind having some alone time," she began. She gazed at Eleanor, her eyes suddenly a little brighter than before, and then looked away quickly. "But I think I'm recharged now. It will be better to travel with you again."

Eleanor's eyes also gleamed. "I am very happy to hear that, Claire."

"Now that you mention continuing to travel," Fable called from behind, "do you three agree that it is best for us to leave this dark place as quickly as possible?"

"Yes. Let's get out of here!" Dax shouted.

"Are you expecting me to say I want to be locked behind a bunch of thorns again until I disappear into a black annihilation?" Claire said. "Yes, we need to leave."

Eleanor looked at Claire. "You were also trapped?"

She nodded.

Eleanor looked in the direction of the Hollow, her face pensive.

"What is it?" Dax asked.

"I am wondering how both of you were able to escape from your..."

"Thorny cells?" Fable suggested.

"Yes," she nodded. "When Fable and I went out to look for something to help you out of your thorny cell, Dax, you and Claire were both already outside."

"Why is that a problem?" Claire asked. "Were you hoping I would languish forever in misery?"

"No, I was simply trying to understand."

"I remember it!" Dax said. "I was sitting there. I was waiting for you to come back, but then I saw some of the wall break off. I went through the hole, and then I was outside. It was great!"

"I'm sure it was," Claire answered.

"Did you have a similar experience, Claire?" Eleanor asked.

"That's correct."

"It makes perfect sense," Fable said, adjusting her paws, so they were next to each other. "Yet, it really is unexpected."

"What do you mean?" Eleanor asked.

Pointing towards the Hollow, she answered, "That boy, Liam, he was the one who let you both go."

"But he put me in my thorny cell," Dax said. "I don't get it!"

Fable wore a slight grin. "I told you it was unexpected."

"Why would he do that?" Claire asked.

"It's not easy to explain how his mind works. I don't really think anyone in all the Togetherwood understands it."

"Whatever," Claire snapped. "Let's just leave here."

"I do not think we should leave here just yet," Eleanor said, standing up straight.

"And why not?"

"Because we need to speak with Liam if we are going to find our way home."

"I really want to go home," Dax said.

Claire appeared as though she were about to speak, but she remained silent, her tail swaying. After a few seconds, she said, "I know you really seem to trust this cryptic owl, Eleanor, but Dax and I have already personally seen what happens when we try to befriend a prince of darkness. We need to just move on."

"I don't want to be in a thorny cell!" Dax exclaimed. "Not a third time!"

"I enjoy cryptic messengers as much as anyone," Fable added, "but perhaps these two are right, Eleanor. Maybe it is time to move on."

Eleanor suddenly felt completely alone once more. Though her three friends all insisted that they needed to change their course, still she believed otherwise. As she looked towards the Hollow and the surrounding valley cloaked in black, she wondered if she was perhaps being foolish. She listened to the silence of the night and affirmed to herself, once more, that she was correct to think that speaking with Liam would lead them to a box out of the Togetherwood and back home at last.

"I hear what you three are saying," she began, "but I do want to go and approach him."

There was a pause before anyone spoke.

"Very well," Fable replied.

"Ugh," Claire groaned.

"Tell him I say hi!" Dax said with a grin.

Eleanor raised her legs and kicked off some of the dust that had been collecting on her shoes. "I appreciate you three being understanding."

"We will wait here," Fable replied. "I think he will be more willing to speak with you if there are not four of us. If after a while we do not see you, we will plan to find you, help free you, and then leave this place once and for all."

Eleanor nodded. She turned towards the Loneliest Hollow, which stood crooked and still. With one final quick look at her friends, she headed towards it.

Feeling unnerved, she looked up at the moon above as she walked. She wondered, too, if somewhere far away her own parents were looking up at it at the very same time she was. Her parents, she knew, must be horribly worried. She longed to be back home in their arms. When she looked down towards the Hollow she started to doubt that this would ever happen.

She stood in front of the Hollow. She turned her head around, hoping she might still be able to see the others, but they were nowhere in sight, having disappeared in the night. Circular and foreboding, the entrance was the same as before. She walked inside and looked to the other side, where not long ago Dax had been imprisoned behind rows of thorns.

Everything around Eleanor felt completely frozen in place, as though time itself had stopped, and she was the only living soul in the entire world. An overwhelming feeling of hopelessness suddenly seized her, causing her to shake slightly. When she looked up towards the top of the Hollow she did not see any sign of the boy. All she noticed was the opening above, the night sky sprinkled with distant stars.

"Are you there, Liam?" she called.

There was no sound except her own breathing.

"I was hoping to talk to you," she continued, "I promise I will not hurt you. I actually think I may be able to help."

Resigned to the fact that he was nowhere to be seen, she lowered her head and stepped back towards the Hollow entrance.

"You didn't run away from me?" a soft voice asked.

Eleanor, jolted by the shock of hearing it, turned around and saw on the other side of the room a boy seated, slumped against the tree wall.

"You're..." she began, still shaking. "Liam?"

The boy stood up and slowly paced across the room towards her. When he was a meter away from her, he looked at her intently. He had tousled, hazel hair, and he stood with his hands hanging at his sides. He looked much like the friends who lived in her neighborhood. But then she noticed something unexpected about him. His eyes were a purple, violet color, and Eleanor thought that they looked weary.

"Yes, I'm Liam," he answered while still staring at her. "Why did you come back?"

"I wanted to speak with you."

"What about?"

Eleanor looked out the entrance of the Hollow, towards the valley slope. She faced him and said, "I was wondering if you might be able to help me and my friends leave the Togetherwood so that we can return home. Is there a cardboard box here?"

255

"That's what you wanted to ask?" he said, his purple eyes eerie.

"I was also hoping to learn why you trapped my friends here in the Hollow."

Liam turned so that his back faced Eleanor. He then walked towards the tree wall, where he sat down, just as he had been before. "I wanted them to understand," he said.

"Understand?"

He placed his head in his hands. "I wanted them to know what it feels like, to be all alone, in a place where no one will ever find you again."

"I am wondering why you would want that. You must have experienced a lot of pain, being here by yourself for so long. Why would you want anyone else to feel that, too?"

Liam looked up and stared at Eleanor once more. "Everyone left me behind, so the only thing I have wanted since then is to be by myself. When I became lost, the world kept going. No one cared."

"I don't think that's t-"

"So now I don't care, either. Now I don't feel anything at all. That dog and cat were stupid. They came here, and they shouldn't have done that." He nodded towards the middle of the room, and Eleanor saw her shadow begin to move, taking several steps on its own. As she looked at it, she felt she didn't recognize it, that it wasn't her.

"When they tried to bother me," Liam continued, "I decided to separate them and let them live here. I wanted them to sink away, just like I did. But then I saw you and that fox. You came down here to my dead tree to rescue them. You wanted to be kind and help others. I knew you were going to ruin what I was doing and then come to talk to me. That's when I had an idea."

"What was your idea?" Eleanor said, trying to ignore the shadow moving in front of her.

"I decided to set them both free. That way, now I can trap you and you alone here, forever. You will waste away here with the knowledge that your friends are living without you, that you could have been with them, but your choice has separated you. It will be your fault. That dog and cat are full of fear now. They will run away and never look for you again. They will forget about you. This is good news for you. You are just like me. You don't want to keep living in a lie."

Eleanor was terrified, afraid that she might fall over. "What lie?"

Liam stared straight at her. "When you feel happy with others, it's a lie that makes you feel better. All of us are really just by ourselves. Today is the day that you sit in this rotten tree and understand that. None of the joyful memories or bonding you had with your friends meant anything. All of that is gone now."

"Those memories with my friends weren't lies, Liam. Feeling happy with others is the most true thing I know," she said with determination in her voice. "Life does not need to be this way for you. You may have had a difficult past, but you can join us and have a new beginning! We will not leave you behind. Octavious the owl told us that you can help us return home, so I need to ask you again: is there a box here?"

"That owl doesn't know anything. You'll never leave here. From now on, this will be your home, a cell covered in darkness." He stood up and looked away from Eleanor, smiling to himself. His hands rested against the tree walls. "They say your shadow will always follow you," he continued. "When the moon is out, your shadow will go wherever you go. But what happens when it betrays you? What happens when you really are completely alone, and you have no one to tell?"

Eleanor gasped in horror. Her own shadow, taking several steps forward, drifted under her, and she felt the same cold, numbing sensation from before. An unbearable feeling of heaviness seized her, a sense that she was no one and that no one had ever loved her in her whole life. She would have done anything to make it stop.

"Now you're home at last!" she heard him shriek, his voice ringing through the Hollow.

She collapsed to the ground, the cold feeling flooding her completely. Just before her eyes closed, she was able to see Liam still staring at her, his purple eyes unblinking.

15.
A VERY GRAND RESCUE

Eleanor woke up suddenly, as though she had been lost in darkness and reality had finally broken through. It felt to her that her lungs were unable to take in enough air as she breathed quickly. Sitting alone in a small space, she saw several rows of thorns nearby. Was this the same place Dax sat in earlier? At that moment, she felt a sharp, cold breeze between the thorns. When she moved closer to them, she realized that she was high up off the ground, sitting in a hole of the Hollow up in the sky. Shivering and clutching herself with her arms, she moved back towards the tree wall. Looking down, she saw the dirt on her shoes.

Why had she been so foolish? When her friends told her to leave, still she insisted on going to him. Why had she thought that she might be able to convince him to help them? Moreover, why had she believed that an owl could direct them in how to return home? She was able to visualize the faces of Dax, Claire, and Fable, all of them looking at her pleadingly to leave the Loneliest Hollow, a rotten wasteland they had been fortunate enough to escape. But still, she had insisted. Eleanor turned her head to look through the gaps in the thorns, hoping to find the bright moon. It was nowhere to be seen.

Perhaps, she reasoned to herself, it was just as well for her to be here, as she clearly deserved it. In refusing to listen to anyone else, she demonstrated that she was wishing to be corrected, and this was precisely what happened. She sighed. At least now, she told herself, she wouldn't be able to misguide anyone else.

It was faint at first, but Eleanor felt startled as she realized she heard something. She rose from her seat and moved towards the thorns. When she looked down, she was met by two beady eyes and some long whiskers, a familiar face.

"There you are, kid," Ryder the raccoon said. "What did you do to get put in the slammer?"

Beaming with joy to be talking to someone else, Eleanor answered, "I'm so happy to see you, Ryder!"

Pulling on his whiskers, he replied, "Now, though I did say I was gonna start behaving, I suppose I should help you, seeing as how you broke me out in a very similar situation just a few hours ago. Besides, I don't think you got to talk to any lawyers before you were locked up."

"If you could do that, I would be very happy," she beamed.

"Come to think of it, getting you out of here is probably the most caring thing I could do for you right about now."

"I think I would have to agree!"

"Alrighty then." He reached into his fur and drew out his small axe. "You will probably want to take a step back."

She nodded and moved towards the wall of the tree. "How did you know that I was here? How did you get here?"

Ryder swung his axe forcefully, shredding the thorns apart. The cool night air filled the tree even more now, causing Eleanor to shiver again.

"Another place with lousy security. Come on over here, kid."

Taking her steps cautiously, she walked out to find she was standing on a gigantic tree branch.

"Why, there she is at long last!" another voice called. Eleanor turned around to see who it was.

Standing next to Ryder was Bradley van Bardsley, the explorer.

"Hi, Bradley!" Eleanor exclaimed, feeling even more happy now.

"It would seem that some misfortune befell you on your venture," he said. He then struck his own chest with a paw. "Never to fear, you will now be rescued by two heroes who are unquestionably brave!"

"Speak for yourself, pal," Ryder said. "I'm just following orders until I can get on with the next job."

Bradley turned towards him and nodded. "Having freed the damsel, I do think it's time to shove off!"

"Where are we going?" Eleanor asked, feeling the cool air against her face.

"Where are we going?" Ryder echoed. "Look, we busted you out, and now we're gonna make our sweet escape."

"We are awfully high up, aren't we?" Eleanor said as she looked down, able to just barely see the ground below.

"Never fear," Bradley said reassuringly. He raised up his wooden oar and then proceeded to hit the wooden floor with it, creating a booming thud sound.

"What are you doing?"

"It's all part of our little operation," Ryder explained.

On and on, Bradley struck his stick against the Hollow, the sound hammering Eleanor's ears. She looked up at the night sky, at the stars sitting in a splendid display. She felt awe as she realized just how many of them were floating above. There certainly was something beautiful, she thought to herself, about how all the glittering stars worked together to create such a view. How could she not have noticed this before?

"Is it working yet, Brad?" Ryder asked.

"Yea, I do think so."

"Is what working?" Eleanor asked. But then she understood.

In the sky, flying in a V-shaped formation, were thirteen ducks. Slicing through the air in unison, moving gracefully, they were descending on the Hollow rapidly.

"It's the 2nd Duck Division!" Eleanor exclaimed, placing a hand to her mouth.

"Sometimes it's good to bring in the guys in uniform," Ryder admitted.

Just as he finished speaking, the ducks all landed in a circle around them, producing thirteen small, squishy sounds. Next to Eleanor, standing proudly, was Captain David Drake. He stuck out his right webbed foot and then slapped it against the other, while the wooden bowl hanging on his head shook slightly.

"Bills up!" he proclaimed.

"Our bills are up!" the others responded.

"Tails straight!"

"Our tails are straight, too!"

Captain Drake finally stuck out his right webbed foot. "Wings loose."

All the others allowed themselves to have a relaxed posture.

"I am so happy to see you and the Division again, Captain," Eleanor began.

Captain Drake marched towards the wall of thorns as he spoke, saying, "Yes, Miss. The last time we knew your coordinates was at 11:00 hours. As you taught us the ways of peace during conflict, I knew it would be an honor for us to assist in this special mission."

"But how did you know to come here?"

"As that information has not yet been declassified, I am not authorized to discuss it."

Eleanor placed her hand at her forehead to salute. "Quackity-quack!"

"So what's the plan now?" Ryder asked.

Bradley unfurled his map, turning it one way and then the other. "It appears that we have reached the tree summit."

"Affirmative," Captain Drake answered. "Now that the subject has been rescued, our next course of action is to descend to the rendezvous point."

"Am I the subject?" Eleanor asked.

"Affirmative. Any other questions?"

"No, sir!"

Bradley turned the map upside down. "It indeed appears we must now make a daring leap into the unknown."

"No kidding," Ryder added. "How were you goons planning for us to get all the way back down to the ground?"

Captain Drake waved with his wing at the other ducks. "My units here will be happy to assist you with that."

"How?"

"No time to delay," Captain Drake replied. He walked towards the edge of the tree and kicked his webbed feet together once more. "Duck Division!"

"We're here, sir!" the ducks yelled.

"Are your feathers ruffled?"

"They're ruffled, sir!"

He stared down into the darkness. "Then deploy!" He soon disappeared.

Eleanor placed her hands on her knees as she stared over the edge of the Hollow branch. "How are we to follow him?" she asked.

The lieutenant duck standing next to her answered, "We will be assisting you, Miss. We will secure your passage, and also that of Ryder and Bradley."

"Is that so?" Ryder asked.

"Affirmative." The lieutenant turned towards Eleanor once more. "When you are ready, Miss, we will begin our descent."

"I think I am ready," she replied, smiling.

"Roger that." The duck jumped into the air, flapping his wings several times, and landed on her shoulder.

"What's this, then?" Bradley asked.

"We are preparing the private's parachute."

Giggling, Eleanor said, "It feels funny to have a duck on my shoulder. Please continue!"

The lieutenant turned towards the others, nodded, and then said, "Operation Duck Drag: commence!"

"Commence!" The others echoed. With that, they each jumped into the air and landed on Eleanor's shoulders, then her head, and several of them wrapped their webbed feet around her waist. Eventually, Eleanor was completely covered with ducks, all of them flapping their wings repeatedly.

Ryder shook his head. "You've gotta be kidding me."

"When you are ready, Miss, execute the jump."

Eleanor nodded. "I know that I am perfectly safe when I have you to support me."

With one final turn of her head towards the hole where she had been imprisoned only minutes earlier, Eleanor ran towards the edge of the Hollow and leapt off.

Terror seized her at first as she felt the air blast against her, watching branch after branch pass by. After feeling the drift caused by the many flapping wings, though, Eleanor knew she would be safe. She moved through the air gracefully like a falling leaf. She extended both her arms and squealed with delight.

"Are your wings flapping?" the lieutenant shouted.

"Our wings are flapping, and fast!" the other ducks responded in unison.

She looked out and saw the edges of the valley, the expanse of trees high above them, and then the moon resting in the sky. She noticed how it filled the blackness with light. The sounds of flapping remained constant, like one continuous gust of wind.

A few seconds later, Eleanor looked down and saw that her feet were about to approach the dirt ground at last. With knees bent, she positioned her feet and landed smoothly. As she stood up straight, she felt the ducks all detach from her instantly, jumping into the air and landing in a circle around her.

"That really was incredible," she said.

"We are only following orders, Miss," the lieutenant replied. "We will need to complete this phase of our mission and go retrieve the others." He turned towards another duck and said, "If we are sighted by the enemy, sound the alert quack."

"Yes, sir! Quackity-quack!"

Minutes later, Eleanor was joined by both Ryder and Bradley.

"These guys sure are organized," Ryder began. "To think of what kind of treasures they could steal."

"Nay, theft is never a noble way," Bradley answered.

"I know, I know. Look, I don't steal, either. All I'm saying is that, you know, if they wanted to do it…"

"What has gone up has now come down. All has been restored," A voice called from a few meters away.

"Who is there?" Ryder asked.

"I think I may know," Eleanor answered with a smile.

Not far off, standing elegantly, was Delilah.

"The universe greets you," she said to Eleanor.

"It really is very nice to see you again."

"Don't forget about me, too!" another voice called from below Delilah.

Eleanor looked down and saw that it was Caleb. "Hello!" she called.

"This deer said she would teach me how to do super-sweet, heroic stuff," he said while slumping over. "So far, though, I haven't seen anything at all. Ugh, I'm so bored."

"With the fullness of time, in a moment of weakness, hero-ism will arise," Delilah said. The orange flower hanging on her head shook slightly as she spoke.

"Do you know where my friends are?" Eleanor asked.

"You mean that little cat and the dog dude?" Caleb asked.

Eleanor nodded.

"This is where your friends are: upon the top of the valley, gazing down, awaiting a reunion," Delilah answered.

"Thank you, Delilah. I was really hoping to find them. I made a terrible mistake when speaking with Liam. I must have said something to upset him, and so I was imprisoned behind thorns."

"Of this we were aware."

"The flower lady's right," Caleb added. "We were told about you doing time back when this plan started."

"What plan is that?" Eleanor asked.

Suddenly, Caleb pointed with his paw behind Eleanor and said, "What is that thing over there? That's super creepy!"

"A being made of pure shadow," Delilah remarked.

Eleanor turned her head around and understood at once. Moving steadily, cloaking the dirt with blackness, was an enormous shadow. Full of curves and round edges, it drifted forwards, moving along the ground like a shark floating in a water current.

"Oh, man!" Caleb squealed. "What do we do?"

With a glint in her eyes, Delilah answered, "Swift and speedy motion guarantees life tomorrow."

Caleb turned to look at her. "Huh? You're kinda hard to un-derstand."

"I think I might understand," Eleanor said. "We need to run quickly."

As she turned to start sprinting, Eleanor saw Delilah standing right next to her. "By riding on my back, I will provide safe passage for you."

"What about me?" Caleb asked.

"You will be safe, for these evil beings seek only her."

Eleanor lifted her left leg so that it was on one side of Delilah and held on tightly. "Do you mean to say that these shadows only want to get me?"

"Yes," Delilah said, "but no time remains for words."

Now only several meters away, the shadow was climbing up the slope of the valley towards them without slowing down. Eleanor looked at it and swallowed.

"I am ready," she said.

"Then we will move with connection," Delilah replied. She sped up the hill, moving like a flash of lighting, just as she had back in the flowery meadow. Eleanor held on with all of her strength, feeling tension in her hands and wrists. She looked down and saw the ground slide away so fast that it disoriented her. Behind her, the shadow was not far off, nearly matching their speed.

"I know that you will help me arrive safely," she said.

"What you say is true. However, to live in truth, I must also mention my fatigue. Brisk running with a passenger is never effortless."

"That makes sense," Eleanor said with a smile. "Do you see that up there?" she asked while pointing.

"The horizon? It is expansive, as it always is."

"Yes, but I mean the ridge."

Placed before them, like a wall ending their trip, was a rocky ridge. Eleanor looked to her left and then her right, wondering desperately where else they might be able to go. But she only had to turn around once and see the approaching shadow to know that there was no time; the ridge was too wide.

"What do we do, Delilah?"

Crouching down, she replied, "Perhaps contemplation may guide us here."

"Hmm... I am not sure."

"I think I know!" a voice called.

Eleanor turned her head in the direction of it and saw Caleb approaching them. In one full movement he jumped onto the rocky ridge, dug in his claws, and climbed up it. He scraped himself up the ledge and then turned down with his paw reaching out.

"You sure are a fast climber!" Eleanor cried.

"Are you just gonna wait and get sucked into that freaky thing? Grab my paw."

Eleanor held on to Caleb's small, furry paw, and felt him pull her up, flinging her over. She stood up on her feet at once and said, "I think we need to continue running."

"Like, duh, lady!"

Eleanor and Caleb sprinted, the sound of their heavy breathing filling the night air. Despite the fear she felt, Eleanor chose to not look behind and check to see if the shadow was close by.

The slope started to flatten as they reached the top of the valley. Eventually, they arrived at a small riverbank. Though she considered herself a quick swimmer, Eleanor knew there was no chance they would be able to cross it and evade the shadow now approaching them.

"This sucks!" Caleb exclaimed. "What do we do?"

Eleanor scanned with her head quickly as she tried to catch her breath. The tightness in her chest was so constricting it was difficult for her to think.

"I am not sure what we can do," she began. "Perhaps-"

"Whoa! Look at that!" Caleb cried.

Eleanor was able to see something approaching them in the distance, though she was not quite sure what it was. She rubbed her eyes with her hands and blinked several times. It was a long log, moving gently in the water towards them. As if moving on its own, the log turned sideways near the bank of the river and came to a halt. It was then that she noticed Frippery, sitting on the edge of the log. He began to hop in the air jubilantly, croaking again and again.

"I must conclude this prototype has been very successful," he said.

"Hello, Frippery!" Eleanor exclaimed.

"What a pleasure it is to encounter you again, my star pupil."

"This boat is pretty sweet," Caleb said, admiring it.

"Not only does it have a pleasant appearance," Frippery replied, adjusting his posture as he turned to the side, "but I believe it will prove exceptionally functional!"

"Will we be using this to cross the river?" Eleanor asked.

"Yes, indeed, we will. However, if my estimates are correct, I do not believe the current capacity is sufficient."

"Huh?" Caleb asked, his mouth hanging slightly open.

"Not much time…" Frippery muttered to himself as he turned to look at the water. "Brigadier!" he called.

At once, there was a splash in the water as another familiar face surfaced.

"Yes, professor. You called?"

The wrinkles in Frippery's face shifted as he smiled. "Would you be so kind as to reengineer the seat so that it is larger? It seems a tad small for Eleanor. You humans certainly do vary in your dimensions."

"Yup, I can do that."

There was another mighty splash as Brigadier Betty jumped out of the water, turned to smile at Eleanor, and then proceeded to gnaw at the log. Her teeth moved continuously and furiously like a spinning drill, tearing at the log and causing chips of wood to spray into the air. Seconds later, she turned to look at the others with her teeth hanging out of her mouth and said, "I reckon that'll do."

Frippery hopped on one side of the hole and then to another. "Marvelous...splendid..."

"Yo, guys," Caleb said. "I'm not trying to rush you or anything, but Eleanor is kinda being hunted by this big shadow thing. She's gotta get going before it shows up."

Frippery wore a thoughtful expression. "Of course, of course. Please hop in!"

Eleanor quickly maneuvered herself onto the log, feeling it press deeper into the water with the added weight. She focused her gaze and slid herself into the hole Brigadier Betty had created for her. Amazed by how deep it was, she felt her legs slide all the way through.

"I think it's a perfect fit!" she said.

"Aw, shucks," Brigadier Betty said. "You really are a sweetie pie."

Frippery began to hop in the air several times while croaking.

"What is it?" Eleanor asked.

"I do believe the youth was correct. That frightful entity is fast approaching."

She turned around and saw the shadow, even bigger than before, approaching the riverbank.

"We will need to activate our engine at once," he continued, looking at the water. "Miss Freya!"

With a small splash, a familiar face broke the surface of the water, looking listless.

"What is it now?" she asked.

"We will need to shove off posthaste!"

Sighing, Freya answered, "I don't know if my swimming makes any difference, but maybe it does. I guess it helped Eleanor out earlier."

"I think having you push the log will be very helpful for us," Eleanor replied with a smile. "I know I would really appreciate it."

"Yup, yup," Brigadier Betty added.

Freya made a small splash with her fin in the water. "OK, then, I guess."

She placed the side of her head against the log and swam with all her might. Brigadier Betty jumped into the water and joined her in the effort. The log started to glide over the water, and within seconds, was sailing at a brisk pace. Eleanor felt a slight breeze against her cheeks. Under the soft moonlight, she was able to see the surrounding area, the rolling rows of trees and gently sloping hills of the Togetherwood. She looked down at the water and saw how the front of the log sliced through it, spraying blue jets to both her left and her right. With the strong river current, the log occasionally bumped up and then sank down.

Eleanor turned to look over her shoulder and noticed that the shadow was nowhere to be seen. "I think we finally escaped it!" she yelled in excitement.

"Certainly a reasonable thought," Frippery replied.

Remaining in silence for the next several minutes, Eleanor felt relief to climb out of the log and step on dry land once more. She turned around and watched the dark water gently lap against the shore.

"I think it fitting for us to remain here," Frippery said.

"I really do appreciate your help," Eleanor said as she placed her hand under chin. "However, I am curious about something. It has been so marvelous to see so many different friends I have made in the Togetherwood, all here at the same time. How is it that they have all shown up at the same time to work together so well?"

Brigadier Betty surfaced from the water. "I don't suppose that's something we ought to explain right about this time."

"I can't believe I was invited," Freya said as she also surfaced. "It really did make me happy, though."

"Yes, indeed on both counts," Frippery said. "Eleanor, I do think it paramount you continue on."

She nodded. "Thank you, again," she said with a smile. "It was wonderful to see you all."

Before her, the ground formed a small hill. Despite the tension she felt in her legs, Eleanor walked with a strong pace. Looking around, she saw nothing except the dirt beneath her feet and the slope in front of her. Everything felt very still, and it caused her mind to race. Where was she going? Where were Dax, Claire, and Fable? Now that she knew Liam did not want to help them, how would they ever leave the Togetherwood? She was still able to see in her mind his purple eyes, the way in which he stared through her, how he had been seated, slumped against the tree wall when he first spoke to her. Restless, she continued to walk, unsure of where she was headed as the summit of the hill finally came into view.

When she reached the top, Eleanor stopped and took a moment to catch her breath. A dozen meters ahead of her, she saw something she remembered at once. It was the wooden branch tied to a rope that looped around a single tree. The swing did not move at all, but remained perfectly still. She tried to imagine someone sitting on it and using it for fun, but was unable to. She approached the rope and held it in her hands. Though it felt rough, there were no signs of it fraying. Curious, she sat on the branch and knew it was secure. She lifted her feet off the ground and drifted slightly. It did feel nice to sit on, she thought. Just as soon as she considered getting off of it, she saw the shadow once more. Only a few meters ahead of her, bigger than ever before, it slowly approached her. Eleanor looked at it and knew there was nowhere else for her to run. The shadow suddenly, quickly slid towards her until she was covered by it. She felt the coldness, the absence of love yet again. It was as though her family and every friend she had ever made had never existed. She wanted to scream, but no sound came. As her remaining strength disappeared, she fell down onto her knees.

A deafening roar filled the night air. Eleanor felt something brush against her, and next thing she knew, she was moving on top of it. The darkness seemed less strong. Disoriented, she sat up and saw Beth Anne standing in front of her magnificently and breathing heavily. The shadow was a few meters away.

"Oh dear, oh dear," she said. "If anything were to hurt you at all, sweetheart… why, I would just be worried sick."

"You saved me," Eleanor said. "Thank you!" She turned and saw that the shadow was moving towards her again.

Though she tried to stand up and run, she was not quick enough, and the cold feeling returned. Even stronger than before, Eleanor collapsed right away. She was prepared to close her eyes and disappear, but something seized her, and she felt as though she was soaring through the air. There was a loud thud sound, and then she felt herself be lowered to the ground. She looked up and saw Gregory holding the wooden swing in his left hand. He let go of it and beat his chest in the rapid, percussive way she knew so well.

"It looked like you were in trouble," he began, "so I thought it would be good to help you out."

"That sure was just the most delightful thing I've seen all day," Beth Anne said. "You really are a sweetheart."

"As long as there is something to swing with, the Bluejay Brothers are here to help," he answered her. "I thought what you did for Eleanor was neat, too. Good job."

"I didn't like that," a voice called.

Eleanor turned her head, knowing at once who spoke. Sitting next to the tree, his purple eyes shining fiercely, was Liam.

"I know you wanted me to feel alone," Eleanor began. "You were wanting me to feel that, and you sent those shadows after me. But I still think there is a better way forward. Would you at least be willing to listen to me?"

He stood up and took a step towards the swing. "No, I think it's time for you to listen to me," he said as he held the rope in his hands. "I never felt like school was a good place. I remember some kids calling me horrible things, treating me like I wasn't even a human. I can recall when one of them told me I was a waste of space and then hit me when I tried to stand up for myself. Day after day, these kids insulted and intimidated me, to the point where I was afraid to even leave my home. Then one morning I ran deep into the woods behind my house. I brought rope along with me, hoping to make a swing. I wanted to wander off and disappear somewhere by myself, and that's what happened when I climbed into a cardboard box I came across near a clay hill. The box closed, and when it opened I found myself lost here, in this place called the Togetherwood."

"It really is an easy place to get lost in," Gregory affirmed.

Liam lifted the wooden branch and let go, watching it glide through the air. "At first I was scared. I still wanted to make a swing, and so I made a few of them as I wandered. I guess deep down I dreamed of sharing one with a friend if I ever had one. That way, we could push each other and see who could swing the highest. But after I finally came here and hung up this branch, I knew I would never have anyone to join me. It was just me, perfectly alone. So I walked with nowhere to go. All it took was one wrong step to send me falling. I slid off the edge near here and rolled down a dirty valley. I rolled deep down. The only thing I found waiting for me at the bottom was this rotten tree, the Loneliest Hollow."

"Oh dear," Beth Anne began. "It's such a sad story!"

Liam crouched down, laying on his back and spreading out his hands and arms as he looked up at the night sky. "I waited. I believed my parents would somehow come find me. The thing is, though, I was wrong. I was foolish to believe that anyone would care, that the world would stop if I needed help. I just lived here, in a dead tree, and after a while I let myself sink into its shadows. I didn't care. When I went out into the woods to run away from the savages at my school, I hoped to discover something better. What I didn't expect to find, in this place everyone calls the Togetherwood, was myself all alone. At least now I don't believe any lies like all of you do."

"I know you have experienced difficulty and pain," Eleanor replied. "That pain is real, too. But take a look around. Don't you see that you are not alone anymore?"

Still laying on the ground, Liam closed his eyes.

"She's there! I see her! She is there and I see her! This is such a great thing!" a voice called.

Eleanor looked past Gregory and Beth Anne, seeing a tail wag in the distance.

"You're right, Dax! I'm over here!" she called back.

Seconds later, a black blur flashed by and then Dax was licking Eleanor as he ran in circles around her.

"Dax, do you have to be so loud? You're going to repel her," Claire's voice followed.

Eleanor, who was petting Dax, looked up and saw her. "There you are, Claire! Did you bring the others with you, too?"

Walking alongside Claire was a big collection of animals all moving as a group: Frippery hopping, Captain David Drake marching with his troops, Brigadier Betty, Ryder ambling slowly, Delilah sprinting and then coming to a halt, Caleb, the members of the Bluejay Brothers soaring overhead, Fable, and Sir Bradley van Bardlsey carrying a bucket that dripped water. Out of the bucket, Freya's head appeared.

"I chanced upon this long ago on a voyage through a distant shore," Bradley said while nodding towards it.

"It's too small," Freya added, "but I guess it could be worse. At least I got to help out."

"Hmm," Gregory said. "I think I should go join them."

"Caleb! You're OK!" Beth Anne ran towards her son.

Beaming, her face lit up with immense joy, Eleanor looked out at them all. They were all the friends she, Dax, and Claire had encountered as they traveled through the Togetherwood that day. Her head was filled with memories, conversations, and adventures.

"I am so happy to see all of you!" she cried. "But how is it you all came together like this? You were so coordinated in rescuing me!"

At that moment, an owl flew past over the group, and Eleanor recognized it to be Octavious. He landed on the ground, looked up with his brows furrowed, and said, "Messenger."

"You told all of them to come here?" Eleanor asked. "But why would all of you do that?"

"They all wanted to help us!" Dax cried. "He flew around and told them that you were trapped in the Hollow. Isn't that great?"

"They didn't make the safest choice, did they?" Claire added.

Still smiling, Eleanor said, "Thank you so much, everyone!"

The other animals all replied with words of encouragement and cheer.

"None of you get it, do you?" Liam said, sitting up now, his purple eyes now somber.

"What do we not get?" Claire asked.

Still sitting, he answered, "All I wanted was to be by myself, just as the world left me." He pointed at Eleanor. "You came here and ruined that, so I wanted to teach you and your friends. Now you come back with even more friends. You bring your cheer and humor, a love for life, and you expect me to join in." He stood up more straight. "Do you really want me to do this?"

"Do what?" Dax asked, tail wagging. "What's he going to do?"

Without replying, Liam looked at the moon intently. Silence followed. He then lowered himself onto his knees, placing his body on the ground so that his face disappeared. A few meters in front of him a shadow appeared, this one even bigger than any Eleanor had seen yet, spreading out dozens of meters in every direction. It moved towards her, and she stumbled to the ground, convinced she was doomed.

"We gotta save her!" Dax called.

"Order received," Captain David Drake replied. "Executing now."

"Though we are many, we are one," Delilah added.

"Everyone here," Fable began, "remember why you were willing to come."

As she felt herself fade away into darkness, Eleanor was able to discern the sound of the others stepping into the shadow with her. She felt something brush against her, and could just barely see what was orange and black fur. Knowing that Dax and Claire were right next to her, somehow, brought her comfort. She prepared to sink into the cold feeling and disappear. But that was not what happened.

A flash of light burst across the sky. Eleanor was able to see perfectly again. No longer did she feel cold, but rather she was very warm. She looked out, seeing all of her friends right next to her where the shadow had been. Everyone appeared joyful, and some were even laughing. When she turned her head to look up, even the night sky appeared brighter now.

Eleanor looked around, but there was no shadow to be seen anymore. "That was incredible," she said. "What happened?"

Octavious fluttered over and landed next to her. "New power..." he said. "Not alone...together..."

"We all went into the shadow with you," Claire explained. "We were able to break through the forces Liam has been using and replace them with something else."

"Truly a marvelous discovery to chance upon," Frippery said.

"Whatever works, huh?" Ryder's whiskers bristled.

"It's true," Fable added. "Eleanor, I think that the curse that has loomed over the Loneliest Hollow all this time, the force of shadows, is healed at last."

"Hooray!" Dax shouted. "We did great!"

"Doesn't look like everyone is happy, though," Claire said, pointing in the distance.

"What is it?" Eleanor asked while standing up.

Laying on his back and hugging his knees, wincing, was Liam.

"Are you all right?" she asked while taking several steps towards him.

She stood next to him and saw that he was in pain. As she looked at him, he did not say anything. The sounds of all the other animals talking and cheering was deafening, but Eleanor continued to focus on him. Without speaking, she crouched down so that she was close to him.

278

"You don't have to say anything at all if you don't want to," she began. "I am here, though, all the same."

The moon rested high up in the celestial sky, stars dotting the spaces all around it. Several patches of clouds were moving away, making the view more clear.

Liam slowly sat up. He turned to look at Eleanor and then at the ground. "Why did all of them show up like this? Why did they jump into the shadow with you?"

"I know!" Dax exclaimed. "It's because we helped them out and became friends! When you are friends, that means you stay together no matter what."

Liam looked at him in disbelief. "I wish I could experience that."

"You certainly can," Eleanor said with a smile.

"There's no way that's true. Who would ever want to invite me?" he asked, staring at the ground once more. When he next lifted his head, he realized everyone else was looking at him. "Could I really be a part of your group?" he asked. "Even after everything I did?"

Eleanor nodded, smiling. "We know you did what you did because you were hurting inside and did not know what else to do. We forgive you."

"Really?" he continued.

"Of course we do!" Dax shouted as he ran into Liam, sitting in front of him, his tail wagging forcefully against his knees. "A new friend! You can be our new friend! Won't that be great, Claire?"

"Does that mean there's someone else you can talk to instead of me?" she asked. She looked at Liam with tender eyes. "It sounds like you were mistreated at school. You do seem to have a good heart deep down. It might be nice to have you around."

"Pet me!" Dax shouted. "You've got to pet me now!"

279

Liam looked at Eleanor and then at Claire, who was shaking her head slightly. As Dax's slobbering tongue collided with his forehead, Liam laughed.

All the other animals turned to look at him and, seeing him now giggling, let loose cheers. Another flash of light filled the area. When Eleanor looked at Liam once more, she saw that his eyes were no longer purple but blue.

"Perfect," Octavious said. He pointed at Eleanor and said, "Rescuer."

"Me?" she replied, appearing surprised.

"I think I may be able to explain," Fable said. "It seems that the reason Octavious led you here, Eleanor, was because he believed you would be able to help Liam leave this shadowy place."

"It's true!" Dax exclaimed.

Blushing, Eleanor answered, "Well, perhaps that is true. However, I would not have been able to do it without the help of everyone else here. It really was a very grand rescue!"

Once more, the sounds of cheers filled the air.

"We're a super-cool crew!" Caleb called.

"Wowsers! They did great!" Larry yelled.

"Wow!" Terry called.

"I think we have great teamwork," Gregory said. "Does everyone understand what I'm saying?"

"New power," Octavious repeated while nodding with his head towards a patch of grass several meters away. A circle of yellow light formed on the ground. A giant cardboard box appeared in the center of it. "Return home," the owl continued.

"Can we finally get out of this place?" Claire asked.

"I think we can," Eleanor answered. She looked at Fable, who nodded.

Taking several steps towards the box, Eleanor turned back to look at Dax and Claire. "You two will go with me, won't you?"

"Is that really a question?" Claire asked.

"I will go, yes I will go!" Dax called.

Eleanor, Dax, and Claire turned to look at the animals of the Togetherwood once more. After saying a final goodbye, they took a step towards the box. Eleanor came to a sudden stop and turned around.

"We can't leave without you, Liam. Will you please join us?"

Wearing a tentative smile, he walked towards them without speaking. They all climbed into the box with joyful hearts and said farewell to the Togetherwood.

EPILOGUE

The orange rays of twilight shone over the neighborhood streets. A slight breeze rubbed a wind chime hanging from a house, creating a soothing and tranquil sound. Liam walked at a steady pace, examining his surroundings closely. Feeling sure he had already looked in every spot he thought could be used, he searched with focus. He stepped under a basketball hoop and crossed the street once more.

Stacey, a girl who lived nearby, stood next to the green wire fence with her hands in her pockets. Liam looked over the fence, to the other side of the yard, and saw no traces of anyone in the bushes. The big oak tree in front of its house did not have anyone waiting in it, either. Where, he wondered, could she be?

Now at the front of a cul-de-sac, he walked down a steady slope and surveyed the houses: one yellow, another dark blue, the one at the very bottom green. He saw James crouched down next to a rock in front of his house. He turned and walked around it, moving through the open fence until he was in the backyard. The grass was astonishingly long and in need of cutting. He wiped several drops of sweat from his forehead. Night, he knew, would soon arrive.

He had an idea of where to look now. Passing another thick tree, He looked up and saw the edge of a forest past the tall grass. Without thinking, he turned to his left and saw it, the shed. He placed a hand against it and felt the worn wood. He let his hand trace it as he walked around the corner and saw her at last.

"There you are!" he cried.

Eleanor was crouched down on the ground, her fingers in the bark.

"You finally found me," she said with a smile.

"I did. This seems like an excellent place to hide."

"Did you find the others yet?"

"Yes, I did. You were the last one I was looking for." He felt proud as he said this. "Thanks for inviting me to play. It's...it's so nice to be back here in this neighborhood again. There's so many more places to hide here than over where I live."

"I am sure I would say the same thing about your neighborhood!"

Liam lowered his head slightly. "I need to thank you again. I really had no idea how miserable I was until I came home and saw my family."

"Of course," Eleanor beamed. "My friends and I were happy to help you. Now they are your friends, too!"

"It is strange to think about. I lived in the Togetherwood for years and spent so much time suffering there. But when I knocked at my front door and my parents saw me, it was as if I had just returned from a morning outside."

"I do remember hearing that the flow of time in the Togetherwood is different from here," she said with a nod. "These first few days back have been peculiar, but it is so good to be home."

"Yes, it really is."

An owl flew by at that moment, perching on a nearby tree. Both Eleanor and Liam looked up at it, aware of who it was.

"There he is again," Liam said as he turned to face the tree canopies of the forest. "It's getting late, isn't it?"

"It is," she agreed. "I think we should go home. I still have to do my homework!"

"Yes, me too."

They walked back towards the cul-de-sac and joined the others. Eleanor said goodbye to them at the street corner and continued down towards her house. Her brother Edward stood in the front yard, raking a pile of leaves.

"Did everyone get found, Sis?"

"Yes. My new friend Liam found me last, over by the shed."

"I remember when I almost broke my ankle after I jumped off that thing. Our parents were not happy with me that day. Anyway, I hope you had fun."

"Thank you."

She walked past him, up the steps to the front door, and turned to her right. Dax was waiting for her, panting and wearing a massive grin. Claire was rolled into a ball and had her eyes closed.

"Where did you say you got these two pets from again?" Edward's voice called.

Eleanor crouched down to pet them before speaking. "I found them far away from here in a very magical place. They are my best friends."

"Sounds good, Sis," Edward answered with a chuckle, continuing to rake leaves.

"Eleanor, sweetheart," a voice said.

Walking around the side of the house was her father. Both his hair and his eyes were dark brown, just like hers.

"Hello, Father!"

Smiling, he said, "I am glad you are back. Would you like to assist me tomorrow with planting some marigolds? I think they will be perfect for the side garden."

"Yes, I would be happy to!"

"Great." He looked at the front door. "Well, I think your mother made apple pie. We better take a look at it before Edward finishes raking."

"It's true!" Edward's voice called. "Only two more piles to go."

Eleanor's father smiled as he trotted up the stairs, kissed her on the forehead, and entered the house.

Looking at Dax and Claire once more, Eleanor opened the door.

"Come in!" she exclaimed.

With a smile, she went inside, her two pets close by her side.

About the Author

Sean Anderson lives with his wife in Everett, WA. He loves reading fantasy books that take him on a journey. In his free time he enjoys open water swimming, spending time in nature, and spoiling his cat, Fancy. He is the author of _The Year of Oceans_ and _The Celestial Life_.

If you feel generous and have a couple of minutes, please leave a review. It makes a huge difference to me. Thank you in advance.

Follow the author on social media
Website: https://seanandersonwrites.com/
Instagram: https://www.instagram.com/seananderson_author/
Facebook:https://www.facebook.com/seanandersonwrites
LinkedIn: https://www.linkedin.com/in/sean-anderson-113528122/

About the Publisher

Sulis International Press publishes select fiction and nonfiction in a variety of genres under four imprints: Riversong Books, Sulis Academic Press, Sulis Press, and Keledei Publications.

For more, visit the website at
https://sulisinternational.com

Subscribe to the newsletter at
https://sulisinternational.com/subscribe/

Follow on social media
https://www.facebook.com/SulisInternational
https://twitter.com/Sulis_Intl
https://www.pinterest.com/Sulis_Intl/
https://www.instagram.com/sulis_international/

Made in United States
Troutdale, OR
06/25/2023

10782448R00166